WITH BOTH FEET

NICOLA KELSALL

Little Studio
Publishing Company

With Both Feet

First published as an eBook 2021

ISBN: 978-0-9956685-4-6

Many thanks to all my friends and family who have inadvertently inspired the content of this book, and a special 'thank you' to Fiona at Fiona McIntyre Designs, for her work on the cover design.

With Both Feet

"Summer is when parents realise teachers are vastly underpaid…"

(Unknown)

With Both Feet

CHAPTER 1

'Soz Babe. Can't make tonight. Work stuff x.'

I read Elliott's pathetic message with the disdain it deserved and turned over to go back to sleep. Then I remembered it was a school day. *Urggh...*

I rolled out of bed and caught my reflection in the wardrobe mirror; mad bird's nest hair, washed-out complexion (shouldn't have stayed up reading all those Year 8 poems last night), blood-shot eyes (same), slightly out-of-shape figure hiding inside a baggy stretch-nightie from BHS Closing Down Sale... not the most alluring of sights first thing in the morning, but hey, it's amazing what a shower and hair-wash can do. Just shove a bit of make-up on and a nice dress, and Bingo! Life's too short for wasting hours of precious time spading on foundation and blow-drying my less-than-perfect hair. A long time ago I came to the conclusion that I am not endowed with elegance or a perfect figure, but I can turn heads with my joie de vivre and a nice lipstick. And, although my wild hair often resembles my mother's rust coloured Cockerpoo, it can look pretty good with a little intervention, if I say so myself. However, this morning I didn't have much time to spend taming it.

'Ah, Laura – quick word…' The Headmistress beckoned me into her office as I tried unsuccessfully to scoot past. She appraised my unkempt appearance with a disapproving sniff, drawing her head back into her skinny neck, as if avoiding an unpleasant odour.

'What do you know about William Parsons?' she said.

'Well, he seems all right, he's lazy like most of them.'

'Anything else?'

'Um. Well, his hobbies include playing computer games, showing off, and chasing girls…' I was trying to be amusing but failed dismally.

'Mm,' she said. 'His social worker rang me this morning…' She peered at me expectantly over her large, red, cat-eye spectacles.

I felt the heat rising in my cheeks. 'I'm not sure what you're getting at,' I said, wondering which of my misdemeanours would be highlighted this time.

The trouble with Evelyn 'The Führer' Ferrier, is that she has absolutely no sense of humour whatsoever. After 30 years, I suppose you've seen all the jokes kids play too often. When Barny Russell glued that fiver onto the floor outside her office last year, it obviously wasn't the most original idea in the world, but watching Evelyn trying to peel it off on the video he took was priceless. She reacted very badly when she found out about it. Barny, not being the sharpest knife in the rack, didn't think twice about putting the footage on social media where her nephew, Gordon, was sure to see it. The end of term is always a bit on the rowdy side. Pranks and high jinks intensify, and none of us gets off scot-free. I am still afraid to leave a drink on my desk and turn my back on the class during lesson time. I didn't even know you could buy Plaque-Detect in liquid form! Bloody kids!

Anyway, I suppose there are worse things than walking around with a blue mouth and matching teeth all afternoon. Mr Enshaw had to remove his trousers in full view of the 6th form chemistry class when he discovered someone had smeared his chair with Superglue. It was a lucky escape – I mean, we've all heard those awful stories of loo seats having to be chipped off bare skin using a rasp to file the glue down…

'Laura…' Evelyn was saying, - 'she's complaining that he doesn't seem to do any homework.'

'Well, he does have some – he just doesn't do it…'

'That's what she means, Laura! She wants *you* to put some pressure on him. For heaven's sake, this isn't a holiday camp.'

'OK, I'll talk to him,' I said, hoping she'd finished.

'You need to step up, Laura. English teachers are *not* in short supply, you know.' She cleared her throat and nodded at me; my cue to leave.

In the staffroom, I found my sensible friend and colleague, Fay, waiting for me with a nice mug of hot tea.

'The thing is, Evelyn's under huge pressure herself to improve this school's performance,' she said. 'Here, have a biscuit.' She thrust a packet of Lemon Puffs in my direction.

'She threatened me with my job though!'

'Oh, don't let it bother you, Laura. You know it's hot air. No one's rushing to work in a school like this, I can tell you. I was the only candidate for my job!' she laughed.

'Chemistry teachers are harder to find, Fay.'

'Well, just make it more obvious that you're trying with these kids, and she'll probably leave you alone. Anyway, you can't leave – I need you! You're the only teacher who makes me look good!' She laughed again, spilling some of her tea on the huge pile of exercise books on the table in front of her. She quickly wiped it off. 'Billy won't notice that stain,' she said, - 'his books are always covered in jam and dog hairs.' Noel Jones looked up briefly from his paper, raising one judgmental eyebrow, and tutting.

'Don't you ever regret going into teaching, Fay?' I said.

'YES! Every day! But on the other hand, I love it too! Go figure! I've got the Year 10s in five minutes – they're my favourite class, except for a couple of them, who I'll be very happy to see the back of next year.'

'Chloe Stevens and Denise Channing by any chance?'

'They're a pain, aren't they! It always makes my day when one of them is off sick.' Fay laughed again and scooped up her books. 'I'd better get going. Some people are actually trying to do some work around here…' Noel coughed and noisily straightened his paper. She rolled her eyes and winked at me.

I stayed and finished my tea, whilst staring out of the window and contemplating my current boyfriend situation.

Should I just dump Elliott and have done with it? I mean, he's not dependable, or durable, or even likeable. Or should I drag it out a bit longer, so I have someone to go to the School Summer Ball with? Decisions, decisions… Apart from the show-off factor, there's not much to recommend this relationship. Elliott is good looking, tall, fit, and smart. He can even make me laugh. However, the plain truth is, he's unreliable, selfish and slightly more misogynistic than is acceptable in this day and age. I think the writing is on the wall.

'Whose idea was this Summer Ball thing?' said Noel, suddenly, as if reading my mind.

'The Führer's – I mean, Evelyn's,' I said, hastily correcting myself. I keep forgetting that she and Noel were an item years ago. They've been friends for years. *Whoops...*

'Mm,' he said, frowning. 'Well, I can't imagine what she was thinking – this isn't the Shires, you know. I would imagine that most of the parents at St. Jude's have never set foot near a soirée of the type she's envisaging.'

'I think you're wrong there, Noel. I bet the mums can't wait to get their glad rags on. It'll be fun. Aren't you going?'

'Certainly not, Laura. I haven't danced since *Kung Fu Fighting* was in the charts.'

'You don't have to dance, Noel. Most people just get drunk and have a laugh.'

'Well, it's not my scene. I'll probably be enjoying a nice glass of Pinot Noir and a lamb cutlet with my wife, after which we'll entertain ourselves by watching an interesting and informative natural history programme on the television.'

'Well, you don't know what you'll be missing, Noel. Your wife might enjoy a night out.'

'She won't, I can assure you.' A faint smile played on his lips. He likes to have fun with us younger teachers. I'm sure he doesn't mean half of what he says.

'Well, I think you should come. It's your duty, Noel. After all, it is a fundraiser for the school. You ought to show your support.'

'Well, if they have a beetle drive, or a quiz, I'll be all in.' He got up, shook his paper, and ambled off to his next biology class.

As I walked along the corridor to my next class, I happened to glance out of the window as something caught my attention in the distance, by the football pitch. I stopped for a couple of minutes and stared at it. Someone had tied one of those blow-up dolls to the goalpost and it was flapping about in the breeze like a big pink windsock.

'Someone should take that down,' said a voice next to me. My friend Dan gave me a wicked grin.

'Has Evelyn seen it yet?'

'Course not! No one's told her.'

'Right...'

'Well, no one wants to be the one to go and get it – the kids will have a field day.'

'Just send Gareth.'

'He's not in yet – dentist, apparently. Why is it that all the caretakers we get here seem to go AWOL just when you need them?'

'I don't know, but someone needs to and get that thing. Go on, Dan – be brave!'

'You know half the school are looking out of the windows with their phones at the ready, to see who goes, don't you?'

'Take a binbag.'

Dan capitulated. 'OK – I'll go. Where shall I put it, though?'

'I don't know… your car?'

'No way! I'm not getting caught with that thing in my boot.'

'You'll think of something, Dan,' I laughed. 'Ooh, I'm going to be late,' I said, as the bell rang. 'Catch you later.'

At lunch time, I nipped into town for half an hour. It's only ten minutes' walk from school. Sometimes I just need to get some breathing space and time to think. My Year 9 class this morning were particularly hard work. The truth is that half the lesson is always spent trying to keep control and get them to cooperate. I'm only just managing to have the upper hand. Over the years, I've discovered that the main way to get the kids' full attention is to tell them a really salacious or gruesome tale of such awfulness that they are literally begging for more. I also promise them sweets and chocolate for making an effort. When I do a class test, I have prizes for the winners. And because I'm a softy, I give them all a present at the end of term, whether they deserve it or not. I should probably have a wholesale account with every sweet shop in town. It's not cheap being a philanthropist, I can tell you. I think the other staff think I'm a bit loopy, to be honest. Evelyn doesn't approve at all. She says it's bribing them, and it'll come to no good. I prefer to call it giving them incentives. My favourite strategy would surprise her, though. A lot of these kids have never had a story read to them and many of them don't read books at all. Quite a few don't even possess books beyond what the school gives them. I discovered that if I pick the right kind of story, they really like being read to – even the Year 11s. Anyway, whether Evelyn is right or wrong, my recent poetry competition for Year 9s, inspired by the theme of '*summer*', achieved some fantastic results. It was the first time that every child in the class handed in a piece of work on time – miraculous! The chocolate bar prize, of obscene proportions, obviously did the trick. There were several contenders, but in the end Harry Beamer's rude but funny poem, 'At the Beach', was my favourite:

At the Beach

When we go down to Brighton beach
My dad turns as red as a crimson peach
He sits in his chair on the burning sand
And falls asleep with his fag in his hand
He thinks he's so cool, when he goes for a dip
With his belly in the air, he looks like a prick
He gets hammered on beer by the end of the day
And my Mum has to cover him with after-sun spray

'Bloody Nora, Laura! A perfect octave that Yeats himself would have been proud of! You must be doing something right! Are you sure he wrote it himself?' My Head of Department, Ray Fletcher, was genuinely impressed.

'I think so. He's a bit of a dark horse, is Harry. He's obviously cleverer than he looks. Shame I can't actually show it to anyone.'

'Get him to write another less offensive one. Tell him he's got a chance of submitting to *Young Writers*. I'll give him a tenner if it's any good. Makes you feel it's all worthwhile, eh, Laura? Shame we can't put it up on the Führer's 'Highlights' board in the staffroom.'

'I haven't put anything up there since Janet Mallet got an 'A' in her GCSE English Lit last year.'

'Well, Harry Beamer is showing real promise - you never know, Laura, you might have another one in a couple of years.'

'You're such a cynic, Ray. I've got at least four pupils in my Year 11 class who are going to do really well this year.'

'Good luck with that, Laura!' he said, chuckling.

Town was busy. Warm June weather on a Friday afternoon, had brought everyone out. I whizzed round and got the things I wanted before scooting back to school. I walked past a holiday shop and couldn't resist looking. It's been a long and tiring year. I needed something to look forward to. I don't know if I've been waiting for Elliott to suggest something, or whether I just haven't been able to summon the energy to think about a holiday. The young woman inside looked up from her computer. Her easy smile encouraged me to go inside. *Well, there's no harm in exploring possibilities.*

'You did WHAT?' said Fay, at the afternoon break.

'I know it sounds a bit mad…'

'That's because it *is* mad!'

'Well, it's not your cup of tea, Fay, but I think it's just what I need. Anyway, you've got your family to go away with.'

'I know. Sorry – I wasn't thinking.'

'It's fine. Listen, it won't kill me to go somewhere on my own for a change. In fact, I'm quite looking forward to it.'

'But it looks so…well…cut off,' said Fay, when I showed her my intended destination. 'There are no other houses for miles, Laura! You won't see another soul. You'll be completely isolated…'

'I know. It'll be wonderful,' I said. 'I can't wait.'

'Well, I suppose it's not as if you're going to live there…you will be coming back, won't you?'

'Yes,' I laughed, - 'I can't escape forever, even if I wanted to. My mother would come looking for me, for a start!'

On my way to class, I was accosted outside the ladies' loo by Morag Turner, Head of PE and self-appointed *wellness* guru. I knew by the look in her eye she was on a mission.

'Laura, just a moment…'

'I can't stop,' I said, - 'I'm in a rush.'

'It won't take a minute…'

I rolled my eyes; 'Please be quick, Morag.'

'I'm starting a relaxation class on Thursdays at lunchtime. It's free. You could benefit from it. I've been inviting anyone who needs to de-stress – anyone who seems a bit, you know, tense…'

'How do you know I'm tense? Sorry, but I don't have time for this now - I'm late for my class already.' I pushed the loo door open, but caught my foot underneath it, causing me to drop the books I was carrying.

'For God's sake!' I said, bending down to pick them up. Then the door swung back and hit me on the head.

'OW!' I yelled, rubbing my head.

'Let me help you,' she said.

'No! I don't need any help. I just need to go for a BLOODY pee in peace!'

Later, when I got back to my flat, I stuck the holiday leaflet onto my fridge. *I'll start that novel,* I said to myself. *No excuses – there'll be plenty of time to concentrate. No people to distract me, no phones ringing. No one coming to the door. Nothing but stillness and the sound of the sea lapping on the rocks, and the salty breeze blowing through the long grass. I imagined myself there – a lone figure striding purposefully along the virgin shoreline. Some lines from Samuel Coleridge's poem 'To Nature' came to mind:* ***…So will I build my alter in the fields, and the blue sky my fretted dome shall be…*** *Ah, yes – it'll be just the inspiration I need. Complete solitude will be my salvation. It was an excellent idea to go to the Outer Hebrides for my summer break. The best idea I've had in ages, I told myself, several times, just to make sure.*

'Is that you, Laura?' My mother's quavering voice sounded louder than normal. It was 7.30pm, and I was just thinking about cooking something.

'Yes, who else would it be?'

'I thought you would be out.'

'Um, well I was supposed to be, but why are you ringing me if you thought I was out?'

'But you are there…'

'You should use my mobile number, Mum.'

'I don't know where it is…'

'It's the big number on the wall by your phone, remember? Anyway, what's all that noise in the background? Have you got people there with you?'

'I just wanted to remind you about your sister's birthday.'

'Ok – I haven't forgotten. It's next year, Mum.'

'And…I need to go shopping for some new lounge curtains.'

'What's wrong with the ones you've got? You only bought them two months ago. Mum, is that an alarm going off? It's really loud…'

'I need new curtains because the ones in the lounge are no good now.'

'What do you mean, Mum?'

'They're a bit, well…burnt. It was a little accident with a candle. I'm so cross, Laura. My curtains are ruined.'

'Good grief, Mum. What are you doing lighting candles, for heaven's sake? It's not the 70's any more. The Winter of Discontent was 50 years ago.'

Well, I couldn't remember where the light switch was. Anyway, there's an awful noise going on here. Can you come and make it stop? I can't hear myself think.'

Once the Fire Brigade had left, I got to work cleaning down the walls and took the remnants of Mum's charred curtains and put them in the bin. Then, I searched the house for any fire-making equipment – even her electric blanket wasn't spared.

'What are you doing?' she said, seeing me remove it from her bed.

'Taking it to the cleaners,' I lied.

'You're a funny one,' she said. 'I couldn't get you to clean anything for love nor money when you lived at home.'

'That was a long time ago. I'll pick you up tomorrow and we'll go shopping for some new curtains. We can't have the neighbours spying on you, can we? By the way, where's Otto?'

'Oh, in the garden, I think.'

'How long has he been there, Mum?'

'Well now, let me think…I let him out this morning…and then I watched the T.V. and then I had a nap…then I went out to the shops. I needed to get some matches you see, for my candle, and it was getting dark…'

I opened the back door and let the poor dog in. 'Mum, do you mind if I borrow him for a while? It'll give you a rest.'

'Oh, well, I suppose that'll be all right. Not for long though. I'll miss him if he's gone for long. Don't forget to feed him and take him for walks, will you?'

'He'll be fine, Mum. Right, see you tomorrow. Come on, Otto,' I said, grabbing his food and toys on the way out.

Things have definitely got worse for my mother. I'm going to have to speak to my sister, Jenny, about it. The fact that Jenny lives 20 miles away doesn't help. Mum could have died this time - it doesn't bear thinking about. Thank goodness her neighbours saw the smoke. This is all I need with exams due to start soon. No wonder I'm getting grey hairs already.

I just finished feeding Otto when my phone pinged.

'Hi! Finished work -shall I come over? Film? Food? Woo's Wok?'

I looked at the time; 9pm. Well, I hadn't eaten, and I was fed up, and Elliott's company would be better than no one's... I caved and responded.

'Yes please. Am starving. Thank God it's Friday. Bring wine' x

CHAPTER 2

Unfortunately, last night was not a great success. Actually, that's an understatement; it was a total disaster. How was I to know that Elliott is allergic to dogs, for heaven's sake! Anyway, suffice to say, until I can find someone else to look after Otto, I am boyfriend-less. There is no way I can let him go back to Mum's, though. Goodness knows what could happen to him. Poor Otto! Left outside all day without a scrap to eat, subjected to a screaming alarm and fire engine sirens outside the house, then taken away to an unfamiliar flat to be yelled at by an irrational stranger. It's amazing he still wants to be friends with anyone.

'There you are,' I said, giving him his breakfast. 'Never mind that nasty shouty man – you're just not his cup of tea.' I stroked his soft, curly fur and thought how nice it would be to have a dog of my own again. 'What am I going to do with you? You can't stay here when I'm at work all day.'

I'd forgotten Otto's lead, so had to improvise to take him out to the park. It was another, lovely June morning – full of sunshine and promise, unlike my relationship, which appears to be going quickly down the plughole. Maybe last night's fiasco was the catalyst. I should just accept that the 'end is nigh'. Otto trotted along happily in his own little world of olfactory paradise, the millions of receptors in his nose telling him that this park was the most exciting place since Mum gave him a proper bone to chew last Christmas. Walking a dog, I discovered, is not only a very good excuse to go out and get some much-needed exercise, but it's also a great way to meet other people. Otto, being a very endearing and friendly fur-person, has only to look at someone and wag his fluffy tail, to get all the love and attention anyone could possibly wish for. He was just in the process of seducing yet another passer-by, when he decided to cock his leg and pee on a man's shoe.

'Oh, I'm so sorry,' I said, mortified by Otto's behaviour. 'He didn't have a very good day yesterday - he might be feeling a bit anxious, what with one thing and another…' I bent down and tried to clean the man's shoe with a tissue.

'He obviously hasn't been trained properly,' said the man, crossly.

'I could get your shoes cleaned for you…' I said, lamely.

'No, thank you. By the way, you should get a decent lead for your dog.' He was scowling incredulously at the pink fluffy dressing gown belt I had tied to Otto's collar.

'Well, thanks for that, Otto,' I said to him as we made our way back to the flat. 'I'm not sure you're going to be the man-magnet I was hoping for.'

My mother had not forgotten we were going out, but she *had* forgotten where Otto was. When I got to her house, there was a Special Constable in her lounge and my mother was showing her endless photos of Otto.

'Laura! You'll never guess what's happened,' she said, tearfully. 'Someone's stolen Otto! In broad daylight! One minute he was in the garden, and the next, he'd just vanished!'

'Mum, it's all right – you've forgotten that I took Otto home with me last night. He's absolutely fine.'

The officer sighed and put her notebook away.

'I hope you haven't been put out too much,' I said.

'Well, I've spent the last hour hearing about last night's drama with the curtains. It's been very entertaining. However, on a serious note, it appears that your mother is struggling on her own here. You might want to think about what's best for her in the long term.'

'What did she mean by 'struggling'?' said my mother as we drove into town.

'I think she just thought that perhaps now you're getting on a bit, you could do with some help…'

'Help?'

'Yes, Mum. What do you think about going to live where there are other people around – you know, for company?'

'I'm not leaving my house, if that's what you mean, Laura. Not over my dead body.'

'OK, it was just an idea.'

'Well, it wasn't a very good one.'

Oh dear. This is not going to be easy. I'll need to involve Jenny. I can't be expected to deal with this on my own. And what to do with Otto?

Jenny works as well, and she's always travelling, so I need to think about re-homing him, but then Mum will keep asking about him. I suppose I'll have to find a dog-sitter. And that definitely means 'goodbye Elliott'.

We traipsed into John Lewis and Mum spent an eon looking at fabric patterns. Eventually she chose some and the shop assistant looked as if he was going to dance for joy. She gave us a fright when she hesitated at the tills, and thought that perhaps she would 'go back and have just one more look…'

'No, Mum. These are perfect,' I said, getting her purse out for her.

I rang Jenny when I got home later, and relayed recent events, culminating in the excruciating shopping trip.

'Well, Jenny, you wouldn't *believe* how long she was in there for. I nearly chewed my own arm off with boredom. And then, after looking at every bloody design in the whole shop, she bought BEIGE ones, Jenny. BEIGE! Two hours we were in there for. TWO HOURS, Jenny!'

'Oh, dear. I'm sorry to hear that,' said my sister, sounding distracted.

'Have you got company?' I asked.

'Um, yes, sorry. I can't be on for long. I'm going out in a mo'.'

'I need to talk to you about Mum, Jenny. Let me know when you're free - it's really important - I mean, who knows what she might do next!'

I hung up and looked down at Otto. 'I suppose you'd like your tea now, wouldn't you? And then you're going to need a walk.'

Otto barked and wagged his tail. Well, at least one of us is happy.

I scrawled a quick advert for the newsagents requesting a cleaner for my mother and went out before they shut. When I got back, my phone buzzed, and I saw there was a message from Elliott:

'Sorry I left so quickly last night - can't be around dogs – hate them - brings on sneezing/ itchy eyes – the lot. Let me know when you get rid. Local animal shelter? xx (smiley emoji)'

'Well, Otto, it's you or him. What do you think?'

After spending two hours ringing round, I finally found someone who could come every day and take Otto out for a walk. He sounded perfect. Loads of experience, and Otto would have other dogs to play with. Having got that worry off my mind, I sat down to mark my Year 10 essays on the theme of 'A Haunted House'. It's always a mixed bag. Rarely is there an exceptional one. To be honest, I would be highly suspicious of anything in that league since Marty Brewster handed in an essay last year that knocked my socks off, and I foolishly praised it to the hilt in front of the whole class, holding it up as a beacon of awesomeness. The next day, I showed it to Ray. He told me I'd been had: *'That's one of Dick King Smith's stories, Laura. I read them all when I was young.'*

Since then, I've acquired a healthy cynicism when it comes to kids and their homework.

On Sunday morning, Jenny rang me back and we discussed at length what to do about our mother.

'She'll have to go into a home,' said my sister, bluntly.

'You try telling her that!'

'Well, I could come over next weekend…'

'The thing is, Jenny, she doesn't think there's anything wrong. We'll have to persuade her to go to her GP first.'

'Well, make an appointment for her and take her to it.'

'I'm glad you think it's going to be *that* easy!' I said.

'What if we get someone to go in every day to do cleaning, but actually they're keeping an eye on her as well?'

We debated how we were going to achieve this without our mother kicking off. She's always been fiercely independent and especially resistant to other people's ideas. When Dad was alive, she wouldn't even let him mow the grass in peace.

'He's not to be trusted with greenery,' Mum used to say, when Dad wanted to make stripes on the lawn. He'll make our garden look like a municipal park if I don't watch him.'

Poor old Dad. We often used to wonder what he was thinking. He never used to say very much. Mum used to say '*still waters run deep*' in a sort of comedy voice, and we used to laugh about it. I used to jokily imagine that he could be quietly planning her demise. Anyway, we'll never know, because ten years ago he got hit by lightning one evening whilst feeding his fish by the pond. Ironic, really. I do miss his quiet presence though. His calming influence was a helpful contrast to my mother's more vociferous self.

After the phone call with Jenny, I decided I needed some propping up and called my best friend, Cath. She's always good company – her cheerful smile and easy-going nature should be bottled and sold. I wish I had her ability to laugh at life after all she's been through. We met at a café in the park, next to the tennis courts.

'There's something very soothing about tennis balls being slapped backwards and forwards on a sunny day, don't you think?' she said, sitting down with me at a table shaded from the sun by a big white umbrella. 'Who's this?' she said, looking down at Otto, who was stretched out by my feet.

'My mother's dog. I think he's going to be living with me now, aren't you, Otto!' He didn't stir.

'Oh, why's that then? What's happened?'

'I think she's got dementia. He's not safe to be left with her. On Friday she nearly set the house on fire. Honestly, Cath, it's really worrying. I'm not sure what to do. I know she won't be persuaded to move.'

'Oh, it's a nightmare, isn't it! My Mum's getting a bit odd too, you know. Only last week, I went over to see her, and she'd bought 52 bottles of washing up liquid. When I asked her why, she said they were on offer. But who buys *that* many all at once, for God's sake! It'll take her twenty years to get through it all! The ridiculous thing is, she's got a dishwasher! AND…she only saved £3.20! Can you believe it! Anyway, tell me, what's going on with your love life – that's much more interesting. What's happening with Elliott?'

'Not a lot. He's allergic to Otto, so it's a bit of a problem.'

'Oh, no! What are you going to do?'

'Nothing. I've realised that I prefer Otto to him anyway. Otto is much better company.'

'Right,' said Cath, laughing. 'Well, that's a no-brainer then. You can have some fun looking for a new replacement.'

'I'm really not sure I can be bothered at the moment.'

'Well, as soon as you feel ready, I've got one or two potential suitors up my sleeve…you won't be disappointed!'

'Cath, you're incorrigible! I've only been single for twenty-four hours, and Elliott doesn't even know it yet. Anyway, I've got too much on my plate right now; my out-of-control mother and exam season at school, both of which are giving me a massive headache.'

'Well, the summer hols will be here before you know it, Laura. How about we go away together for a few days? Somewhere chilled – Greece? Italy? You name it.'

'What are your summer plans?'

'Matt and I are going to Ireland for two weeks. He wants to go fishing. I'm taking a load of books with me and enough wine to sink the Armada.'

'Teaching does that to you, doesn't it!'

'I wouldn't do anything different, though, Laura. Would you?'

'Not sure. I'm on the fence.'

'Well, let's get some lunch and you can give me all the school gossip. I've missed it!'

Cath's been my friend and confidante since we both qualified ten years ago. We were over the moon when we both got jobs together at St Jude's (until we realised that they were biting our hands off to go and work there!) Then two years ago she became ill and ended up having to leave. I was so upset about it, I thought about leaving myself. It's a tough school and you need friends to keep your sanity (except for Noel, who seems to be Teflon-coated). She's in remission now and ready to go back to work, although not to St Jude's. She probably needs somewhere less challenging. A quieter, calmer environment.

'Any luck on the job front?' I asked her when we sat down again.

'I've got an interview tomorrow, actually. Teaching French to primary school kids.'

'That sounds ideal.'

'I have to get it yet! Anyway, things are going in the right direction. Matt got a promotion too. I told him, next year we're going somewhere really amazing for our trip away.'

'You deserve it Cath; something exciting to look forward to.'

'What about you?'

'Well, I'm going up to the wilds of Scotland for a couple of weeks. Hebrides. Just on my own. I thought I'd start working on the book…'

'Ah, yes, *The Book*. Has it got a title yet?'

'No.'

'Well, you'll get some inspiration hopefully. Sounds a very romantic location. Is Otto going?'

'Oh, I hadn't thought about that. I suppose so. I'll have to ask them if I can bring him. I'm not sure if I've done the right thing, now. It feels a bit impulsive. I've had to organise a dog-walker for him while I'm at work.'

'Are you really going to keep him, Laura?'

'I don't know what else to do at the moment. It's quite nice to have someone to come home to at the end of the day, even if it's only a dog.'

'Well, we need to work on that,' said Cath.

'As long as you don't set me up with any more gym bunnies or OCD nutters.'

'That's not fair, Laura! You were the one who said you wanted someone fit. I was responding to your specific requirements.' Cath grinned.

'I just wanted someone fitter than Henry, who was lazy and lived on pizza and Chocopuffs.'

'Well, I thought Jason was rather gorgeous. I don't know what you were complaining about, Laura. Most women would chop their own arm off for a few hours with an Adonis like that.'

'He thought carrots grew on trees, Cath.'

'Well, you could have overlooked his lack of observational skills…'

'And then there was Fanatical Farouk…'

'How was I supposed to know he was fanatical – he seemed normal to me when I met him at Matt's work do. I knew he cycled everywhere, but it didn't occur to me he had a problem. If I'd known he wore his cycling gear to bed, I wouldn't have suggested he asked you out.'

'Haven't you ever been in his flat, Cath?'

'No. Why would I go to his flat? I don't make a habit of visiting Matt's workmates at their homes, you know!'

'Well, if you had, you would have known what a complete saddo he is. Everything in his place has a bicycle on it, including the toilet roll holder.'

'But he was fit, Laura! You can't deny that.'

'There's 'fit', and there's 'obsessed', Cath. He had a peddle exerciser next to his bed, and who the hell has a duvet cover with a massive photo of Bradley Wiggins on it!'

'Oh my God, Laura, that was *soooooo* funny. I nearly wet myself when you told me that the first time.'

'Well, just don't organise any more blind dates for me. I'm quite capable of arranging my own disasters, thanks very much!'

'Now you're spoiling my fun, Laura!'

'The Scottish Islands will be very therapeutic for me.'

'Well, I must say, I'm quite jealous. Two weeks of not having to think about anyone else, surrounded by stunning scenery and time to be all creative, all alone. Sounds like bliss to me!'

I should be feeling excited about my trip but being 'all alone' isn't really what I was dreaming of a month ago. I suppose I was hoping the Elliott thing would turn out to be more of an actual relationship. In the end it's just been a string of dinner dates with nothing substantial keeping it together. Ever since Henry and I broke up six years ago, I just can't seem to click with anyone. And now it's going to be really difficult with my mother getting more reliant on me. Men will have to go on the back burner, along with hobbies, fun weekends away, and life in general... Which reminds me, I must ask Jenny to be on standby for Mum while I'm up in Scotland.

Around 5pm the doorbell went, setting Otto off.

'Sshhh,' I told him, opening the door.

'I'm here for the key – we spoke yesterday. I'm Gabriel, your friendly dog-walker,' he said, smiling.

'Oh, yes, of course! Sorry, you surprised me! I'll just get it for you.' He made a fuss of Otto before he left and promised to let me know how things went.

'Wow, Otto, things are looking up for both of us! Gabriel seems very nice, doesn't he? And good-looking too. Probably spoken for, though, so don't get too excited, Laura. Mind you, how I'm going to conduct any sort of love-life with a demented mother to look after is anyone's guess.'

CHAPTER 3

'Did you see Evelyn's notice, Laura?' said Dan, catching up with me in the corridor.

'No, I was just on my way to get a coffee…'

'I'll get one too. There's an emergency meeting in the staffroom in fifteen minutes.'

'I wonder what that's about then?'

'No idea, but she looked like thunder earlier.'

Last time we had an emergency staff meeting was a month ago. Gareth had found ten packets of weed in the boys' toilet block, hidden in one of the cisterns. We all had to go on drug awareness training, AGAIN.

'What do you reckon it is, then?' said Dan.

'Who knows! Were you caught smoking again, behind the science block?'

'Haha, very funny! I've given up, by the way.'

'How long?'

'A week. I'm chewing these things instead.' Dan showed me a pack of gum.'

'If you can keep that up through exam time, I'll be really impressed. By the way, Dan, what did you do with the rubber doll?'

'Not so loud,' he said, as some Year 10 girls went past. 'I put it in the cleaner's cupboard,' he whispered in my ear.

'You what!'

'Ssshhh!'

'Dan, that's asking for trouble!'

'Well, I had to put it somewhere.'

'Where is it now, then?'

'No idea. I looked on Monday morning and it was gone.'

We made our way back to the staffroom and found a couple of empty seats next to Fay.

'I could do without this,' she said, - 'I've got lesson prep to do. I hope she keeps it short.'

We heard Evelyn's heels clacking down the corridor and waited for the door to swing open.

'Right, everyone, listen up. There has been a serious breach of security within the school premises.' Evelyn looked round at us all, her eyes appearing bigger than usual behind the thick lenses of her glasses. 'On Monday morning I arrived at my office at around 8am, and when I got there, I discovered my door was unlocked and my chair was occupied.'

We all looked at each other.

'What's she talking about?' I said to Fay.

'I was both shocked and disgusted to find *this* sitting at my desk…' Evelyn beckoned someone to enter the room. From behind the door appeared some pink feet, followed by the rest of the body being carried sideways by Gareth. It had lost some air but had gained a painted-on toothbrush moustache. He set it down beside Evelyn.

'Oh my God! I don't think I can keep a straight face,' whispered Fay.

'Don't look at it,' I said, - 'or anyone in the room.' I clocked quite a few members of staff struggling to stop themselves from laughing.

'I'm going to lose it…'

'No, Fay, think of something horrible or sad…'

'Like *that,* you mean…'

'Sssshh,' said Evelyn. 'I know some of you think this is funny, but I can assure you, I do not. If anyone in this room knows anything about this, please come and see me ASAP.' She marched stiffly out of the room with Gareth shuffling behind her carrying the offensive toy. Everyone managed to keep it in for about 10 seconds, until Fay burst out laughing, followed by almost everyone else.

'Oh, God, I can't believe she just did that!' said Fay, tears streaming down her face.

'Was it you?' I said to Dan, straight away.

'No! It wasn't! What sort of person do you think I am, Laura?'

'Who do you think did it, then?'

'Well, no one except the cleaners has a key to her office, do they? So, I'm guessing it was one of them.'

'There's a key in the main office, Dan. It could have been a member of staff, but I think it's more likely to be one of the kids, don't you?'

'They would have had to get a key and sneak back in after the staff had all gone home.'

'Well, whoever it was we'll probably never find out. Another unresolved mystery to add to the long list. I don't have time to ponder on it, anyway – my chemistry class awaits,' said Fay, drying her eyes. 'That was the best bit of entertainment since my father's wig blew off on the Helter-Skelter at Brighton last year.'

The sad thing is, Evelyn actually thinks it was one of us! I know there are some members of staff who can be a bit childish, but I honestly don't think any of them would pull a stunt like that. Bloody funny, though! I would feel sorry for her if she wasn't so miserable all the time.

'Have you seen what they're doing in the main corridor?' said Fay at lunch time.

'I saw a couple of men up ladders.'

'They're installing CCTV, Laura.'

'Oh, I see. Big Sister will be watching our every move, now.'

'Well, as long as she doesn't put it in here,' said Fay.

'I know who would be particularly annoyed if she did.'

'Noel?'

'Yes! How did you guess! He spends more time sitting doing crosswords and reading his newspaper than actually teaching.'

'I suppose that's one of the perks of being a part timer. To be honest, I'm quite envious!'

'By the way, Fay, has Morag buttonholed you yet?'

'No…'

'Well, beware. She's on the prowl for staff to join her stress-buster circle at lunchtimes on Thursdays.'

'I don't think I could fit it in, anyway.'

'It's only twenty minutes. You never know, Fay, it might do you good!'

'Are you going, then?'

'Well, Morag said she thought I was tense. I think she might be right. I've decided to try and be less negative about all that crystal healing stuff she goes on about. Anyway, I can just ignore that part - as you know, I'm a committed cynic, but I don't mind a few visualisation exercises and a bit of soothing music...'

'And what, or who would you be visualising about, then?'

'You're supposed to imagine yourself floating on a lilo in the sea, or lying in a summer meadow, listening to birdsong. You know the kind of thing, Fay.'

'I'd be visualising my lunch and a big glass of wine.'

'It doesn't matter what you think about, does it? As long as it works for you.'

'I tell you what would really work for me – a romantic liaison with Denzel Washington on a beach in Bora Bora.'

'Come on, then, it'll be a laugh.'

'Well, I suppose it would take our minds off teaching for a bit.'

My Year 10 class were tricky this morning. Denise and Chloe were sitting together giggling and distracting the class. As usual, I separated them.

'Miss, that's so unfair,' moaned Denise. 'We weren't doing nothing.'

'It's 'we weren't doing *anything,*' I said.

Denise gave me a pitying look, sighed heavily and sat down noisily in the spare chair at the front of the class, where I had to spend the next forty minutes looking at her miserable expression, and terrible eyebrows. *Why do they do that to themselves?*

'Right, please continue: Act 1 Scene 7…'

Fergus Garbet was about halfway through Macbeth's momentous soliloquy, when one of the boys let off and the whole class erupted. When I went to open the windows, Chloe Stevens thought it was funny to shout: 'We can see up your dress, Miss!' causing even more of a furore. I took a deep breath, banged my copy of the play on the desk to get their attention, and gave them a lecture about Shakespeare's legacy, which fell on deaf ears of course.

'This play is about all the things you love,' I said, hoping to inspire them. 'It's about murder, intrigue, betrayal, passionate love…It's about the power of persuasion and the destructive consequences of jealousy and ambition. It's a tragedy of epic proportions. Now, where were we before we were so rudely interrupted…Fergus, carry on, please.'

He tried again: '…*upon the sightless couriers of the air shall blow the horrid deed in every eye…*'

At the end of the class, I held William back and tried to talk to him about his lack of completed homework.

'Why aren't you doing your homework, William?'

'Dunno.'

'Well, you won't do very well next year in your GCSE's if you don't make an effort. Don't you want to do well?' William shrugged, and looked at his feet.

'I'm sure your parents want you to do well, and so do I. Is there anything you'd like to ask me about? I can help you if you're stuck with anything.'

He shook his head.

'What do you know about William Parsons?' I asked Ray at the end of the day.

'Quite clever. He was in my class last year.'

'Did he hand in homework?'

'Sometimes. Why?'

'Evelyn has asked me to keep an eye on him. I wondered if you might be able to do the same?'

'OK, I'll see what I can do.'

As I walked home, I got another message from Elliott:

'BTW forgot to say can't meet up this weekend – 7k mudathon. You should try it! I'll sign you up for the next one! x (hysterical laughing emoji)'

I found a note from Gabriel on the kitchen top when I got home:

Hi Laura!

Great walk with Otto. He's really good fun.

Got on fine with the other dogs.

It'll be no problem taking him out.

G. 😊

'Sounds like you had a lovely time, Otto! Pity I couldn't come too! I'd much rather go for a walk with you and the rather attractive Gabriel, than be in that madhouse they call 'school'.'

Suddenly, there was a knock at the door which made me jump.

'Cath! What are you doing here?'

'Well, I know it's a work night, but I wanted to celebrate! I've brought wine.'

'You got the job?'

'Guessed it in one!'

I got out two glasses. 'Brilliant news, Cath!'

'So, have you ditched Elliott yet?'

'Um, no.' Just as I said this, my phone pinged with another message from him.

'What does it say, Laura?'

I read it out: '*Are you Ok? Am thinking you've fallen off a cliff… call me!*'

'No time like the present.'

'I should speak to him directly – it's a bit off to send a text, isn't it?'

'No one wants drawn-out goodbyes, Laura. He probably wouldn't bother, would he?'

I typed back:

'*Hi! I've been thinking things over and decided not to continue with this relationship. Sorry Elliott. No hard feelings. All the best L x*'

'It's a bit stark,' I said, looking at it.

'Give it here,' said Cath, grabbing my phone and pressing 'send'. 'Now, let's celebrate!'

CHAPTER 4

'I had a word with William,' said Ray on the way into school on Thursday morning.

'Oh, good.'

'Couldn't get anything out of him, though.'

'Oh, well, thanks for trying. Do you think he's got problems at home?'

'I have no idea, Laura. To be honest, I've got a lot on with exams coming up. I don't really have time to investigate any further.'

I decided on a whim to put Harry's poem up on Evelyn's board and take the consequences. I knew some of the staff would appreciate it. I wasn't really prepared for Evelyn's rather extreme response, though.

'Laura,' she said, stalking into my classroom before class started, - 'what on earth do you think you're doing putting this up?' She was flapping Harry's poem about as if it was a dirty rag.

'Well, I thought it was rather good, Evelyn.' I tried to stand my ground.

'I don't care how 'good' it is. It's crude, Laura. We don't encourage vulgarity at St Jude's. There's more than enough of that sort of thing going on everywhere else. I am trying to the best of my ability, to drag this school OUT of the gutter, not put it back there!'

At morning coffee break, I mentioned it to some of the other staff members.

'She's really got the hump this week!' said Dan. 'After the porno doll incident, she's on the warpath. You should have waited till she calmed down…'

'I suppose you're right. Oh, well – I'll have to keep a low profile for a bit!'

'By the way, Laura – would you sponsor me? I'm doing a charity mudathon this weekend.'

'I think my ex might be doing that.'

'I'll look out for him. What does he look like?'

'Six foot two, short blond hair, fit…'

'Sounds like my type!'

'You've got no chance, Dan. He's strictly hetero. Anyway, he's a bit of an arse, so I wouldn't recommend him.'

'Like I said, sounds like my type…'

'Dan, be quiet!'

At lunch time Fay and I just made it in time to Morag's class.

'Right, now everyone's here,' she said, slightly sarcastically, - 'take a mat and lie down. Don't worry if you can't do some of the stretches,' Morag said, looking at me and Fay, - 'just do your best.' She was in her element, instructing us all. 'This breathing exercise will help you to heal those chakras, people,' she said, counting while we took lots of deep breaths. Whilst lying there, in the Corpse pose, I drifted off and was in the land of nod in no time.

'Laura, wake up!' Fay was thumping me on my arm. 'Morag's finished.'

'Oh, sorry, was it good?'

'It was until you started snoring,' said Fay, sniggering.

'You need to work on your Drishti,' said Morag, as everyone was leaving.

'My what?'

'Your third eye is clouded – you're unable to focus, Laura.'

'What should I do?'

'Get rid of those negative toxins. Meditation will help. You need to supercharge your blocked chakras. Why don't you come along to my evening class? You would really benefit. I can feel your negative energy – your Chi just isn't flowing well at all. In fact, it's stagnating. You can practice what we did here today, at home. Here's something to help…' She gave me a box of incense sticks and some Patchouli oil.

She's probably right. My ***life*** *has stagnated, never mind my Chi. I've been doing the same job for years. I've had a string of shallow, one-dimensional boyfriends and I'm not doing anything meaningful. I'm not getting any younger, either. No wonder my chakras are blocked – it's my own fault. I need to focus, like Morag said. I hate to say it, but* *she's absolutely right. I need to grasp the nettle, bite the bullet, take the bull by the horns. Basically, I need to decide what I want from life and be more proactive about achieving it. But what is this elusive '****it****', and how will I know when I've found it?*

There was another note from Gabriel when I got home:

Hi!

We went down to the river today. Otto had a great time. He really loves swimming, doesn't he! I had quite a hard time getting him to come back. Maybe I could do some individual training with him to improve his recall. What do you think? No pressure at all – just a thought.

G. ☺

'Well, Otto, what do you think about that? Shall I give him a call? I mean, it can't harm, can it!'

Friday has come around superfast, thank goodness! Another message from Elliott last night has put me in an agitated frame of mind, though. I'm not sure what to make of it, apart from finding it extremely irritating:

'Hi Laura, just to say no hard feelings either! I'm fine with it - tbh, I've been seeing someone else, so it's all good! Elliott x (big grinning emoji)

'What a tosser!' said Fay, when I showed her, at break time.

'I suppose I had half an idea he was not being honest with me, anyway. I'm not going to let him bother me, Fay. I'm going to take Morag's advice and really think about what I want from life.'

'Well, in the meantime we've got a staff meeting at lunchtime, so don't forget to turn up this time.'

'What's this one about?'

'Exam planning – the usual stuff.'

'Urggh. I don't know how I got through last year. It's so stressful. You spend all year trying to motivate these kids to do their best and then something always goes wrong. Last year six of them didn't even show up from my class.'

'It could be worse, Laura. My cousin works in a school in north London. What goes on there would make your hair stand on end. He says he barely manages to teach them anything – never mind crowd control, it's all about self-defence there. Every day is a battle to survive flying missiles, foul-mouthed insults and gang fights. He told me last week that two boys threw all the exercise books out of the window, while he was talking to another teacher outside the classroom. And the week before, someone locked their teacher in a store cupboard, and she was stuck there until the cleaners came in on Saturday morning.'

'How on earth do they keep their staff?'

'They don't. Every second one is a supply teacher. Anyway, my point is, things aren't too bad here, are they?'

'Well, not if you are comparing crocodiles and alligators!' Noel butted in.

'And how are your little hatchlings, Noel?' I asked.

'Same as usual. Mostly active at night and asleep during the day. Occasionally one of them comes to life when they spy a tasty morsel. Most of them are only interested in impressing the opposite sex. Did you know that the male alligator's penis is permanently erect?'

'Er, no, Noel, we didn't.' Fay raised her eyebrows.

'Thanks for that most interesting fact, Noel. I'm sure it will come in useful one day.'

'Animals are fascinating, Laura. Much more interesting than humans.' He went back to reading his book.

'Have you got your dress yet?' asked Fay.

'Dress?'

'You know, for the Ball.'

'Oh, no I haven't. Have you?'

'No. Let's go tomorrow. I could do with your opinion.'

'What about Scott?'

Fay snorted. 'You *are* joking, aren't you? He's as much use as a chocolate fireguard when it comes to shopping for clothes.'

'OK, that'll be fun. We can have lunch out.'

'Have you had any luck finding someone for your Mum?'

'Only one so far.'

'Any good?'

'I don't know – I'll ring her back this weekend. She sounded a bit odd…'

'What do you mean?'

'Well, she said she would have to bring her friend, Betty, with her to Mum's, as she goes everywhere with her.'

'That sounds a bit strange.'

'There's nought so strange as folk,' I said, directing my eyes at Noel, who was sitting reading his paper, oblivious.

Fay smiled. 'It takes all sorts to make a world.'

'It certainly does. Right, I've got class in five minutes. See you at lunchtime.'

My year 9 class were surprisingly well-behaved for once. That was until the fire alarm suddenly went off and all hell broke loose.

'FILE OUT IN A CALM AND SENSIBLE MANNER,' I shouted, to an already half-empty classroom.

'Is it a drill?' I asked Ray on my way passed his classroom.

'No. There's a fire in the school kitchen.'

In the playground, I quickly counted the kids in my class, once I'd yelled at them to get in line. One was missing.

'It's Jake Wilson, Miss,' said one of the girls.

'Damn it!' I said. 'Where the hell is he?'

'I'll go and look for him,' said Dan. 'Keep an eye on my lot, please.'

Evelyn came out, blowing her whistle very loudly and more than was necessary, in my view.

After ten minutes, Dan reappeared. 'I can't find him anywhere,' he said.

'OK, kids, any ideas? This is really important,' I said to them. They all looked at each other.

'He said he wasn't well yesterday, Miss.'

'Could he have gone to sick bay?'

They all looked a bit blank.

'He isn't in today, Miss,' said one of them.

'For goodness' sake!' I said, rolling my eyes. 'OK, we've got everyone, then.' This was just in time for Evelyn to come along and check the register.

'Phew!' I said to Dan, when she'd moved on. 'I've already blotted my copybook once this week.'

'What did you do now?'

'Well, one of my kids wrote this really good poem – only it wasn't very PC. I put it up on the Highlights board anyway. Evelyn didn't really appreciate his mastery of the iambic tetrameter construct, or the social realism of his chosen subject matter.'

'I'm not sure I would, either…'

'I'm not going to let it get me down, though, Dan. I've made a promise to myself to try and rise above negativity.'

'Good for you!'

'Yes, life's too short for dwelling on things that go wrong.'

Evelyn blew her whistle to indicate everyone could go back inside.

There wasn't much time left of the lesson, so I decided to go round asking each of them what they wanted to do when they were older. I got a few silly comments from the usual suspects:

'Drug Lord,' said Riley Munro.

'Wizzard,' said Blake Harness.

'Horse Whisperer,' said Adelle Clarke.

'Zombie,' said Lizzie Fisk.

'Rich Bastard,' said Riley.

There was uproar in the classroom.

'OK, calm down, you lot. Now what do you think all these things have in common?'

'They're all stupid,' said Barny Russell.

'Apart from that? I'll tell you – all jobs require you to have good reading and written English. You need to be able to communicate effectively. You have to be able to fill in job application forms and later, you need to be able to understand your tax and household bills so you can pay for things without getting into financial difficulties…'

'Like Barny, Miss. He owes me a fiver!' piped up Charlie Taylor. 'He told me he'd pay me back ages ago!'

'It was *your* idea to prank Mrs Ferrier,' shouted Barny, across the room, at Charlie.

'No, it wasn't!'

'YES! IT WAS!'

'That's enough,' I said. 'Why don't you agree to go fifty fifty…'

Charlie thought for a moment. 'OK, but he *has* to pay me back on Monday.'

'OK, deal,' said Barny, reluctantly.

'Right, can we get back to the subject of 'effective communication'?' I smiled at them, but they looked at me blankly.

'Can anyone tell me what *elucidation* means?'

'Miss, Miss, I know!' said Ollie Drabble, putting his hand up. 'It's what happens when people smoke drugs and stuff.'

I was saved by the bell.

'Quick, Laura,' said Fay as we went into the staffroom, - 'grab something before the best fillings go.' Evelyn had provided the usual spread of uninspiring sandwiches and fruit for the meeting.

Morag grabbed a paper plate and filled it with fruit. 'I'm a vegan,' she said when Dan pulled a face. 'You should try it, Dan. Maybe you wouldn't look so knackered all the time!'

'Look at Noel,' said Fay, to me, pointing. 'He's so funny. He's got his own lunch box. He won't touch school food.'

'Why?'

'He says it's contaminated with what he calls the school's 'aroma'.'

'What's that supposed to mean?'

'He says it tastes of cheesy socks and floor polish.'

'Oh…' I put my cheese and ham sandwich back down on my plate. 'I think I've lost my appetite.'

'Sorry,' grinned Fay.

Evelyn's heels made their presence known, and the door swung open. She had the look of a prison guard on a bad day.

'Don't poke the bear,' whispered Dan.

'Well, I suppose it was the usual drill,' said Ray, when it was all over.

'Apart from the bit where she said we all have to be here an hour earlier EVERY day from next week.'

'You'll have to learn to stop burning the candle at both ends, Laura!' said Ray.

'I should be so lucky! I'm just not a morning person, Ray. And I've got to walk Otto before school.'

'Ah, I see. Well, as Aristotle said, we all have to make sacrifices for the greater good.'

'Yeah, well, Aristotle didn't have to do his own washing, cooking, cleaning or dog-walking…'

'No, he had his slave women to do all of that. Things have moved on a bit since 350BC.'

'I'm not sure if they have, Ray.'

'Ah, well, roll on the summer holidays, eh? By the way, could you take my class on Tuesday, please? I've got the afternoon off.'

'Have I got a choice?'

'Not really! Sorry! I'll take one of yours for a swap. That's fair, isn't it?'

'It would be if it actually happened.'

'It will, I promise! Right, must go.'

'You let him walk all over you,' said Fay when he'd gone.

'I know. I need to go on assertiveness training or something. He owes me at least five Tuesday covers. It's not in my nature to be confrontational.'

'Just say 'no',' said Fay.

'It's not that simple. I've tried. Somehow he always gets round me.'

When I arrived home, I got my usual mad greeting from Otto, who jumped up furiously wagging his tail. After I'd taken him to the park and fed him, I settled reluctantly down to some Year 8 marking. Around 7pm, the doorbell rang, and I remembered I'd invited Mum's only job applicant round.

'Hi, my name Mrs Wang,' said a little middle-aged woman, when I opened the door. 'I here for clean job…'

'Oh, yes, come in.'

'Is OK to bring dog?'

'Yes,' I said, looking round for it.

'She here!' She pointed at her chest. A tiny little ginger face appeared from beneath her cardigan.

'What sort of dog is it?'

'Chihuahua,' said Mrs Wang. 'She call Betty.'

'Ah, I see…'

'She not any trouble.'

'Do you think she'll play with my dog, Otto?'

'Maybe, as long as Otto not eat her!' said Mrs Wang, very solemnly.

Luckily, it was fine. Otto was delighted to have a new friend.

'So, Mrs Wang, this job is not just a cleaning job. I also need someone to keep an eye on my mother – you see, she's getting a bit forgetful in her old age...'

Mrs Wang looked at me quizzically. 'You no need cleaner?'

'Yes, we do, but my mother lives by herself and she is not very good at looking after herself now she is older.'

'Ah, yes, I see. But old horse know better the way home…'

'Sorry?'

'Old Chinese proverb! It mean old person wise and more knowledgeable.'

'It doesn't quite work in this case though. My Mum has dementia, you see…'

Mrs Wang shook her head and frowned. 'In China we fight demon with peach stick. I can help you...'

'Oh, no, you don't understand – not demons – she has an illness…'

'Ah, I make her chicken noodle soup – it very good - make her feel better!' She smiled and I noticed she had several teeth missing.

After she'd left, I wondered if I'd done the right thing hiring her. She's certainly a bit eccentric, but she seemed very nice. I don't know what my mother will make of her. Still, you never know until you try something, how it will turn out. It will be nice for my Mum to have a regular visitor. I hope she doesn't take offence at me arranging a housekeeper. Mrs Wang agreed to meet me there tomorrow afternoon for her first introduction. I'm crossing all my fingers and toes.

I rang my mother to tell her the good news. 'I'm coming round to see you tomorrow afternoon, Mum.'

'Oh, good. Can you bring me some lettuce?'

'OK. I'm bringing someone to meet you, Mum. She's called Mrs Wang.'

'Mrs who?'

'Wang.'

'That's a funny name.'

'It's Chinese. Anyway, it's no funnier than ours, Mum.'

'There's nothing wrong with 'Blewitt' – it's a very old established English name. Very distinguished. It goes back centuries.'

'Well, you try teaching a bunch of teenagers with a name like ours. It's made my life *very* difficult I can tell you!'

You can imagine what a field day the kids have had over the years with my name, can't you! If I'd known how bad it could get, I don't think I would have gone into teaching. I was so naïve! When you apply to become a teacher, they should warn you about these things. Poor old Dan should definitely have thought twice before becoming a teacher with a name like 'Longbottom'. Mind you, kids will make something out of anything. Fay told me she heard some of them call her 'Gromit' the other day. When I looked perplexed, she reminded me her name is Cheeseman. It's a bit of a stretch, but kids will do anything to knock you off your pedestal! She can't complain, though – my nicknames are far worse. 'Blue-tits' is the least offensive of them.

CHAPTER 5

My phone pinged with a message while I was making a cup of coffee. I had a lazy breakfast with a good book in mind this morning. Surprisingly, it was from Elliott:

'Hi! Wish me luck! Just met your teacher mate from school. He's a right laugh! Gave me all the goss! Hahaha!! You never told me what the kids called you – you should use that as your Twitter handle!!!' (4 hysterical-laughing emojis, followed by 2 blue balls)

'Right, I'm blocking you, Elliott Guthrie, you complete prick!'

I messaged Dan: *'Please don't tell my prat of an ex-boyfriend anything else about me if you want to live!'*

Honestly, I thought Dan would have more sense than that! He doesn't even know Elliott! I can't believe he told him. Just goes to show, you can't trust men to behave properly – they are *so* puerile. Thank goodness I'm going out with Fay today. I'm really looking forward to it. But first I have to persuade my mother to agree to Mrs Wang's services. This could be tricky.

'Right, Otto,' I told him after breakfast, - 'it's a quick walk round the block today. I'm a busy woman, I'm afraid, but I promise I'll make it up to you later.'

At my mother's I was half an hour early, just to get her used to the idea of a stranger coming to visit.

'She's very nice, Mum, you'll like her,' I said. 'I've checked her references. She seems ideal.'

'Why is she coming?'

'I just told you. She's going to do some cleaning and tidying,' I said, looking round at the messy lounge. 'By the way, Mum, why have you put potatoes on all the windowsills?'

'They keep your windows from fogging up, Laura. I saw it on *How Clean is Your House* last week.'

'I think you are meant to cut them in half and rub the juice on the window…'

'What? Well, I'm not going to waste a perfectly good potato doing that with it!'

'I'll make us a nice cup of tea, shall I?'

'Oh, yes, that'll be lovely. Did you bring some lettuce?'

'No, sorry Mum, I forgot.'

'Well, we can't have tea without lettuce…'

I went to the fridge and discovered it was milk she was out of. 'I'll text Mrs Wang and ask her to get some.'

'Mrs who?'

'Mrs Wang, your new cleaning lady.'

'I don't need a cleaner, Laura. I can manage perfectly well.'

'Mum, you've put all the dirty dishes back in the cupboards,' I said, going to get two cups out.

'Well, I don't know how that happened,' said my Mum. 'It must have been my new cleaning lady. I told you not to get anyone.'

'How could she, when she hasn't even been here yet?'

'She doesn't sound very reliable, Laura…'

When Mrs Wang came, I was a bit worried about how my mother would react, but it went better than expected.

'My name Doreen,' said Mrs Wang. 'Please, you call me Doreen.'

'Oh, that was my mother's name!' said Mum.

I left them to chat and had a look round the house. If there was any doubt about my Mum needing help, it was quickly dispelled. In the bathroom, I found 20 packs of loo roll stacked up in the bath. I went to look in the cupboard and found 10 more. In her bedroom, there was a huge pile of clothes including hangers, on her bed. I looked in her wardrobe and sure enough, there was another mountain of loo rolls filling every corner.

I rang my sister.

'Jenny, look at this!' I said, slightly tearfully. 'She's gone mad!' I said, showing her Mum's excessive loo roll collection.

'Maybe she's just worried she'll run out,' said Jenny.

'This is serious, Jenny!'

'No, well, what do you want me to do about it?'

'I don't know. We need to stop her going shopping…'

'Good luck with that! She's always been a compulsive shopper, Laura. It'll be impossible. Did you get someone to help her?'

'Yes, they're chatting now. She's called Doreen Wang. She seems OK.'

'Well, look Laura, I need to go, but let me know how it works out.'

'What are you up to today?'

'Just a country outing with a friend…'

'A 'friend'?'

'Oh, all right, I've got a new chap, if you must know. He's called Jack.'

'And?'

'I haven't got time to go into details, Laura. He's an investment banker: No ex-wives, no kids, no dark secrets, seems solvent.'

'Sounds perfect, Jenny,' I said. *Typical of Jenny to find a rich man with no baggage.*

'We'll see. Anyway, I've only been seeing him for a few weeks.'

'Well, have a nice time this afternoon.'

'I will. And try not to worry about Mum too much. Bye.'

Of course, what she really means, is 'don't worry HER *about Mum!' She's conveniently miles away with her new love-life going on and she's not going to want to get involved unless she's forced to. She's always been like that. When we were little, she was an expert at wriggling out of her responsibilities. I'll never forget the time she was supposed to be looking after next door's cat while they were on holiday. She bribed me with bubble gum to do it for her. I found out years later she was paid handsomely by them,* AND *they bought her a present! That's typical of my sister, though. She hasn't changed much – last Christmas she'd agreed to have Mum and me over but at the last minute she cancelled it, saying she wasn't well. She admitted later that she'd been invited to go skiing in St Moritz with some of her glamorous friends. I sometimes wonder if she's really my sister…*

'Look,' said Mum, when I went back downstairs, - 'Doreen's got a little dog! Isn't she sweet!'

'She is!'

'I had a dog once,' said Mum, to Mrs Wang, - 'called Otto. I don't know what happened to him. Some terrible dog-thief took him one day – in broad daylight! Can you believe it!'

'I've got him, Mum. He's safe with me at the flat.'

'Oh, thank goodness you found him.' said Mum, - 'What a relief!'

Mrs Wang has agreed to go to Mum's three times a week and take her shopping once a week. She seemed to understand what she might be dealing with, when she saw me re-loading the dishwasher with stuff from the cupboards and removing all the potatoes from around the house.

'Not to worry, Laura. I keep good eyes on your Mum.' She smiled, got into her bright blue Nissan Micra, and disappeared down the road. I turned and looked at my mother's little semi with its slightly neglected front garden and wondered how much longer she'd be able to stay there. I didn't want to think about it. My mother's been there for over 40 years.

'Oh God!' I said to Fay, in the changing rooms at *Favola's*, 'I look like a sausage in a tutu…'

'Mm,' she said, looking me up and down. 'Agreed.'

'I need to lose at least a stone to wear anything like this!' I looked at myself in the mirror. What has happened to me in the last year? How did I go up two dress sizes without even noticing?

'We'll find something more, um…generous. More your style,' she said, tactfully.

'What do you think of this?' she said, posing in front of the mirror. Her hourglass figure looked stunning in the fitted gold lamé dress.

'Beautiful! The Cowl neck really suits you, Fay. And it looks great with your afro hair. You look a million dollars!'

'It's a done deal, then,' she said, happily. 'Now it's your turn.'

I must have tried on every dress in the shop, until eventually I settled on something simple.

'Black is a very good choice for someone like you,' said the shop assistant, - 'and the tummy-flattening panel is nice and discreet with this front ruffle hiding it,' she said, tugging it in place. I saw Fay trying not to laugh.

'It's a bit low-cut,' I said.

'That's a good thing,' said the assistant. 'It will take the eyes away from this area,' she said, waving her hand in the general direction of my middle. Fay sniggered.

'Thanks, friend!' I said, as we left the shop.

'I'm sorry, Laura, but that was pretty funny! Anyway, you did look great in that dress – especially the top half.'

'Hahaha.'

'Now for shoes, bags and accessories,' said Fay, enthusiastically. 'We're going to knock 'em dead!'

'I don't know who I'm going to take,' I said, as we perused the accessories in Hancock's.

'Not Elliott, then?'

'No, he's cooked his goose.'

'I might know someone…'

'No, thanks Fay, but my friend Cath keeps trying to set me up, and you know how awful most of those dates were.'

Back at the flat, Otto was overjoyed to see me, having been on his own all afternoon. I threw my bags on the bed and took him out for a walk.

It was really busy at the park, with lots of other dogs for Otto to play with. I let him off the lead so he could run free and sat on a bench soaking up the afternoon sun.

'Helloooo…' said a voice in my ear, jolting me awake.

'Oh, cripes, I must have nodded off!' I said, looking round frantically for Otto.

'It's OK – I've got him,' said Gabriel, smiling.

'Thank goodness! Oh, I feel terrible now! The sun was so nice and warm. I only closed my eyes for a moment…I don't usually do that,' I said. *A voice in my head guiltily reminded me of Morag's yoga class.* 'What time is it?' I shielded my eyes from the sun, as I tried to look at his face. He sat down next to me and removed his sunglasses and I found myself staring at his pale smoky-grey eyes for just a little too long.

'6:00pm,' said Gabriel, still smiling.

'I've been really busy at work,' I said. 'It's quite stressful at the moment…'

'Oh, don't worry, we all get tired sometimes.' He grinned again.

'I didn't realise how late it was. I'd better get Otto home and give him his tea,' I said, - 'plus I've got piles of stuff to get through - books to mark, papers to assess, reports to complete…'

'Sounds like you're a very busy person…'

'I am…well, quite busy…at the moment…you know how it is!'

'Not really. I'm not busy. Particularly at the moment – I'm not busy at all, actually,' he said, giving me a sideways look.

'I meant work-wise…'

Ah, well, I'm between jobs right now. Dog-walking is just a temporary thing. Don't get me wrong – I really enjoy doing it. It gets me out of the house, and I meet some interesting people…' He flashed me another easy smile.

'So, what do you normally do, then?' I tried to deflect his slightly flirtatious remark and reverted to chit-chat, trying to pretend what was happening here wasn't happening.

He was about to tell me, when three very excited black Labradors charged up to him and he took the opportunity to put them all on their leads.

'These are some of Otto's companions,' he told me. 'Fritz, Cleo and Monty. Cleo is my dog,' he said, giving her a hearty pat. 'I'd better let you get on, then. Give me a ring about Otto's training, won't you? I'd be happy to spend some extra time with him. Maybe you could come too?'

Before I'd had time to say anything else, he'd gone. I sat on the bench for a bit longer, still inhaling the smell of the Armani aftershave I vaguely recognised, and wondered if he was married or not. I'd glanced at his left hand while we talked, and noticed he wasn't wearing a ring, and he hadn't mentioned a girlfriend or a wife…

When I got home, there was a message from my mother:

'It was lovely to see you today, dear, but I'm not sure about your friend. She said she wants to take me to see a 'doctor of pins', Laura. It sounds very unpleasant. Why would anyone have pins put into their head? I don't like the sound of it… And she said she is going to put roots in my tea. She showed me a photo – it looked like parsnips, Laura. I don't want parsnips in my tea…'

I called her back. 'Hello, Mum! I got your message.'

'You weren't in…'

'No, I was out shopping with my friend Fay. We're going to a dance next month. I needed to buy a dress.'

'I would have come with you if you'd asked me,' said my mother, sounding slightly disappointed. (*I was instantly transported back to my youth when shopping for clothes with my mother was a difficult and disappointing experience. She definitely wouldn't approve of my rather racy frock, and even less of the shoes I intend to wear, which are totally impractical and verging on tarty.)*

'What did you buy?'

'Oh, just a plain black wrap-over,' I said. 'Nothing to write home about. Anyway, about Doreen: She's only trying to help you, Mum. I think she's talking about acupuncture – it's really good for you. Lots of people have it done. It's very beneficial…'

'Well, I'm not going to some quack doctor and I'm certainly not drinking anything made with a root vegetable…'

'OK, Mum, no one's going to force you to do anything you don't want to do. Give Doreen a chance though, please? Once you get used to her, you'll like her, I'm sure.'

I hope Mrs Wang is thick-skinned enough to persist with my mother. She was difficult enough ***before*** *she started getting ill.*

CHAPTER 6

'I think she's talking about Ginseng tea,' said Fay, when I told her about the parsnips. 'It tastes awful, mind you. Your mother would probably prefer the parsnips!'

'Oh dear! Well, I'd better warn Mrs Wang not to give her any.'

'Morning, ladies,' said Dan, limping into the staffroom on crutches.

'What happened to you?' I said.

'Bit of a mishap at the mudathon.'

'What's a 'mudathon'?' said Fay.

'It's a marathon with lots of mud involved. Basically, by the time you've completed the course, you look like a clod of earth yourself. Plus, it's one of the most killing thing I've ever done,' said Dan, easing himself into one of the softer chairs.

Fay sniggered. 'I don't know why you do these things to yourself, Dan. It's nothing short of masochism, if you ask me!'

'It's good for the soul,' he responded, wincing as he moved his foot to let Noel go past. 'By the way, I met your boyfriend.'

'He's not my boyfriend, Dan. And thanks for telling him my nickname – really appreciated!' I said, sarcastically.

'On to pastures new, then?' Noel piped up. 'No one has staying power any more, do they? In my day, things were much simpler. Young people now are so flighty – they don't take relationships seriously enough.'

'That's right Noel,' laughed Dan, – 'the good old 'Flower Power' days, when the Summer of Love was youth's dream come true…do you mean those days? I bet you were one of the beautiful people, Noel, weren't you? With your kaftan and beads and acid trips…'

'Not everyone was a hippy, you know, Daniel. Some of us were hard-working ordinary folk who had morals – we knew the difference between right and wrong. Nowadays it seems to be a free-for-all. No one has standards any more.' He sighed and went back to his book.

'What are you reading, Noel?' asked Fay.

'*The End of the World as we Know it,*' said Noel, stonily.

'He's a bundle of laughs today, isn't he?' whispered Dan.

'Well, it *is* Monday,' I said. 'We're entitled to be miserable – there's a whole week of stress and struggle ahead.'

'Talking of which…' said Fay, nodding towards the staffroom door. Evelyn marched in and made a brief but distressing announcement about an impending Ofsted visit the next day. She told us we would be expected to stay two extra hours after school for planning. She looked even more thunderous than usual.

'That's all we need,' said Ray, joining our little group.

'You're not even going to be here tomorrow,' I said. 'Can't you cancel whatever it is? I need you!'

'Sorry, Laura. You'll have to hold the fort, I'm afraid.'

'I had a feeling this week was going to be painful,' said Dan.

'In more ways than one…' I said, watching him limp out of the room.

'Well, Noel,' I said, getting up, - 'that book says it all, doesn't it! I'd better get to my class too. See you all later.'

On my way along the corridor, the Deputy Head, Bryce Colston stopped me. He looked worried.

'Laura, sorry but just a quick question…'

'Yes…'

'Buffet or sit-down?'

'Is this the Ball?'

'Yes. Caterers have pulled out. I'm thinking a buffet would be easier to arrange. Do you know anyone?'

'No. It's a bit short notice, isn't it! How about asking the school kitchen to help?'

'We don't want school dinners, Laura!'

'No…well, what about the cookery teacher, Jean Carter? You could ask her…'

My class took a while to settle, as Bryce made me late.

'Right, I'm handing back your essays. Some were good, some were just OK, and some were non-existent.' I read out a list of pupils who needed to 'see me' after class.

'Aw, Miss, I can't – I've got netball,' said Denise Channing.

'I've got netball too,' piped up Chloe Stevens.

'Don't worry, I've already spoken to Mrs Turner and OK'd it with her.' They both looked seriously hacked off. William Parsons just stared out of the window, Ollie Drabble laughed and jeered at Adam Fisher, but when his own name was read out, he looked surprised.

'But I did do an essay, Miss.'

'Well, Ollie, *you* might call it that, but I beg to differ. An essay requires a beginning, a middle, and an end. Yours, I'm afraid to say, does not conform to that general rule, plus half a page doesn't really cut the mustard.'

It was Adam's turn to jeer at Ollie.

'That's enough! Your homework for next week is to find an example of an essay you really like and write 200 words on why you liked it.'

'Urrgh,' they all groaned.

The staff meeting after school was, as expected, extremely tedious. Despite various people's best efforts, it dragged on until 7pm. An Ofsted inspection is the last thing anyone wants right now, just when we have exams starting. We're already stretched to the limit. It's at times like this when I wonder why on earth I stay in this profession.

When I finally got home in the evening, I decided to bite the bullet and ring Gabriel. We arranged to meet on Wednesday evenings at a field on the edge of town, where Otto wouldn't have too many distractions. I felt strangely exhilarated about the prospect of it. In fact, I felt so pleased with myself that I decided to go to Morag's evening yoga class.

I found the little community hall round the back of the chip shop, just as Morag had described, and joined about six others.

'We're going to start with a relaxing Cactus Position, Laura. No falling asleep this time!'

Morag's students were obviously experienced and accomplished yogis, which made me feel inadequate and very unfit. I stayed at the back where no one could see my red face puffing away.

'I thought yoga was supposed to be gentle exercise,' I said at the end of the session. 'That was quite hard work!' I wiped away the sweat from my face and took a big swig of water.

'That *was* a gentle session. Laura. Next week we'll be ramping things up a bit,' said Morag. 'No pain, no gain!'

The chip shop was extremely tempting, and as I left, it took all my willpower to avoid going in. Especially when I knew all I had waiting for me at home was a ready-meal curry of indeterminate age, a couple of eggs and a stale packet of crackers. I really should go shopping…

'Blimey,' said Cath, when I told her on the phone later, - 'you actually went? I thought you said Morag was a fitness fascist. You said you wouldn't be bullied by someone wearing pink lycra and a matching sweatband…'

'Well, I know, but I've revised my opinion, based on the fact that my expanding waistline isn't helping my self-esteem. Plus, I can't touch my toes any more…'

'Well, I'd join you if I could, but as you know, I'm still in recovery. So, what else is happening? How's school?'

'Terrible. We've got an Ofsted Inspection tomorrow. Evelyn made us all stay two hours after school to get everything ready. I'm on my own tomorrow because Ray is absent. Honestly, Cath, I'm thoroughly pissed off!'

'No wonder you went to Morag's yoga session to de-stress. Poor you! What a useless Head of Department you've got. How come Evelyn didn't tell him he had to be there?'

'I don't know, but there's no point in worrying about it. Anyway, it's two days, so he'll be there on Wednesday. But more importantly, I've got a sort of date that evening, or rather, Otto has…'

'What? What do you mean? Who with?'

'Otto's dog-walker. He's called Gabriel.'

'Ooh, you've kept that quiet! What's he like, then?'

'Well, he's tall, dark, and handsome…'

'And?'

'That's all I know.'

'Well, it's a good start! I expect to be updated regularly on how it's progressing, Laura. I need every detail!'

'Well, after the last string of boyfriend fails, I'm not holding my breath. Anyway, I know nothing about him.'

'Be positive, Laura! You never know – he could be the perfect man for you!'

'I'll have to go,' I said, - 'I've got a ton of lesson plans to do for tomorrow. Got to be prepared for the day from hell.'

'Good luck, Laura. Stay calm and remember – there's more to life than work.'

The next two days went past in an adrenalin-fuelled blur. I barely ate anything – even the wine in my fridge remained untouched, and that's unheard of. Dan tried to cheer us all up with his jokey repartee, but even Noel didn't take the bait. We were all in a state of high anxiety, due in part to sleep deprivation, but mostly because Evelyn was stalking us like the ubiquitous grim reaper, and the kids were wired like coiled springs. By the time Wednesday evening came, I was bone tired, and in no mood for dog-training.

'The problem is, he's got into some bad habits, and it'll be hard to break them,' said Gabriel, as we watched Otto take off after a squirrel. We'd only been in the field for five minutes. We called him and I waved his favourite snacks. It was hopeless.

'Well, this is a good start!' I said, embarrassed.

'How old is he?' asked Gabriel.

'Mum has had him for five years, but she got him as a rescue dog. I think he was two…'

'Ah, well, this isn't going to be a quick thing. He's going to take a while to catch on.'

'Sorry,' I said, - 'you can say if you don't want to continue…'

'I don't give up that easily, Laura!' he said, laughing. 'Anyway, it'll be a challenge.'

'Oh, good!' I said, - 'although at £40 a session, I might have to re-consider at some point.'

'Are you saying I'm expensive?' he said, grinning.

'Um, no, not at all. It's just, you know, a teacher's salary doesn't stretch very far.'

'Ah, yes, but a very admirable and rewarding occupation, isn't it?'

'Well, I don't know about 'rewarding' – you should meet some of the kids I have to teach. And some of the adults I have to work with too! You haven't told me what you do, Gabriel…'

'Well, I'm currently taking a sabbatical – it's complicated. The work I do now is not what I ever really wanted to do - I sort of ended up falling into this career by accident. Sometimes, it's better to take a risk with something, rather than stick with what you know. I've decided to re-evaluate things. Hey, we should go and find Otto…'

There was no difficulty in locating him, since his barking could be heard echoing all around the woods. The squirrel he'd chased sat on a branch above him, nonchalantly nibbling on a pinecone while Otto whizzed round and round the tree underneath.

'Perhaps we should abandon the lesson today,' said Gabriel. 'I think he's a bit distracted. Would it be inappropriate to invite you to go for a drink? I know a very nice little pub not far from here…'

CHAPTER 7

'Did you see the local news last night?' Fay asked me at lunchtime.

'No, I was out. Why?'

'Go online and check it out. You won't be disappointed!' She laughed.

'I haven't got time now, Fay. I'll do it later. I am intrigued, though…'

'You'll laugh your head off!'

'Well, I could do with some cheering up after the last two days here – it's been hell.'

'We got through it though, didn't we? Anyway, it's not too bad getting a Grade 3 rating, is it? We've gone up in the Ofsted world!'

'I think I can hear Evelyn coming down the corridor…'

'Coming to tell us it wasn't good enough, I expect.'

The door to the staffroom swung open and a much brighter and happier-looking Head addressed us, with a smile on her face, would you believe!

'I just wanted to congratulate you all and say thank you for all your efforts over the last two days. It's been hard work, but worth it in the end. I'm sure you've all heard that we've finally gone up in Ofsted's estimation. There's still a long way to go, but let's continue to work together to improve our standards even more. Thank you, everyone….'

'Well,' said Dan, when she'd gone – 'I've never seen her smile before! Slightly unnerving, wasn't it!'

'I don't know why she's so chipper,' said Noel, - 'we've only gone from 'inadequate' to 'needs improvement'. In my book that's the same thing, isn't it?'

We all looked at him.

'Trust you to be less than enthusiastic, Noel,' said Fay.

'Well, I'm right, aren't I? Laura, you're the English teacher – what do you say?'

'Um, well, Noel, you're being pedantic, as usual.'

'By the way, Laura, did you see the local news last night?' Dan asked.

'No,' I said, - 'Fay just asked me that, too. It must have been unusually gripping!'

'It was,' said Dan, laughing.

'Don't spoil it,' said Fay.

'Oh, OK, right, I'd better go. Swimming Gala this afternoon.' He got up and limped off, just as Bryce came in and made himself a coffee.

'Ah, Laura – just wanted to ask you for a favour. We need to do something fun at the Ball. You know – like a quiz or auction, or something. Do you think you could come up with something?' He was looking hopefully at me.

'I don't know if it's really my forte…'

'Oh, I'm sure you could manage something, Laura…'

When he'd gone, I kicked myself (metaphorically, of course).

'I'll help,' said Fay. 'It'll be more fun if we do it together. By the way, did you hear about William Parsons?'

'No…'

'You know the fire in the kitchen? Well, apparently, William was involved in it…he's been suspended.'

'Oh, no! I didn't know. I thought the fire was caused by an electrical fault.'

'Well, according to Jean Carter, he was seen going into the kitchens just before it happened. Evelyn questioned him this morning and sent him home.'

'Oh, dear. He hasn't done anything like that before, has he?'

'Don't think so. Just goes to show, you can never really know what's going on with these kids…'

I caught up with Ray on my way to class to see if he knew anything about it. 'I've only heard the same as you, Laura. Sorry.'

I went to my class feeling quite troubled. It didn't take the kids long to comment on William's absence.

'Miss, Miss, did you hear about Will – he's an ARSONIST, Miss!' shouted Chloe.

'He tried to burn down the school, Miss. Will he go to prison?' said Charlie Pinnock.

'No, he's too young,' I said. 'Anyway, we don't know all the facts yet, do we, so no one should be commenting. He could be completely innocent…'

'No way,' said Fergus. 'He definitely did it.'

'And how do you know that?'

'Connor McCan said he heard him say he was going to torch the school…'

'Well, he might have misheard him, Fergus.'

'Nah, he definitely said it. You can ask Connor.'

'I'll let Mrs Ferrier deal with it, thank you, Fergus. Now, let's get on with our work, shall we!'

I spent the rest of the lesson being acutely aware of the empty chair where William usually sat. I decided to go and see Evelyn before I went home.

I hovered by her door, hoping to find her in a good mood. She looked up, aware of me standing in the doorway.

'I just wanted to ask you about William, Evelyn.'

'What do you want to know?'

'Well, it just seems strange that he would deliberately cause a fire.'

'He's refusing to say anything, Laura, so I've had to assume the worst. He wouldn't answer any of my questions, apart from denying having anything to do with it.'

'How did it start?'

'In one of the rubbish bins.'

'I think there's more to this than meets the eye, Evelyn.'

'Well, if you've got time to investigate, be my guest. I certainly don't.'

'What will happen to William?'

'He will be allowed back to school next week. There's nothing else I can do. I can't keep him off for ever. We don't have enough evidence to prove he did it.'

'I see. Do you have any objections to me going to visit him at home?' I asked, tentatively.

'I suppose that would be OK. Just be careful not to upset his mother. She can be a tricky customer.'

Evelyn wasn't wrong. I stood with Otto, on the doorstep of a scruffy little bungalow on the outskirts of town, waiting and wondering if there was anyone in, when William's mum, still in her dressing gown, finally opened the door with the chain attached.

'Hello, Mrs Parsons,' I said to the darkness behind the small gap, - 'I'm William's teacher. Would it be possible to speak to him?'

'What for?'

I guessed she hadn't heard about his suspension yet. 'It's about his approach to his school-work. I thought he might be able to talk outside of school more easily.'

'WILLIAM!' she yelled up the stairs. 'Come down and speak to … what's your name?'

'Miss Blewitt,' I said.

'That's a funny name, isn't it?' she said. 'WILLIAM!! It's your Miss Blewitt at the door. Hurry up.'

I heard a door go upstairs. Mrs Parsons undid the chain as William appeared looking miserable.

'Shall I come in, or would you like to go for a walk, William?' I said, hoping he'd agree to the walk. 'I've brought my dog, Otto. Do you like dogs?' His eyes lit up when he saw Otto.

'He likes dogs, but he's not getting one,' said Mrs Parsons. 'I can't stand animals in the house.'

'Shall we go to the park?' I said to William. 'Just for an hour…'

He nodded. 'I won't keep him long,' I said to his mother. She looked at me with cold, humourless eyes and shut the door.

We walked to the park further away than his local one, to avoid bumping into any of his mates from school. He walked beside me with his head down inside his hoodie and his hands thrust into the front pocket.

'I know there's something wrong, William,' I ventured. 'What's going on? Please let me help you. You can talk to me in confidence. I won't share it with anyone without your permission. I promise. That is, unless you've murdered someone, chopped them up and stuffed the bits in a suitcase under your bed…that kind of thing. Otherwise, you can trust me.'

That did raise a smile from him. I decided to keep quiet and let it sink in. We got to the park and I gave him Otto's ball so he could play with him.

'So, how did that go, then?' asked Cath, later, when we were on the phone.

'I'm just trying to gain his trust at the moment.'

'He didn't spill the beans, then?'

'No. He did ask if he could take Otto out for walks, though.'

'Do you trust him?'

'I think so. His mother's not very friendly, though.'

'Maybe there's something going on at home, Laura.'

'Well, I'm hoping he will confide in me. I'm using Otto as an inducement!'

'And how are things going with Gabriel?'

'We had a drink at the pub the other night. I'm not sure if you could call it a date, though. It was, you know, spontaneous…'

'They're the best dates, aren't they? So, what happened?'

'Nothing, Cath. We hardly know each other. I think I did most of the talking. He's been here for a couple of years. Moved down from Leeds for work. Says he had a long-term relationship that went wrong around that time. He doesn't have any children. Anyway, he's a bit elusive. I can't get out of him what he actually does for a living. When I asked him, he just said it was quite boring and I wouldn't be interested. Don't you think that's a bit odd?'

'Ooooh, that's mysterious, isn't it! I could do some sleuthing for you…'

'No, thanks! I'm sure I'll get to the bottom of it eventually.'

There's no way I'm letting Cath do any such thing. Part of me wishes I hadn't mentioned him at all to her, because now she'll be asking me about it every five minutes. Anyway, I've decided not to expect much from men at the moment. I'm still feeling upset about Elliott's behaviour.

After taking Otto round the block, I opened the fridge for food inspiration. I needed to have something to look forward to after Morag's gruelling yoga class. Then I realised I still hadn't gone shopping. How I wish I had my own Mrs Wang! I got changed into my lycra sports gear and went out. At my local shop, the choices are limited. However, I like to feel good about supporting the local economy…that's what I tell myself, anyway. The truth is, that by the time I get home from work and walk Otto, I can't be bothered to go further afield. I was just wrestling with the shop's freezer door that always jams, when I heard a familiar voice behind me.

'Hi!'

'Oh, Gabriel! Hello!'

'Let me get that,' he said, shutting the door with ease.

'Oh, thanks. It always sticks! Well, for me anyway…'

He smiled and looked down at the slightly embarrassing contents of my shopping basket. I quickly moved the giant bag of fries and two bottles of wine, so he could see the salad bag underneath.

'It's on offer,' I said, pointing at the wine.

'Oh, good. I thought maybe you were planning on drowning your sorrows this evening, or have you got company?'

'I have my yoga class this evening, so I'll have to be good. Anyway, it's a school night!' I suddenly became very aware of my exceedingly unflattering outfit. I clutched the basket higher up and moved towards the till.

'What are your plans this weekend?' he said.

'Um, well, I don't know… I'll probably have to go and see my mother. She has dementia, and well, she's getting worse, and I need to start searching for a suitable place for her to go…*(Why on earth was I telling him all this, for heaven's sake!)* I rambled on a bit more about the lack of support for elderly people like my mother. Gabriel just carried on smiling and waited for me to run out of things to say about demented mothers.

'How about dinner on Saturday?'

CHAPTER 8

'Did you see it?' said Fay the next day.

'See what?'

'The news story.'

'Oh, no, I forgot. I was busy last night – it was Morag's class.'

'How's that going?'

'Painfully.'

'Must be working, then!' She got out her phone to show me the video.

'That looks like Elliott…' I said, squinting at an assault course in a sea of mud. Everyone was covered in brown sludge. Halfway up a rope-net someone was dangling upside down by their feet.

'What's he doing?'

'He's stuck,' said Fay. 'Look, he had to be rescued!'

'This new craze for extreme physical challenges is not for the faint-hearted…' the presenter was saying. The camera zoomed in on Elliott's contorted mud-spattered face, as he was rescued by two fifteen-year-old girls.

'That's hilarious!' I said, hooting with laughter. Then I felt a bit guilty. 'Do you think he was all right?'

'Dan saw him afterwards and said he was fine, except for a bruised ego.'

'Oh, good! Mind you, there's nothing like a bit of karma to cheer one up in the morning!'

'By the way, we need to talk about the entertainment at the Ball for next Saturday. What should we do?' said Fay.

'Well, we don't have time to organise an auction. We can't ask the parents to fork out any more money, anyway. Let's just do a quiz with a prize. It would be nice to get a really good one, wouldn't it!'

'OK, I'll start asking around. Hey, Noel, have you got a secret luxury holiday home anywhere?'

'No, I certainly do not,' he said. 'Muriel and I have a caravan in Wales, if that's any good?'

'Not glamorous enough, Noel. Sorry!'

'No one appreciates the simple pleasures in life, any more,' he said, sighing.

'I'm sure we'll come up with something,' said Fay. 'Right, back to work- see you all later.'

My Year 7 class were particularly rowdy this morning, and rude. I mean, where do they get the idea that it's OK to call a teacher by their first name? Cheeky blighters! I swear the Year 7s get worse every year. I decided to give them a fun thing to do for homework in an attempt to win them over.

'Names can be really interesting,' I told them. 'For instance, the name Laura comes from a plant called Bay Laurel and means 'victory', because the first Olympic athletes and Roman Emperors wore laurel wreathes on their heads like a crown. And 'Blewitt', (*lots of sniggers*) comes from the French word 'bleuet' meaning 'blue', and when the Normans invaded England, it was given to people with blue eyes…'

'But you've got green eyes, Miss,' said Gillian Spratt (*not the sharpest knife in the rack).*

'Well, one of my ancestors would have had blue eyes, Gillian. A long time ago. The Norman Conquest was in 1066 and that's when the French invaded England… What famous incident happened in 1066 at the Battle of Hastings? Anyone?'

'King Harold got shot in his eye, Miss,' said Martin Drew.

'That's right, Martin. And William the Conqueror, of Normandy in France, crowned himself King of England. So, for your homework, I'd like you all to research your own names and write down what you found out about them. You could ask your parents to help if you want.'

'What's 'ancestors'?' asked Gillian.

'It's all the people in your family that lived before you – so, your great, great, great, great, great grandparents…'

'Oh,' she said, looking blank. 'I've only got an uncle…' The class started laughing.

'Don't worry, Gillian. Why don't you ask him to help?'

'Nah, I'm not allowed to speak to him, Miss. My Mum says he's a crackhead.'

At the end of the school day, I rang my mother to remind her I was on my way to fetch her for her doctor's appointment.

'Mum, it's me, Laura.'

'Yes…'

'I'm coming down now to take you to see Dr Flanagan.'

'But I'm not ill. Why do I need to see a doctor?'

'It's routine, Mum…' I fibbed.

'Well, it's very inconvenient. I'm just getting ready for bed…'

'But, Mum, it's only 5pm!'

'My clock says it's 10 o'clock …'

'It's wrong, Mum. Please can you get dressed or we'll be late.'

'I don't like that Dr Flanagan. Can't I see someone else?'

'Why don't you like him, Mum?'

'I can't understand him, Laura. He's got a funny accent. I think he might be foreign.'

'He's Irish, Mum. Could you get dressed now?'

When I got to my mother's house, she was still wandering around in her dressing gown.

'I haven't had my breakfast yet,' she complained, when I asked her again to get dressed.

'You mean 'tea'.'

'Stop trying to confuse me, Laura,' she said, crossly.

I finally managed to persuade her into the car. We got to the surgery fifteen minutes late. I tried to explain to the receptionist how difficult it was to get my mother to cooperate but was met with a rather stony response. My mother didn't help things, either, by telling the woman I'd always been poor at being on time for things.

'Laura's never been one to worry about punctuality, have you, dear! Always in a world of your own. Remember when you used to take all your clothes off just as we were about to leave the house? Goodness me, you were a holy terror for that!' My mother recounted this, gleefully, to the po-faced woman behind the desk. The woman told us to take a seat in the waiting room.

Dr Flanagan was perfectly charming, and luckily, my mother let me go in with her.

'Well now, what's brought you here today then, Mrs Blewitt? Feeling a bit under the weather, are we?' My mother looked confused.

'I've brought her in to see you, doctor, because she appears to be suffering with memory loss and …'

'What are you talking about, Laura!' she said, abruptly. 'There's nothing wrong with my memory. It's you who doesn't seem to know whether it's night or day! Honestly doctor, she wouldn't let me eat my breakfast before coming here. I'm starving!'

Dr Flanagan smiled and told her not to worry about it. 'Well, you're here now, which is the important thing. I just want to ask you a few questions…'

'What's so funny?' said my mother, as we got back in the car.

'I'm sorry Mum, but it was quite funny when he asked you what year it was, and you said 1976.'

'Well, I just got in a muddle, that's all. I mean, you can hardly understand what that man says! Of course I know it's not 1976! When we get home you can ask your Dad. He always knows everything.'

Oh dear! I hope the medication Dr Flanagan has prescribed will help. Forgetting that Dad is dead is very worrying. She seems to have deteriorated at an alarming rate. I'm not sure how I'm going to persuade her to go to more appointments, though. Jenny, where are you when I need you?

I made Mum some tea and settled her down in front of the TV to watch a travel programme about Africa. I also got her to take her medication, which was no easy job. I'll have to ask Mrs Wang to make sure she takes it.

Back in my flat, I was greeted very enthusiastically by poor neglected Otto. I gave him a big cuddle and some food. Gabriel had left me another note…

Hi Laura!

Forgot to ask you if you have any food preferences or allergies? Thought I'd book early!

Looking forward to it!

G. ☺

'So, it's a date, then!' enthused Cath later, on the phone.

'Well, yes… I suppose it is...'

'You could sound more enthusiastic!'

'Well, I'm just not sure – it's a bit unexpected. I've only just finished with Elliott. That reminds me, Cath – the funniest thing happened to him last weekend…'

Just before I went to bed, I realised there was a message on my phone.

'Laura. I'm coming up on Sunday to see Mum. We can talk then if you're free? OK. Byeee…'

That's my sister for you, 'short and sweet'… well not so sweet, in reality. I suppose it's something, that she's coming over to see us. She needs to see for herself how bad Mum is getting. I'm intrigued to hear about the new man in her life, although they never seem to last very long. I personally think it's because she's so insensitive. I mean, what man wants to be told how to drive his car (Angus), or, given a book for his birthday called *How to be a Better Lover* (Giles), or, told to 'grow some' when he gets a bad performance review at work (Wyatt), OR, (and this is the most heinous of crimes) informed that his mother is 'a bigoted, brainless, busybody' (Vince). Diplomacy has never been her strong suit. I don't know how she keeps her job, to be honest. Maybe it's in her job description to cut straight to the point… Anyway, I'm always slightly nervous when I know she's visiting. At least she won't want to stay overnight, so that's a blessing.

'Coffee?' I said to Ray the next morning. I found him in the staffroom sitting next to a pile of exercise books.

'Thanks, Laura. This is my last one,' he said, chucking it on top of the pile.

'You're in early, then…'

'I had a meeting with Evelyn.'

'Oh…'

'Yes. I couldn't tell you before. I'm leaving, Laura. At the end of term.'

'Oh, I see,' I said, not sure whether to be sorry or not. 'Why?'

'New job. Starting in September.' He smiled happily. 'Can't say I'm sorry to be leaving here, but I'll miss you lot.'

'Well, that's a bit of a surprise, Ray. I had no idea…'

'Sorry I didn't mention it, Laura, but I've had a few interviews this term and this is the only one that came through for me. You should think about pastures new yourself, you know. It gives you a new lease of life. You can get a bit stale staying in the same place for too long.'

Later, when I told Fay, she didn't seem surprised. 'He always said he'd give it five years, you know. You should apply for his job. It's probably yours for the taking…'

'Oh, really? I don't know about that. I mean, Evelyn doesn't rate me very highly. I don't think I'm her ideal employee by a long shot.'

'Well, I still think you should try for it, Laura. By the way, I heard William Parson's mother is coming up today. She's furious, apparently, about William being sent home.'

At 4pm, I got a message from Evelyn asking me to go to her office. Actually, it was more of a command. She could do with a few lessons in effective communication herself. I mean '*need you in my office ASAP*' is neither polite nor appealing, is it! I did consider ignoring it and pretending I'd left my phone somewhere. When Mrs Parsons marched into Evelyn's office, red-faced and already shouting abuse, I wished I had.

'Please calm down, Mrs Parsons, and take a seat,' Evelyn said, pointing at the seat furthest away from us.

'It's an outrage!' shouted Mrs Parsons at us. 'He didn't do anything! You can't send him home for something he didn't do! You've got no evidence!'

'As I've already explained to you, William was the only person seen in the vicinity of where the fire started. We have it on CCTV,' Evelyn said, strongly emphasising 'CCTV'.

'That doesn't prove anything. Anyway, I know my rights,' said Mrs Parsons. 'You can't suspend him without evidence…'

After Evelyn had explained the school policy on discipline and suspensions to her, William's mother finally gave in and got up huffily, to leave.

'Thank you for attending,' said Evelyn, as I got up to go as well.

'I didn't really do anything…'

'No, but I needed a witness,' she said, - 'just in case things got out of hand.'

'She's quite a character, isn't she!'

'You can say that again, Laura. The main reason she's annoyed, of course, is because she doesn't want William hanging round the house all day long when she's working. It'll be cramping her style.'

'What do you mean?'

'She's a sex worker, Laura.' Evelyn spoke in hushed tones. 'Didn't you know?'

'No, I didn't…'

'Unfortunately, she's all he's got.'

'What about his dad?'

'Prison.'

All the way home, I was thinking about William. I couldn't help feeling sorry for him. No wonder he's going off the rails. It's amazing he hasn't already. What sort of future does he have when the odds are stacked against him like that? Such a shame, when he's a clever lad with a chance of doing something with his life.

When I got in, there was a message from Mrs Wang.

'Hello Laura. I just tell you – your Mum – she is putting lot of nets over garden. She say it because of bad wocuss…'

I rang my mother. 'Mum, I just got a message from Doreen saying something about nets in the garden…'

'Yes, Laura. It's terrible! They eat everything in their path - huge swarms of them. I've only just planted my strawberry plants.'

'Swarms of what, Mum?'

'Locusts, Laura. Millions of them!'

'But, Mum, we don't get them here.'

'I saw it on the TV. They can fly hundreds of miles – it's frightening.'

There was no dissuading her. I can't wait to see what her back garden looks like! With hindsight, perhaps I shouldn't have left her watching *Natural Disasters of Eastern Africa,* the other night.

Gabriel was fifteen minutes late this evening. I was just thinking he must have forgotten when he turned up with his dog Cleo in tow.

'Sorry Laura, I got caught up with something. I thought I'd bring Cleo – Otto might get the idea of obeying instructions if he sees my dog doing things.'

Watching Gabriel trying to train Otto was quite entertaining. I couldn't help laughing when Otto repeatedly refused to cooperate. Even Cleo's exceptionally good example did nothing to encourage Otto to fall into line.

'I'm really sorry, Gabriel,' I said, - 'He's proving a hard nut to crack!'

'Oh, well, it's not going to be a quick fix,' he said, smiling. 'Anyway, it just means you'll have to keep coming out with me,' he laughed. 'By the way, have you had any thoughts about what you want to eat on Saturday?'

'Um, no. I don't mind. I'm not fussy. Just book whatever you fancy.'

'OK. How about Karim's Kebabs'? Or Tony's Fry-up?' he said with a straight face.

'Well…'

'I'm kidding! I think I can manage something a bit more up-market than that for a first date! I'll pick you up at 7pm. Is that OK?'

'Well, Otto,' I said to him as he trotted home with me, - 'it looks like Cinderella might have a partner for the Ball after all!'

CHAPTER 9

'When's Will coming back?' said Denise as soon as I walked into the classroom.

'Next week, I think.'

'He shouldn't be allowed back,' said Chloe. 'He's insane…'

'Yeah – he's a psycho,' said Ollie, twirling his fingers round and pointing at his own head.

'You must be his twin, then,' said Denise, guffawing.

'Shut your face *Disease,*' retorted Ollie.

'Shut YOUR face *fathead',* Denise shouted back.

The class erupted.

'QUIET!' I shouted, just as Bryce knocked and entered.

'A bit on the lively side today, I see,' he said. 'Sorry to interrupt you, but I just wanted to tell everyone we've got a special assembly on Friday morning, with a VIP coming to speak to you all.'

'Who is it?' said Chloe.

'Ah, well, it's a surprise guest. I don't want to spoil it for you! Right, that's all. Thank you, Laura.'

'Who is it, Miss?'

'I honestly don't know, Denise. I'm as intrigued as you are.'

'I reckon it's the Queen,' said Fergus.

'Hahahahaha,' laughed his classmates.

'Don't be stupid!' said Ollie.

'You'll just have to wait and see,' I said. 'Can you all hand your homework in, then we'll carry on with Macbeth.'

'So, who is it?' I asked Noel at lunchtime.

'No idea, Laura.'

'Come on, Noel, you always know what Evelyn's plans are.'

'Not this time.'

'It's probably some boring old councillor or business magnate…' said Dan, - 'or someone off *Eastenders*…'

'It could be a sports hero, like Anthony Joshua or Christiano Ronaldo,' I suggested.

'I doubt it,' said Dan.

I joined Morag's lunchtime yoga class with Fay for some chill-out time, after quickly scoffing a bean salad I'd made last night.

'I'm trying to eat more healthily,' I told Fay when I saw her looking at my Tupperware box. She raised her eyebrows and said she knew me well enough to guess there was something I wasn't telling her.

'So, what's his name?' she said, as we laid our mats down on the floor.

'I'll tell you later, but there's nothing much to tell – not yet anyway…'

Morag put on some soothing music and I found I had to fight the urge to fall asleep again.

'I don't know what it is about lunchtime yoga, but I just can't stay awake,' I said to Fay after the session. 'I think I'll just have to stick to Monday evenings from now on.'

Walking back to the staffroom, I spied Connor McCan shambling along the corridor with some of his mates.

'Could I have a quick word, Connor?' He moved away from his grinning friends and sheepishly approached me, hands in pockets, eyes cast down. 'I just wanted to ask about William Parsons. Some of the kids say you heard him threaten to 'torch the school' – is that true? Because if it is, then I might have to get the police involved…' Connor looked down at his shoes. 'Well?'

'Um, I'm not sure, Miss. I thought he said something like that…but I'm not really sure…'

'I see. Well, Connor, I think you need to be very careful about saying something that may not be true. Do you understand me?'

'Yes, Miss.'

Dan was in the staffroom resting his leg up on a stool and reading the paper. I made us some coffee. 'How are you managing to teach PE?' I asked him.

'Badly.'

'When will you be fit again?'

'Well, the doctor said in a couple of weeks. It's a real bore. I was supposed be going surfing this weekend down in Devon. The weather's going to be perfect for it. What are you up to?'

'Not much. My sister's coming on Sunday. She's a bit of a pain, to be honest. I'm not looking forward to it. My mother's got dementia. It's all very difficult. I never thought I'd be having to cope with this at my age. It's not fair, Dan!'

'I tell you what,' said Dan, - 'how about getting together for lunch on Saturday? We can cheer each other up.'

I accepted Dan's invitation happily. It's been ages since I went out and had a laugh with him.

My Friday afternoon lesson with year 7 was as rowdy as ever, made ten times worse by the antics of a Year 11 pupil called Jake Saunders who was running around the soccer pitch outside the class, distracting everyone.

'What's he doing?' I said, going over to the window.

'He's chasing a dog, Miss,' said Sanjay Chatterjee. 'He's trying to catch it.'

Jake was unsuccessfully trying to catch up with a black and white whippet which was going like the clappers round the field. 'He's got no chance,' I said, hoping it would run off out of view. 'Come on kids, focus on what we're doing.' I switched the TV on which usually gets their attention. A video with some rapping poets got their attention for a while, but Jake's antics with the escapee dog was more interesting.

'Honestly, Ray, it was hopeless!' I moaned to him afterwards.

'I wondered what all the commotion was,' he said. 'I saw Jake running after it in the carpark. Dan nearly ran it over. Thank God it's Friday! I'm off home now for a beer in the garden. What about you?'

'Dog walk,' I said, - 'followed by binge-watching something vacuous on telly, eating a cheese omelette and drinking too much wine.'

'Living the high-life, then. OK, well, have a good weekend,' he laughed. 'See you on the other side.'

When I got home, there was a message from William – a slightly hesitant, rambling one asking if he could come on Saturday to walk Otto.

I wasn't really sure if I'd done the right thing suggesting this idea to William, but it was too late now. I rang him back and told him to come round the next morning at around 9.30am.

After walking Otto and stopping by the shop for some essentials, I filled up a big glass of wine and settled down to read my Year 7 class's contribution to the theme '*what's in a name?*' Some of the kids had really got into it and written a couple of pages, and others, like Gillian Spratt, had barely managed a few lines. Anyhow, they made fascinating and entertaining reading. The whole gamut of social and political history was here; arrow-smiths, musicians, bakers, shepherds, servants, innkeepers, outlaws, vagabonds, drunkards, farmers, warriors, landowners, noblemen and kings. It was all here, in one classful of kids. Amazing!

David Fogarty: *My name is from Ireland and it means banished or exiled. There are lots of famous people called Fogarty – one is Carl Fogarty and he is a racing driver. We have got our own castle in Tipperary called Castle Fogarty. Mum says we can go there one day if I save up enough. I've only got £32.50 at the moment, though. Especially if we stay in a hotel. I've never been in a hotel. My Mum says we would have to stay in a B&B because hotels are for toffs.*

Philip Chambers: *My name comes from when rich people had servants in their bedrooms who looked after them and cleaned their clothes and polished their shoes and did their ironing and stuff like that. It comes from the French word 'chambre', so maybe I've got French blood which could be true because I really like cheese a lot.*

Andrew Slack: *Google says my name means lazy, but I'm not lazy, so that's obviously wrong.*

Ryan Sherbourne: *Sherbourne used to be 'Shiteburne' in old English. My Mum said that means 'shit-stream'. She says it's a good description of our dad because he talks rubbish all the time.*

Gary Mallory: *Mallory means bad luck which is weird because why would anyone want to be called that? George Mallory was a famous climber who fell off Mount Everest and they found his dead body 80 years later cos it was frozen in the ice and no one knew where it was. So, he obviously had REALLY bad luck!*

Susan Flack: *Flack means 'sod' which is like turf and soil and stuff.*

While I was reading them, it occurred to me that Gabriel hasn't told me what his surname is. I hope it isn't something awful. Mine's bad enough…I mean, what if it's 'Dick', or 'Aycock', or 'Beaver' or something? Or something silly, like 'Fish', or 'Crisp'? Or impossible to spell or pronounce - like 'Tjarnqvist', or 'Achtymichuk', or 'Gwalchmai'?

Stop it, Laura, I told myself. It's not as if you're marrying the man, for heaven's sake! Otto's barking brought me to my senses. I'd forgotten to feed him his tea.

William turned up the next morning right on cue and took Otto out for an hour.

'No taking him to friend's houses, William – OK? Just take him for a walk. You have to watch he doesn't run off. Keep him on the lead for now,' I said, suddenly thinking of worst-case scenarios and slightly regretting this idea of mine.

'Yes, Miss,' he said. 'I'll look after him.'

When he returned, I offered him a drink and a biscuit and to my surprise, he accepted, scoffed it down and asked for more. I asked him how he'd got on.

'Great! We went to the park by the Co-Op. I got him to bring the ball back nearly every time!'

'That's really good, William! He's learning. By the way, I've marked your class's homework, but I didn't see yours…'

William looked at his feet.

'You can talk to me, William – maybe I can help…'

He chewed his lip.

'It's OK. It won't go any further. Is it too noisy at home, perhaps?' I ventured.

'No…it's not that…'

'Because I could think of a way to help…'

'I'm not allowed in the house in the evenings,' he blurted out.

'Oh,' I said, stunned. 'Where do you go, then?'

'Friends. In the park, McDonalds is open late…'

'Goodness,' I said, lost for words. 'Your mother shouldn't be doing that – it's your home too, William.'

'Please, don't tell her I told you,' he said, - 'my Mum will make me go to my Dad's if I tell anyone…'

'But isn't he …um…away somewhere?'

'Yes, but his girlfriend lives there. I hate her. She doesn't want me there anyway.'

'William, I'm so sorry…' I looked at him and suddenly realised how thin he looked. 'Are you getting proper meals at home, Will? Come to think of it, I haven't seen you in the canteen at lunch time.'

'My Mum can't afford to buy food because of all the bills and stuff. I get fed at my mate's house sometimes…'

Then I suggested something rash and mad. 'If you had somewhere nice to stay as an alternative and you could still go to school and meet your friends in the evenings and at weekends, what would you say?'

'There's no way…how?' I looked at his confused, flushed, spotty face. 'Do you mean…?'

'Yes.' I finished the sentence for him. 'I mean, here. I'm not expecting an immediate answer, William. I'll show you my spare room and then you can think about it. None of your mates need to know. OK?'

'You did WHAT?' said Dan, as we sat outside Café Rouge in the midday sun.

'He's got such a miserable home-life, Dan.'

'So have half the kids in the school! Honestly, Laura – it's madness! You're going to get yourself into hot water.'

'Well, I've thought about that…'

'Have you? Really?' Dan took another swig from his pint of cold, frothy lager. I laughed.

'What's so funny?'

'You've got a white moustache.'

He wiped it off. 'Seriously, Laura – you can't just take in a teenage boy. I mean, you could be accused of all sorts…And what about the small problem of fire-starting. Have you thought about that?'

'I don't believe he did it. I think there's another explanation for that fire. William doesn't have it in him. Really, Dan, he's not a trouble-maker.'

'Well, I hope you know what you're letting yourself in for. I know what teenage boys are like.'

'What were you like, then, Dan?'

'Terrible. I made my Mum's life a misery,' he laughed. 'I was always staying late in the library and spending hours in my room, tidying up after myself – that kind of thing.'

'Are you being serious?'

'Yes, actually! I was a very well-behaved lad. I used to clean the house for my Mum as well. She was devastated when I moved out.'

I laughed. 'I never knew you were such a mother's boy, Dan!'

'I wasn't typical, I can tell you. Most teenagers are the opposite of that. They're selfish, noisy, rude, messy, and they smell really BAD. You should know this already, but at least you can go home at the end of the day and regain some sanity! Really, Laura, think hard about what you're taking on – you're not used to anyone else being in your space.'

'Well, Dan, just because you would struggle with someone in your space re-arranging the cushions on the sofa and messing up your colour-coded CD collection, doesn't mean I wouldn't cope with another person in *my* flat.'

'We'll see!' joked Dan. 'I can't wait! I'm going to want a blow-by-blow account, Blewitt!'

'You're funny. Anyway, keep it under your hat for now, please, Dan.'

'So, what's happening in your love-life, then?' Dan was smiling.

'Ah, I'm guessing Fay told you…'

'Well, spill the beans.'

'Nothing to tell you yet. He's called Gabriel. He likes dogs. He's nice. We're going on our first proper date tonight. That's it. What about you? What's happening with Freddy?'

'History, I'm afraid.'

'Oh, I'm sorry to hear that.'

'I'm not!' Dan laughed. 'He turned into a royal pain in the neck. He was so fussy. You know, he took TWO HOURS to get ready to go out! I couldn't stand it any longer. He was *so* vain, and *so* obsessed with himself. He spent half the time we were together looking at himself in the mirror. I wanted to KILL him, Laura! Seriously, I don't know how it lasted so long.'

'Oh, well, onto pastures new for you, as well, then,' I sniggered.

'Looks like it. Or maybe I'm destined to live alone forever…'

'Come on, Dan, you're only 33!'

'Now, Otto,' I said to him as I got several items of clothing out of the wardrobe, - 'which of these should I wear?' I looked at the limited selection and wished I hadn't eaten so much for lunch. It was all Dan's fault, ordering those chocolate sundaes with extra cream. In the end, I plumped for a long white shirt, dark green skinny jeans and white pumps. 'How do I look?' I asked Otto, when I'd showered, done my hair and got dressed.

'Woof.'

'Good. Thanks, Otto. It's always nice to be appreciated.'

I put the TV on to distract me from getting nervous and waited for my date to turn up.

'I've booked Zizzi's,' said Gabriel, as we climbed into his silver Mercedes.

'Nice car,' I said, admiring the red leather interior.

'I've had this a long time,' he said, patting the steering wheel affectionately. 'I got it in my twenties. It's a classic car. Cost me all my savings. My parents weren't impressed,' he laughed. 'They were right, of course. It took me ten years to save up a deposit for a flat, but I wouldn't sell my Lucy for anything,'

'Lucy?'

'Yeah, after my first girlfriend.'

'Oh. What was she like?'

'She was a sweet girl. Dark, curly hair, big blue eyes, always smiling. I loved her more than anything; her short, fat legs, her red chubby cheeks, her toothless grin! We were six…' he said, seeing my confused expression.

'Very funny,' I said. 'You nearly had me there. Do you know where she is now?'

'No, we moved away. What about you, Laura? Who was your first love?'

'Apart from our dog, Badger, there was a boy called Ben who I sat next to at school – I was infatuated with him because he knew his 2 times table off by heart. Then the teacher split us up. I was very upset about that. I reckon my mother had a hand in it…'

'I'd better watch out for her, then.' Gabriel smiled. 'We're here,' he said, pulling up. 'I hope you like Italian…'

'So?' said Cath the next morning, on the phone, hardly giving me enough time to wake up.

'Mm?'

'Your date! How was your date? I'm dying to know, Laura…'

I laughed. 'Cath, your life can't be *that* boring!'

'Oh, I'd swap with you in an instant right now!' she said. 'Married life can get pretty dull, I can tell you! You should put it off as long as possible!'

'What do you think I'm doing, Cath? I mean, spinsterhood is just a hair's breadth away, in case you hadn't noticed. I'm 35 next month!'

Cath laughed. 'Come on, though, tell me – how did it go?'

'Well…do you want the unsullied version or the warts and all one?'

'The latter, of course!'

I gave her a blow-by-blow account of the meal; the tomato sauce spillage on foolish choice of white shirt moment, the laughing too loudly moment, the prattling on about past boyfriends too much, my unnecessary mentioning of my own expanding stomach moment, and then the 'in the car outside the flat' moment which was almost too painful to recount.

'So, you didn't invite him in, then?'

'No. The evening was a failure. I made a complete idiot of myself.'

'But he did ask you out in the first place!'

'Well, he'll be regretting it now.'

'That's ridiculous, Laura. It can't have been as bad as you think.'

'I shouldn't have accepted his invitation. I wasn't ready – I don't have the confidence at the moment. I want to get more in shape and feel good about myself.'

'Dating isn't an Olympic sport, you know!'

'I know, but I've let myself go a bit in the last year or so.'

'Well, for what it's worth, I think you look fabulous,' said Cath.

'Thanks. That's why you're my best friend – I can always count on you to sugar-coat the truth.'

'So, did you find out his surname?'

'Yes – it's 'Shape'…'

'No! That's really funny!'

'Well, it's unusual...'

'Mrs 'L. Shape' has a certain ring to it...'

'Oh, my God, Cath, that's terrible! That didn't occur to me at all! It's a non-starter, then! How can I possibly see him again! Actually, I'm not expecting it to really turn into anything much, so I think I'm pretty safe at the moment.'

'So, *are* you going to see him again?'

'Well, after I dodged his goodnight kiss, I think that's probably a 'no'.'

CHAPTER 10

How I wish I could rewind last night's thoroughly regrettable night out. God knows what Gabriel thinks of me now. It all went downhill when I foolishly ordered spaghetti Alle Vongole. Honestly, it's impossible to eat that and look sophisticated and refined at the same time. Clams are slippery beggars at the best of times, and it's just not acceptable to chop up your spaghetti with a knife in a posh restaurant, especially on a first date. I think Gabriel thought it was amusing to watch me struggling. He was smiling more than is customary, if you ask me. Anyway, he, of course, had the sense to order something he could eat with aplomb and dexterity, whilst managing to continue looking handsome and charming. And then, I probably drank my wine too quickly, because he asked me if I wanted another bottle when we were only half way through our starters, and I realised he'd only had half a glass himself.

'I'm driving,' he said, - 'but please go ahead if you want to…'

'Oh, no, it's fine,' I said, embarrassed. 'I'll stick to water now, I think.'

And then, I know, I did most of the talking. I'm sure Gabriel didn't really want to know about past relationship fails, disappointing sisters, mad mothers, and the disaffected youth of today. I nearly knocked my chair over on the way out, got my coat stuck in the car door when I tried to close it, and then remembered I'd left my bag behind. And THEN, I was so eager to put the evening's debacle behind me, that I didn't realise Gabriel was leaning in after we parked up. He told me he'd had a fun evening and I mistook his sudden proximity to me for a gentlemanly move to open my door for me and turned to get out. Then I caught a glimpse of my stained shirt in the wing mirror as I got out. Honestly, it couldn't have been a more humiliating end to the evening. I thanked him for a lovely evening and practically ran inside my flat and shut the door. I then spent the next hour agonising over what a bad job I'd made of the whole thing, and swore I'd never go on another date EVER again. Anyway, at least I'll never be known as 'Mrs L. Shape', so that's a bonus.

I didn't have time to sit and dwell on yesterday's dating debacle this morning. My sister rang me at 11am to say she'd arrived at Mum's house, and did I want to bring lunch over because Mum appeared to have thrown all the bread out onto the garden for the birds.

When I got there, I could hear Jenny remonstrating with our mother in the back garden. I went to investigate.

'The birds don't even need bread in the summer, Mum,' Jenny was saying. 'They've got plenty of seeds and worms to eat. And they don't eat vegetables… or cheese…' she was saying, pointing at the ground which was completely covered in what looked like the entire contents of Mum's fridge.

Mum was covering her ears. 'Don't shout, Laura, I'm not deaf.'

'I'm not Laura,' said Jenny.

'Who are you, then?' Jenny looked at me in disbelief.

'I told you things were bad, Jenny.'

'I didn't realise it was as bad as this, Laura.'

'Well, this is why we need a plan for Mum. It can't go on,' I said. I could tell Jenny was genuinely upset by this sudden and dramatic change in our mother's behaviour. I tried to explain that it was taking a while for the medication to take effect, and that she might improve.

'Cripes,' said Jenny, when we went into the kitchen to prepare lunch.

'She's not safe on her own like this at all.'

'I know.'

'She needs to go and be looked after somewhere.'

'I know.'

'It's terrible…'

'I know.'

'Where's Doreen?' said Mum, coming into the kitchen.

'She doesn't come today, Mum.'

'Who's Doreen?', said Jenny.

'Mrs Wang – Mum's cleaning lady and helper. She's very good at keeping an eye on things. Remember, I told you about her…'

'Oh, yes. Well, it looks like Mum needs someone at the weekend too.'

'We could take turns, Jenny…' *I knew this idea would go down like a lead balloon.*

'Oh, no, I couldn't do that. I've got too much going on, and I'm too far away,' she said, predictably, - 'whereas you're here all the time, so you could just pop over, couldn't you?'

'I do already…' I was starting to feel very irritated with my sister. 'It's not enough, though,' I said, opening a cupboard expecting to see mugs, but instead encountering a large frozen chicken.

'Oh, I wondered where that was,' said Mum. 'I was going to cook it for my daughter coming. She's coming for Sunday lunch, you know.'

Jenny and I looked at each other. 'We're making something, Mum, it's OK.'

'Well, put it back, then. We don't want it de-frosting all over the place.'

Jenny rolled her eyes and opened the freezer door. 'Mum, why have you got all these bags of peas?' All three drawers were stuffed with them.

'I'd better speak to Doreen,' I said. 'I thought she was supervising Mum's shopping trips.'

'Your Dad likes his peas,' said Mum, wandering back into the lounge.

'We need to arrange a few visits to some nursing homes, Laura,' whispered Jenny. 'Are you free next Saturday?'

'Yes, but I'm helping with an event at school from 5pm.'

'Great. I'll leave it to you, then.'

'You *are* coming too, aren't you?'

'I'll do my best.'

'What's in my sandwich?' said Mum, poking at it suspiciously.

'Lettuce and ham,' said Jenny.

'I don't like ham,' said our mother, childishly. 'I wanted corned beef.'

'There isn't any. In fact, your fridge is almost completely empty. You gave it all to the birds, remember?'

''Well, they're starving. I saw it on the TV. They've got nothing to eat. Hundreds of birds are just falling straight out of the sky. It's so sad!'

'That was in America last year, Mum.'

'The trouble is,' I said to Jenny, - 'she sees things on the telly and gets confused. She thought locusts were descending on us last week.'

'Oh, dear. She'd be better off watching old black and white movies.'

'She'd probably think she was back in the 1940's again and start going on about the war…'

'We'd better go and get her some more food,' said Jenny. 'She can't be safe using the microwave or cooker, can she?'

'No. Doreen and I disconnected them. When no one's here she has cold food. It's the only safe thing to do. Can you imagine what would happen if she was allowed to cook!'

'We'd better take this chicken away and stick it in the bin. We have no idea how long it's been in that cupboard, and we don't want Mum getting salmonella poisoning.'

When I got home and switched my phone back on, a message from Gabriel popped up immediately. I hesitated to open it, assuming the worst. I waited three minutes, before looking.

Hi Laura! I hope you enjoyed our evening out as much as I did. When can we do it again? Or would you prefer something in the daytime, perhaps? Saturday again? If you have plans, that's fine. I guess I'll see you on Wednesday as usual?

Love, G x

'Love…' I repeated. 'It says 'love', Otto! Not a smiley face! Phew, I think I got away with it! Let's go out and celebrate!'

'You seem cheerful for a Monday morning!' said Dan. 'I'm guessing your date went well?'

'Let's just say that despite the fact that I failed to dupe the man into thinking he was out with someone really cool and sophisticated, he's going to give me another chance…'

'What?'

'I was clumsy, self-conscious and nervous. Honestly, Dan, it was NOT a dream date. Anyway, unbelievably it seems he's still interested.'

'Of course he is, Laura! Don't be so self-critical. I bet it wasn't as bad as some of my first dates.'

'I'd rather not know, Dan.'

'I would,' said Fay. 'I need cheering up this morning. My weekend was terrible. My father-in-law came to stay. It was torturous. Honestly, I never want to see another car showroom again.'

Just at that moment, Evelyn made a sudden appearance.

'She's looking very chipper today,' whispered Dan. 'Something's up…'

'Good morning, everyone. I just wanted to let you all know I've arranged for a special visitor to come to the school on Friday morning. I think you might be both surprised and delighted to learn that we've got celebrity chef Larry Largo coming. He's a very inspiring speaker and he's agreed to give a short talk during assembly, and then visit some of the classrooms. Now, to make this fair, I have put everyone's class on a piece of folded paper in this bowl, because he will only have time to visit a few, as I'm sure you realise…'

'Ooooh, how exciting,' said Fay. 'I love Larry's programme on the telly. Scott bought me his new book for Christmas…'

'I've never heard of him,' said Noel.

'Oh, I have,' I said, - 'isn't he that Scottish cross-eyed bloke who's really fat, with ginger hair?'

'That's the one,' said Dan.

'Oh my God! The kids will have a field day.'

'Noel, could you come up and draw out three names, please?' Evelyn smiled at him in a particularly syrupy way.

'Right you are,' said Noel, looking less than enthusiastic.

Evelyn read out the chosen few. 'The lucky classes are – Mr Dodden: Year 8 Maths, Mrs Gardener: Year 7 Art, and Miss Blewitt: Year 9 English.'

'That's you, Laura!' said Fay, - 'Oh, I'm gutted!'

'Think of it more as a lucky escape,' said Noel, sitting back down.

'I wonder how she managed to get Larry Largo to agree to come here… I mean, it's quite a coup, isn't it!'

'Maybe she's related,' said Fay.

'No,' said Noel. 'They aren't.'

'How do you know?' said Dan. I gave him a look to shut him up.

'Well, anyway, at least it's something to look forward to, isn't it!' said Fay.

'If you say so,' said Noel. Fay rolled her eyes.

'I'm going to bring my book in and get his autograph,' she said, happily.

My Year 10s were a little bit overcharged when I walked into the classroom. William was back in his usual seat and enjoying a bit of notoriety himself.

'Oi, Will, did you enjoy your holiday, then? Where did you go, Will? Fire Island maybe, or was it Burnham-on-Sea?' Charlie Pinnock was enjoying himself. The class hooted and bellowed with excitement.

'Shut up, Pinhead,' said William. 'You're such a prick!'

'That's enough! You've had your fun, so settle down NOW!' I shouted at them all. 'Right, after marking your homework, it seems to me that you ALL need to focus on less SHIRKING and more WORKING! Right, CHARLIE?' Charlie feigned ignorance. 'Well, you don't appear to have given me your homework…'

'It accidentally caught fire Miss,' he said, guffawing.

At lunch time I decided to escape to town for my own sanity. I took a short cut through the kitchens, where some of the staff were huddled together just outside the door having a quick smoke before serving lunch. When they saw me, they stubbed out their cigarettes and went back in. One of them, however, stubbed her fag out on the wall and threw it in the waste bin just inside the kitchen, still smouldering.

'Excuse me,' I said, - 'but do you always do that?' I pointed to the waste bin. 'Where's the Manager?' I said, - 'I need to speak to her.'

I found Olga tucked away in her little dark office, surrounded by invoices and staff rotas.

'I think I've found our fire-starter. It wasn't William. I'm pretty sure it was one of your staff, throwing a lit cigarette into the bin in the kitchen. I've just witnessed her doing it.'

'They know they're not supposed to do that. I've told them so many times.'

'Well, to be honest, they aren't supposed to be smoking on school grounds at all,' I said. 'I'll have to inform the Head, I'm afraid. It's important that people know it wasn't William Parsons who was responsible.'

Olga sighed. 'I don't want to have to sack anyone. It's so difficult to get reliable kitchen staff these days.'

I looked at her incredulously. 'Well, Olga, it'll be up to Evelyn anyway.'

I felt so pleased about William being off the hook that I almost went back into school to look for him, but the sunshine and fresh air was so inviting, I carried on walking into town.

Sometimes I wonder what it would be like to be able to go into town and be completely anonymous. What bliss that would be. No one watching you or noticing where you go, no one calling out in the street or sniggering behind their hands, or laughing loudly and pointing at you… honestly, it's a wonder us teachers don't all turn into agoraphobics or end up suffering from a host of other mental disorders, for that matter. So far, I've managed to avoid being seen with any boyfriends in town – that would cause consternation and horror, to be sure. I mean, how could their teacher possibly have another life outside of school?

To my great satisfaction, I managed to do my shopping and go to the bank incognito – particularly as I had to nip into The Babyland Store to use their loo. I think I got away with that! It's not so long ago that there was a rumour going round at school that Noel Jones was a cross-dresser because Denise Channing and Chloe Stevens saw him entering a dress shop called *Pretty in Pink* and re-emerging with a large carrier bag. These kids are brutal, I'm telling you! They were calling him 'Mrs Jones' for weeks afterwards. When I just started here at St Judes, there was a young teacher who was foolish enough to think that it was a good idea to tell his Year 9 class that his hobby was flower-arranging. He had *Tiptoe Through the Tulips* ringing in his ears until the day he left. It's even worse if they can't find anything about you to hang an insult on – they will make something up. Poor old Mr Clement was permanently cast as a Nazi sympathiser and the kids used to give him the Nazi salute behind his back just because he taught German. As my old college tutor used to say, "*all we can do is try to instil in these kids a sense of moral responsibility, but don't forget... you can't teach a crab to walk straight*".

Back at school, I found Evelyn in her office and told her about my Dinner Lady discovery.

'Well, we still don't know why he was in the kitchens, Laura...'

'I think I have a possible explanation for that, Evelyn. I think it's quite simple, actually. I've been noticing he doesn't eat any lunch. He's really very thin.'

'Boys his age are always thin, Laura...'

'I know, but I don't think he's getting enough to eat at home. He was probably hoping to find some food in the kitchens here. He won't admit that, of course.'

'OK, well, if you're right, I don't know what we can do about it.'

'Well, I've been meaning to mention this to you, Evelyn...' I took a deep breath, - 'I've kind of offered him a room in my flat...' I waited for the inevitable response.

'What? You did WHAT?' Evelyn's eyebrows threatened to disappear completely into her widow's peak, her thin face blanching simultaneously.

'Yes, Evelyn,' I said, trying to stand up straight and look confident.

'Good God, Laura! Have you lost all sense of reason? It's a completely ridiculous idea. What will his parents say? Have you spoken to his social worker? I don't think you've thought about this properly at all. It's typical of you. It's irresponsible and impulsive.'

'Well, you're entitled to your opinion,' I said, fighting the desire to punch her on the nose.

Evelyn threw her hands in the air. 'Well, I'm telling you not to do it, Laura. It could have serious repercussions for you, for William, AND for the school!'

CHAPTER 11

I *sooooo* needed my yoga class last night. My stress levels were through the roof. I'm still fuming about Evelyn's reaction to my plan for William. It was completely uncalled for. Strange that she went into teaching, when she has so little empathy or understanding for some of these kids. I'm the first person to complain about them, I'll admit it, but there are times when you need to step in and do something to help. I am really surprised she was so upset about my proposition – it's not as if I'm doing anything illegal or dangerous… at least I don't think I am. Anyway, William hasn't agreed to it yet – he might decide against coming here. It would be quite a big decision for him. For me too. I mean, Evelyn is quite right – I haven't thought it through properly at all. I need to speak to his social worker ASAP.

Otto loved his walk this morning. We went via the bakery, and they always give him a treat (usually a left-over sausage roll). It's a great way to start the day, and today I felt much better about my clash with Evelyn. I'm not going to let it get to me. When I rang Cath, last night, feeling really down, she was a great help.

'Sounds like she's got her own agenda going on,' she said, suspiciously. 'She overreacted massively don't you think? I mean, I still think you're bonkers, but it's your choice. If I were you, I'd just plough on regardless - it's nothing to do with her anyway. It's between you and William and the social worker.'

Cath is so sensible. Thank goodness for friends. It's far too soon to discuss this with Gabriel of course. I wonder what he'd say about it…Probably that I'm crazy, like Cath says.

Before going to school this morning, I left a note for Gabriel asking him if he'd like to come to the School Ball with me on Saturday. I'm not sure if I did the right thing because it feels a bit soon, but, anyway, I've taken the plunge.

'Miss, Miss,' said Sanjay in class this morning, - 'can I have a new jotter?'

'Why?'

'Because Ryan threw my bag in the pond on the way to school.'

'Is this true, Ryan?'

'No, he's lying. I never touched his stupid bag…'

'Yeah, you did,' said Gillian. 'I saw him, Miss. He chucked it off the bridge.'

'Why did you do that, Ryan?' I said, looking him straight in the eye.

'Ryan scowled and said, - 'he started it!'

'I didn't!' shouted Sanjay.

'Right, both of you stay behind after class, please.'

Honestly, it's a wonder any teaching gets done in this school. By the time you've dealt with all their altercations and gripes, you're tearing your hair out. It's like swatting wasps at a picnic – you just get rid of one, and another comes along. Over the years I've heard everything:

Miss, Gary keeps kicking my chair; Miss someone's flicking spitballs; Miss, Susan's sticking her ruler in my back; Miss, Martin stuck chewing gum in **my** *hair; Miss, there's a bee in* **your** *hair; Miss, there's a stink bomb in Martin's bag; Miss, can we open/close the window; Miss, I need the loo; Miss, I forgot my pencil case/books/lunch; Miss, I feel sick; Miss, I've* **been** *sick…*

The list is endless. I'm pretty certain that if you added up all the time that they actually did any work, it would amount to a very small percentage of the day's activities.

At the end of the session, Ryan and Sanjay stayed behind as requested. I discovered that they'd been fighting over whether Man United should have been awarded a penalty kick after the final whistle…

'Did you knock their heads together?' asked Fay at lunch time.

'I wish,' I said, - 'honestly, Fay, I sometimes think I'm living in a parallel universe of insanity.'

'Yep, that's because you are. By the way – I've done a load of quiz questions for Saturday. Could you manage to photocopy some celebrity faces for a 'guess who' game? We can cut the faces in half and stick miss-matching ones together. It's quite fun, trying to guess which two people they are.'

'Oh, OK. I'll need to get some magazines…'

'You could ask Noel – he'll have plenty of newspapers.'

'So, Laura,' said Fay, changing the subject, - 'are you still coming alone, then?'

'Don't know yet. I've asked him. He hasn't had a chance to reply yet.'

'OK, well, I hope he comes – we're looking forward to meeting him, aren't we, Dan?'

'Are you bringing anyone?' I asked him.

'Well, I asked my sister, Beth. She said she'd love to come.'

'Noel says he's not coming,' I said, in his earshot, as he sat down opposite us. 'He says he'd rather stay at home and watch TV.'

'It's not my cup of tea.'

'We're having a quiz, Noel,' I said, hoping to entice him.

'You won't persuade me,' he said, getting his book out.

Fay smiled. 'He's a right old stick-in-the-mud,' she whispered.

My phone buzzed and I checked my messages.

'Is it *him?*' said Fay.

'Yes. He says *yes*, and *is it black tie?*'

'Tell him it is…'

'No, Fay! No one else is wearing a dinner jacket!'

'Oh, but he'll be so handsome!'

'How do you know?'

'Just guessing!'

'I thought I'd wear my Dame Edna outfit,' said Dan.

'That would be really funny,' said Fay. 'I dare you!'

'Well, I can't sit here having fun all day,' he said. 'I've got a football match to referee.'

'How on earth will you do that?' I said, pointing at his gammy leg.

'It's table football down the pub,' he said, laughing. 'I've got the afternoon off.'

'Ooooh, I wouldn't mind a pint right now,' said Fay. 'My Year 11s have their Chemistry GCSE exam this afternoon. I feel as if I'm sitting it myself, I'm so anxious for them. I'd better go and check everything's OK. See you all later.'

When I got home, I found a note from Gabriel cancelling tomorrow's dog training session. I felt strangely relieved. It wasn't that I didn't want to see him exactly, just that I was hoping to redeem myself and I need more time to prepare, especially since this week has been very taxing, to say the least. It was a nice note, though, which cheered me up, and he'd left me a little bunch of freesias. They smelled divine. I showed them to Otto, who was not remotely impressed.

By the time Friday came around, I'd managed to avoid Evelyn's razor-sharp tongue, but I'd spoken to William's social worker, Orla, who was not much better and wasn't very enthusiastic about my idea. She commented several times that being single wouldn't be the best thing for William, and that he needs a male role-model. I had to bite my tongue when she said that – I mean, what sort of role-model does he have at the moment, for heaven's sake! She said she'd speak to William and get his 'perspective' on it, but not to expect anything because his mother would probably refuse to allow it. I said I thought that his mother probably couldn't wait to get rid of him, which didn't go down very well. '*It's not for us to comment*,' she said, haughtily.

Assembly this morning was the most exciting thing to have happened since the fire in the kitchens. Whole school assemblies are a rarity, as there isn't really enough room for all the pupils in the main hall. However, this morning was an exception. Evelyn was in her element, beaming with pride at her own achievement. The local reporter from the Gazette was there, with her photographer snapping away as Larry enthused about his meteoric rise to fame and his small beginnings here in our town.

'Did you know he was from here?' whispered Morag. I shook my head. The kids were enthralled, not with his tales of cooking exploits, but with his eyes which roved around independently of each other and were fascinating to watch. He spoke for twenty minutes, and then Evelyn allowed some well-chosen questions from the floor (hand-picked reliable Year 10s). It didn't stop some of the other kids shouting out, though.

'Mr Lardo – how much money do you make?' said Adam Fisher.

Evelyn quickly stepped forward. 'It's *Largo,* Adam. And that's not the sort of question we ask people.' She smiled painfully at Larry.

'Well,' said Larry, - 'I don't mind telling you that I've been lucky to make a good living doing something I love, and if you kids work hard enough, you could do very well too…'

Adam looked disappointed with Larry's response. 'Have you got a Porsche?' he asked.

Evelyn scowled down at him from the lectern. Larry just smiled and said he didn't drive because of his eyesight. Before anyone could ask anything else, Evelyn directed us to go back to class.

Once the kids were all sitting down, I told them Larry would be along soon to meet them. I emphasised to them that personal remarks and questions are not acceptable.

'OK, Adam?' I said, making sure he'd heard me.

'Yes Miss. But, Miss, how does he see with cross eyes?'

'Um, I don't know…'

'He probably crashes into things a lot,' said Fergus.

'How does he do cooking?' said Chloe. 'Do you think he has a white stick?'

'Maybe he's got a dog to help him…' said Ollie.

'Dogs can't cook, stupid!' said Denise.

'I didn't mean that!' said Ollie, scowling.

Their conversation was interrupted by Larry making an appearance at the door. I shushed them and opened it. He walked in smiling happily.

'Do any of you like cooking?' he asked them, leaning casually on my desk. A few of them put their hands up. 'What do you like to cook?' he asked.

'Noodles,' said Frankie Beaston.

'Toast,' said Jane Flynn.

'Cakes,' said Denise.

'Brownies,' said Chloe.

Larry looked impressed. 'What recipe do you use?' he asked.

'Well, it's Betty Crocker, innit,' she said.

'OK, well…I like to cook things from scratch with fresh ingredients. It's better for your health that way. He looked around the class, and I could see they were all mesmerised by his roving eyes, which were pointing in opposite directions. I was struggling not to stare at them myself.

Adam could no longer contain his curiosity and blurted out, 'Mr Lardo, how can you see recipes and stuff with your wonky eyes?'

Larry smiled graciously and, putting his hand in his pocket, drew out an eye patch. 'Like this,' he said, putting it on over his right eye. I gave Adam a hard stare to try and shut him up.

'What's it like being cross-eyed?' said Ollie. 'Can you see down both ends of a road at once?'

'What about football,' said Barny. 'Can you, like, run ahead and see the ball behind you at the same time? I mean, that would be so cool!'

Larry continued to smile, although it looked a bit forced now. 'That's right, son,' he said, - 'I'm like a chameleon - I can swivel my eyes in any direction. It's really useful if there are any snakes around…'

'Wow,' said Ollie. 'I wish I could do that!'

'He's joking with you, idiot!' said Denise. Ollie reddened and scowled at Denise who promptly stuck her tongue out at him. Before things spiralled out of control, I thanked Larry for taking time to come and chat with them.

'That's no problem. I've enjoyed meeting you all,' he said, making a quick exit.

'I've got these for you,' said Noel at lunchtime. He handed me a pile of newspapers and magazines.

'Oh, brilliant! Thanks Noel.'

'It's the least I can do, since I'm not coming,' he said. 'Have fun cutting some of those people in half – I must say I'd relish doing that to some of them…'

I sometimes wonder whether Noel gets any joy out of life. Mostly he seems a bit of a misery guts.

'Do you think he's always been like that?' I asked Fay, as I sifted through the photographs for likely victims.

'Probably,' she said. 'People don't change that much, do they! By the way, I got a great prize for the quiz tomorrow.'

'Oh, what is it?'

''Well, when I asked Larry for his autograph, I also asked him if he would be willing to donate a prize. He was very generous. He's offered us a meal for two at his restaurant in London, a signed book and tickets for his TV show in August!'

'Oh, wow! That's just brilliant, Fay! You're a star!'

'I know,' she said. smugly.

There was a message from Mrs Wang on my answer phone when I got home. I pressed 'play' and opened a window for some fresh air.

Hello, Laura…I am just calling to say your Mum is missing today, but she found now, OK…police have got her and bring her back…she OK now…

I tried ringing her back but got no answer. I closed the window again, grabbed my bag and went straight out.

When I walked into Mum's house, Mrs Wang was talking to a couple of policewomen, and Mum was sitting quite happily watching TV.

'Are you Laura?' they asked.

'Yes. What's been going on?'

'Well, it appears that your mother went shopping with Mrs Wang here in town and wandered off out of sight. Mrs Wang couldn't find her…'

'I look everywhere,' said Mrs Wang, - 'but she nowhere to see…'

'We sent out a search party. Luckily, someone spotted her walking along the dual carriageway ten miles away and reported it. When we caught up with her, we found her shopping in Romford Market…'

'How on earth did she get there?'

'We don't know. She's not making much sense. Anyway, she's home safe now.'

'Yes. Thank you so much,' I said. 'I can't thank you enough. Thank goodness you found her.'

'We'll be off now. But it might be a good idea to put some phone numbers in her coat and bag, in case she goes wandering off on an excursion again!'

CHAPTER 12

Poor Mrs Wang was very upset about losing Mum, and said she didn't feel she could take her out any more. I don't blame her. I asked her if she was still willing to come to the house. Luckily, she said she didn't mind doing that. She did point out that Mum quite often forgets who she is, though. Apparently, the other day, Mum thought she was the next door neighbour and told her to stop her cat from coming over the fence. Mrs Wang thought she meant Betty.

'But Betty not jump that high,' she told Mum.

'Your cat is digging up my flowers,' complained Mum.

'But Betty in house whole time...she good dog...'

'Not dog. CAT! Your CAT!'

This went on for some time until Mrs Wang realised Mum meant the neighbour's cat. It just happened to come into the garden during this conversation. 'There it is!' shouted Mum, rushing into the garden to shoo it away.

I'm still completely dumbfounded as to how my mother managed to get to Romford from Sheppington. She has no idea herself. In fact, she doesn't even recall what she did five minutes ago, never mind yesterday. Maybe it'll come to light later. The main thing is, she came to no harm, thank the Lord. Jenny rang me this morning to say she's going to be late, and could we start without her. Typical! I got up early, walked Otto and hot-footed it to Mum's, hoping that she hadn't decided to go out for a midnight stroll last night.

'Mum, we're going out soon,' I said, seeing that she was only half dressed.

'Where?'

'Somewhere nice. It's a surprise.'

'I don't like surprises, Laura.'

'OK, well, we're going to visit an old friend of yours,' I lied.

'Oooooh, is it Margery Dunlop? I haven't seen her for ages.'

'Um, yes Mum, it is.' I cringed inside. Margery Dunlop has been dead for six years. It did the trick, though. Mum was ready in double quick time. We got to the first place on my list (Cherry Tree Lodge), rang the buzzer and waited.

'It's very big,' said Mum. 'I don't remember Margery's house being as big as this…'

'She must have moved, Mum.' My mother looked round suspiciously as the expansive front gardens, large shrubberies and sweeping flower borders.

'Ah, do come in. It's Laura Blewitt, isn't it?' said the receptionist. She was carrying a clipboard and wearing a lanyard round her neck.

'This is my mother, Rose. We've come to visit Margery,' I said, winking at the woman and hoping she understood what I meant. She gave me a funny look and waved us inside. She started to recount the long history of the building and its various uses. I looked at her lanyard for her name. 'Janet,' I said, 'do you think you could show us round fairly quickly, please. I've got two more to see today.' Janet gave me a rather cold look and marched ahead.

'This is nice, isn't it Mum?' I said, as she showed us the lounge and dining area, where a few people were playing cards and doing puzzles.

'Where's Margery?'

'We don't have any residents of that name here,' said Janet, curtly. She showed us a couple of rooms with elderly people asleep in chairs and we made our way back to the front door.

'Let's try another place,' I said to Mum. 'Margery might be at the next home, I mean house…' Jenny rang me while we drove to the next address and said she'd meet me there.

I parked up at *Sunnyside Villas,* just as Jenny pulled up next to me.

'Great timing,' she said.

'You missed the first one,' I said, slightly narked.

'Well, you can tell me all about it,' she said.

'Margery wasn't there,' said Mum. 'She's moved.'

'This looks nice,' said Jenny, as we looked up at the massive Victorian building before us. There were bars on all the windows, disabled ramps and wheelchair walkways all around it.

'I don't think Margery lives here,' said Mum. 'She's not disabled – she's a champion runner, you know. She always wins the 100 metre sprint at school…'

We were let in and shown around by a nice friendly man in a nurse's uniform.

'Who's he?' said Mum, loudly.

'He works here,' said Jenny. 'He looks after the old people who live here.'

'I knew this wasn't Margery's house,' said Mum, crossly.

I looked at Jenny. 'Well, you can't keep the pretence up for ever,' she said.

'Let's have a look round anyway, since we're here, Mum,' I said.

She grumpily tramped round as we inspected the social areas and some of the private rooms. Suddenly, as we went past an open door, an old lady called out: 'There you are! I've been looking for you for ages!' She darted out and took Mum by the arm and asked her if she'd like a cup of tea.

'Margery, how nice to see you,' said Mum, sitting down next to her. The old lady chatted away to Mum for ages. After a bit, the nurse told her we needed to go.

'Do come again,' said the old lady. 'Any time!'

'That's Grace. She's a bit doolally - lovely though – always happy and cheerful,' he said.

'She's such a chatterbox, is Margery,' said Mum. 'You can't get a word in edgeways.'

'That was Grace, Mum,' said Jenny.

'No, it wasn't. I'd know her anywhere. That was definitely Margery. Don't you think I know my own friends!'

The next place we visited wasn't so good. It smelled of wee and boiled cabbage.

'I don't think any of my friends are in hospital, are they?' said Mum, looking anxiously round.

'It's not a hospital,' said Jenny.

'Well, it looks like one. They've got no curtains or carpets. And look at that awful plastic furniture! Whoever owns this place ought to do it up and make it look nice. They should put some nice lights and pictures on these bare walls,' said Mum, looking up at the tatty Health and Safety posters hanging up. The Manager looked a bit po-faced and showed us out.

'Well, I liked *Sunnyside Villas*,' I said as we drove back. 'It's like a hotel there. What did you think, Mum?' I looked across and saw that she was asleep.

'It's expensive,' said Jenny, looking at the brochure when we got back to Mum's.

'She can afford it, though,' I said. 'She's got her own pension, and Dad's. The hard thing is going to be persuading her to go.'

'Well, we can get her to go for a short break first.'

'I feel terrible, Jenny.'

'We don't have any choice, Laura. She can't manage on her own any more. And going AWOL like that yesterday is just the last straw.'

'What if she hates it there?'

'She might actually enjoy it, Laura. They've got lots of activities going on, and she'll have people to talk to and keep her company.'

'I suppose so…it's just…I don't know, it's all happened so quickly.'

'Laura, we have to be practical. It's the best thing for everyone.'

After we'd given Mum some lunch and tidied up, Jenny and I went our separate ways.

'I thought you were staying a bit longer,' I said.

'No, I can't. I'm meeting Jack later – we're going down to the coast for the rest of the weekend. He's got some friends in Bournemouth. We're staying over.'

'That sounds nice.'

'Well, they say you can judge someone by the company they keep, don't they? So, we'll see…'

I watched Jenny get into her smart red convertible and drive off quickly down the road. She obviously couldn't wait to get away. Poor Mum. At least she won't really notice anymore.

'Doreen is coming in half an hour, Mum,' I told her. 'Shall we have a cup of tea?'

'Yes, please. And one of those chocolate biscuits that nice lorry driver gave me…'

'Lorry driver?'

'Yes. He was so helpful, Laura.'

'Oh my God, Mum! You got into a strange man's lorry?'

'He wasn't strange. He was very friendly.'

'But Mum – he could have been an axe murderer…'

'What ARE you talking about, Laura! He was on his way to market with some veg, that's all! Anyway, I'm fine.'

'Good grief! Please don't do that again. No one knew where you were!'

'I knew where I was. I don't know what all the fuss was about.'

'How did you think you would get home again, then?'

'Your Dad would have come, Laura. Now he's retired he's…' She stopped and looked around the lounge at his empty chair. 'He's not here, is he?'

'No. Mum, he isn't, but Jenny and I are. We'll always be here for you.' She got a tissue out of her pocket and wiped her eyes.

'Look. Mum, Doreen's here,' I said, seeing her little car pull up outside. 'I've got to go now. I've got an important date tonight.'

'I hope it's not that awful boy from up the road…what's his name?'

'You mean, Dexter.'

'Yes, that's the one. I really don't think you should be seeing him, Laura. He's got a shaved head *and* an earring…'

I smiled at the memory of my mother's past mortifications. At the time I refused to give him up. I wondered if Dexter still had a bald head and an earring, and what he would be doing now.

'That was seventeen years ago, Mum. And, no, it's not Dexter. I've got to go now.'

Back at the flat, Otto was overjoyed to see me return to him. What it is to have such a welcome every time I go home! I honestly don't think he can tell the difference between half an hour and four hours, bless his little furry socks! I was just getting his lead on when there was a tentative knock at the door. I looked out of the side window and saw William standing there with a large holdall, a rucksack and a carrier bag.

'You said it was OK to come…' he said, as I let him in.

'Yes, of course, William,' I said, trying not to let him see how surprised I was. 'Come in and tell me what's happened.'

He kicked his trainers off and plonked himself down on the sofa in the lounge. 'Orla came round,' he said.

'Right…'

'My Mum had some dodgy people in the house, and well, Orla didn't think they should be there. They were doing drugs and stuff. My Mum told her to 'f' off. When she'd gone, my Mum told me to 'f' off as well. She was drunk as usual. I dunno, I'm just sick of it all, to tell you the truth…'

'OK, William. I'm sorry that happened to you – you are very welcome to stay here this weekend, but I'll need to speak to Orla about it on Monday to make sure she agrees.'

'I don't care if she doesn't. I hate it. I'm not going back there again.'

'OK, William. Let's put your stuff in the spare room. I was just about to take Otto out…would you like to come with me? We could get an ice-cream at the park.' He nodded and mumbled a *thank you.* I patted his arm. 'It's going to be all right, you'll see.'

Thank goodness for Otto, I thought, as we went round the park. William was enjoying himself chasing the dog round and throwing his ball for him. The timing of his sudden appearance couldn't have been worse, though. I'm going to have to leave him alone in the flat all evening. Oh God! What have I done! What if William's mother comes looking for him, along with her dodgy friends? And then, later, if things go well, I won't be able to invite Gabriel in – I mean what a passion killer this is! Damn it! I really don't want to have to explain it all to Gabriel this early on. It could put the kybosh on any further progress. And what if he hates children…or in this case, teenagers? I don't even know if he's got any of his own – I mean, I haven't asked him straight out…Oh, I have got myself into a bit of a pickle here…

Back at the flat, I explained to William that I was going to the school do, and I needed to go and get ready. 'Do you like pizza?' I asked him. He nodded. 'OK. I'll put one in the oven for you while I get ready. You can put the TV on, or do stuff in your room – whatever you like, OK?'

'Thanks, Miss.'

'Um, so, William, while you are here in the flat you can call me 'Laura'. It's 'Miss' at school, but *Laura* otherwise. OK?'

'Yes Miss, I mean, *Laura.*'

Getting ready, I realised that something else was going to have to change. Normally, I wander between the shower and my bedroom completely starkers. Suddenly, my personal freedom has been seriously curtailed. I'm going to have to be very careful from now on. As I got dressed, Gabriel texted me to ask if I wanted to be picked up. '*No thanks*', I quickly responded. I told him I needed to be there early to help set things up. I ended my message with an 'x', then took it away, then put it back, then removed it again. Oh, the agony of the early days of dating! I put it back and sent the message.

I could tell William was taken aback by my appearance when I went into the kitchen to retrieve his pizza from the oven.

'Teachers do dress up sometimes, William,' I laughed. 'Some of us can even manage to look glamorous occasionally.' He did smile when I said that. 'Right, William, I'm going to have to go now, but I just want to say a few things. Please don't let anybody in – I mean NOT ANYBODY AT ALL. Here's my phone number if you need to speak to me. Here is a spare door key if you have to go out. And here is where I keep the snacks,' I said, opening a cupboard to show him. 'Help yourself, OK?'

'Yes. Thanks.'

'I've put a towel on your bed if you want to shower. Are you going to be OK by yourself?'

He looked at me as if I was a bit mad. 'Yes, I'll be fine.'

'OK. Give me your number and I'll see you later. Oh, one more thing – don't let Otto out by himself. He can get out of the garden easily, as I haven't made it escape-proof yet.'

'Wow! Look at you, girl!' said Fay when I arrived in the dining hall.

'And you!' I said. 'You look stunning. Where's Scott?'

'He's coming later. Right, we've got stuff to do. Let's have a drink first,' said Fay.

'But the bar's not open,' I said.

'I've brought my own supply,' she said, bringing out a bottle and plastic cups from a bag secreted underneath the prize table.

'Haha, Fay, you're like a naughty schoolgirl! I can't get too drunk tonight, by the way.'

'Oh, I know – It's a bit boring having to be responsible adults,' said Fay, meaning in our roles as teachers in charge.

'No, I mean I've got a teenage boy taking up residence, as we speak.'

'You haven't!'

'Yes. He turned up this afternoon, I couldn't turn him away.'

'Oh, my goodness…'

'Don't tell anyone, though. Particularly not Gabriel. He might think I'm a bit nuts, if he finds out.'

'OK. Mum's the word. How will you keep it quiet, though?'

'Well, I know I'll have to tell him, just not yet.'

The next hour was spent sorting out the quiz and the prizes. Larry's took pride of place on the table.

'Which team have you put Gabriel and Scott on?' I asked Fay.

'With Dan and Beth.'

'OK. Although Dan's a bit of a liability where my boyfriends are concerned. He'll probably tell him all sorts of things. Speak of the devil!' I said, as Dan came tottering in on heels and wearing a ridiculous sparkly dress that looked as if it came out of his grandmother's wardrobe. He was hardly recognizable with his massive purple wig and huge glittery Edna glasses.

'I thought you were joking about coming dressed as Edna Everage,' I said.

'You should know me well enough by now!'

'Oh God, Dan, you look hilarious. Can you dance in those shoes? I mean, you're still recovering from your accident. I can't wait to see Evelyn's face when she sees you. Who's she bringing, by the way?'

'No idea. Does she have a partner?'

'I've never seen one. Not since her divorce from Greg.'

'Ah, yes,' said Fay, - 'I've got her down as part of Bryce's team. So, his wife is called Jo.' She looked down her list of teams. 'That means Evelyn is with someone called Tim.'

'I can't imagine anyone putting up with her, can you?' I said.

'Well, you won't have to imagine any more…' she said, nodding her head in the direction of the entrance. Evelyn was dressed in a plain but tasteful blue satin dress and matching jacket. Beside her was a thin, balding man with a pale complexion. Wearing an old-fashioned black suit and a tired expression. We waved at them but only got a vague response. Then she saw Dan.

'You're for the high-jump,' said Fay.

'Tell her you did it for charity – she can't tell you off, then.' Dan laughed. 'I don't care if she doesn't like it – it's time the old boot grew a sense of humour.'

'Where's your sister?' I asked.

'Late, as usual. She'll probably get here half way through the meal. What about your date?'

'Here in fifteen minutes.'

'I'm looking forward to telling him all about you,' said Dan.

I gave him a hard stare. 'It's OK – all your secrets are safe with me,' he said, revising his comments.

'Dan, I mean it!'

'The parents are starting to turn up,' said Fay. 'We'd better go and start welcoming them in.'

I'm not sure what to think about the events of last night, but I don't think Evelyn will wish to repeat the experience in a hurry. The PTA's choice of DJ was (with hindsight) not perhaps the most sensible idea they've ever had. *Jumping Jack Flash* might be the right bloke for a stag or hen night, but not really suitable for an occasion where a more tactful and civilised entertainer is called for. Having said that, some of the parents threw themselves wholeheartedly and without restraint into his suggestive balloon games. At the behest of Evelyn, the PTA Chairwoman, Belinda, had to step in and caution him when he started waving a packet of condoms around and producing a bag of courgettes.

'I don't think that's a good idea at all,' she said, signalling furiously to Belinda to stop him going any further.

The food was stodgy and dull, but no one seemed to care much, since most of them were availing themselves of copious amounts of discounted wine and vodka. Fay and I managed to run the quiz without anyone getting into a fight, which was quite an achievement, given the amount of male testosterone flying around, fuelled by booze and bravado. Once the dancing started, the evening began to seriously deteriorate. Gabriel was charm itself, but he must have thought the whole thing was a tremendous farce. One of the parents tried to climb up onto the table of desserts and promptly stood on a pavlova, sending it flying onto the dance floor, someone stole Larry's book and used it to prop up a wobbling table, Beth pulled Dan's wig off and threw it across the room during a drunken Conga dance, knocking Evelyn's drink down her dress, and Belinda had a meltdown when Morag threw up in the raffle-ticket bucket.

At the end of the night, Gabriel gallantly offered to help some of us clear up.

'You don't have to stay,' I told him.

'It's fine. I love sweeping up broken glass and spilt food,' he said, laughing.

'Well, you're a keeper,' said Fay, winking at me.

'How do you think it went?' said Scott, with a straight face.

'Well, I'm guessing that's the first and last Ball the PTA will hold, don't you think?'

'I enjoyed myself,' said Scott. 'It was most entertaining. What did you think, Gabriel?'

'Well, apart from the awful food, terrible music, inappropriate games, warm drinks and doubtful guests,' said Gabriel, looking at Dan, - 'I thought it was a huge success!'

'Well,' said Belinda, - 'the parents seemed to enjoy themselves…'

'Most of them could barely stand up at the end of the night – I think we need to re-think the alcohol selection and perhaps not serve spirits next time,' I said.

'I don't think there'll be a 'next time',' said Dan. 'Did you see Evelyn's face when *Jumping Jack* announced that twerking competition? It was epic!'

'Does she even know what that is?' said Fay.

'I think timid Tim did,' said Dan, grinning. 'I saw him smirking, and when she saw him he switched to serious face mode instantly. It was so funny! Hey, Gareth, that reminds me – what happened to the blow-up doll?'

'I put it in the rubbish by the kitchens, like she told me to,' he said, looking embarrassed.

'Any idea who did it?' said Dan.

'Who did what?' said Gabriel, intrigued.

'I'll tell you later,' I said.

'I think we've finished here,' said Fay. 'Time to go home. I'm shattered.'

Gabriel walked me to my car. 'Would you like to come back for a nightcap? You could drop your car at your flat first, if you like, and I'll run you home afterwards…'

I looked at his handsome face and disarming smile, and was more than tempted, but how could I accept? I thought of William's miserable face and his little pile of belongings, and knew it was impossible.

'I'm really sorry, Gabriel, but I can't stay up any longer. I have something on in the morning and I need to get to bed. Maybe next time?'

CHAPTER 13

William had gone to bed when I got back last night, and I got my first glimpse of life with a teenager in the house. Shoes and socks were left lying around, an empty packet of crisps with crumbs spilling out all over the sofa, the remote control was shoved down the side of the cushions, a chocolate wrapper was stuck to the rug in front of the TV…

'I hope you didn't eat that!' I said to Otto. I took him out for his midnight pee and went to bed, exhausted.

There was no sign of life from William when I got up the next morning. I pottered about, tidying and cleaning and then took Otto out again for a proper Sunday walk. I left a note for William in case he thought I'd abandoned him.

Help yourself to whatever you can find for breakfast. I'll be back in an hour. Don't set the place on fire!

L. 😊

As I was walking along the road, I realised he might take that last bit to heart, even though I'd told him we pretty much know he wasn't responsible. Oh, well, I hope he's got a sense of humour, or this living together business will be very trying. I sat in the park while Otto ran round with some other dogs, and called Cath.

'Are you free to chat?'

'Yes,' she said, - 'Matt's gone out on a bike ride, so it's just me here. So, how was the Ball?'

'Well, depending on your viewpoint, it was either a raging success, or an absolute fiasco.'

'Haha, that sounds fun! I wish I'd gone, now. Did Gabriel enjoy it?'

'I think he did, from an amused observer's perspective.'

'And is there anything else to report? Any progress on the romance front?'

'Not really – there could have been if William hadn't turned up just as I was getting ready to go out.'

'Oh, no! That was bad timing!'

'You're telling me! I couldn't believe it! Anyway, he's now ensconced in my flat for the foreseeable future.'

'Are you there now?'

'No, I'm out with Otto. William's still asleep.'

'Laura, what are you going to do? I mean, you can't just have him there permanently…'

'Well, it is my own fault. I felt sorry for him.'

'Does Gabriel know?'

'No. I had to give him the cold shoulder last night. Goodness knows what he'll think when he finds out.'

'Well, you know about the third date rule, don't you?'

'Haha, Cath, you know I don't follow rules! Anyway, the truth is, if having a teenage boy in my flat is going to put him off, then he's not worth bothering about, is he?'

On my way back to the flat, I picked up some croissants from the bakery. William was in the shower, which was a relief. I mean, you hear terrible stories about teenagers not washing and their rooms becoming fetid caves of pestilence and contamination. It was the opposite in our house - my parents were always complaining about the reek of perfumes, hairsprays, body washes and shampoos of various assortments. My father was forever opening windows and doors and telling us we'd ruin our lungs breathing it all in. Little did he know we were already practicing ruining our lungs with borrowed cigarettes behind the pavilion at the local park. I look back on those days with a mixture of horror and nostalgia. We were naïve, impetuous, and impatient to be older – hanging around waiting for something exciting to happen. Jenny, being older, was always trying to get rid of me. *'You're spoiling my fun,'* she'd say, when I was an annoying gooseberry to her illicit liaisons with various boys she liked. '*Go AWAY, Laura,'* was always ringing in my ears. She must have been delighted to be able to leave home to go to university. But at least we had each other, unlike William, who seems to be completely on his own.

'Look what I got us to eat!' I said to him, when he finally appeared.

'Great!' he said, seeming to be genuinely delighted.

'What do you want to do today?' I asked him. 'Are you going to meet up with some of your friends?'

'They want me to play football this afternoon,' he said.

'Well, that sounds like a good idea.'

'I can't, though.'

'Why not?'

'I don't have any football boots. My last ones split, and my Mum wouldn't buy me another pair. She said it was a waste of money.'

'I see. Well, can't you play in your trainers?'

'No, it's a proper match. No one wears trainers…'

At the retail park I found a space to park near the sports shop, and we went in. I must say, I was blown away by the overwhelmingly vast choice of trainers and football boots, and somewhat shocked by the price of them too. I didn't even know Louboutin made football boots! At £985 they'd better be good!

'Look, William,' I said, - 'I can't afford most of these.' He shrugged and we surveyed the cheaper ones. I felt completely out of my comfort zone here. Having had no brothers or male cousins, I really didn't have a clue about anything to do with boy-stuff, and it showed. 'How about these?' I said, pointing to what I thought were perfectly good. William's expression said it all.

'Nah, they're done out.'

'Pardon?'

'Done out – it means, like, dead…'

'I assume you mean they're not trendy enough?'

'Yeah,' he said, smirking.

When we came out of the shop, William looked happier than I'd seen him in ages. I almost felt like a proud mother. Not that I know what that's like, but I did feel quite pleased that I'd made him happy, even if it was short-lived. I dropped him near the football pitch and went home feeling quite gratified. This feeling didn't last long, unfortunately. While I was out, Gabriel had sent me a message and I hadn't noticed it pinging.

'Hi Laura! Just to say thanks for the 'Ball' experience! It was good fun. I'm away now for a couple of weeks. I hope you don't mind, but I've asked my sister, Isla, to walk Otto for you. She's really good with dogs and very reliable. Sorry about this, but I'll explain when I'm back. Gx'

I made myself a cup of coffee and sat down in the kitchen, feeling deflated. *TWO WEEKS!! Where is he going for TWO weeks? And why didn't he mention that yesterday? Maybe I have inadvertently put him off…*

I decided to distract myself by marking all the homework piling up. At least there's only two weeks left of having to read and assess classwork until the end of the summer term. I read through Year 9's efforts to describe a scary experience. In fact, they were pretty entertaining and a good tonic. I photocopied some of the funniest extracts to show Ray:

'My scary experience was really, really, really, scary. It was so scary, that I can hardly manage to write about how scary it was… (Harry Beamer)

'When I broke my arm. it was quite scary. I was jumping on the trampoline with my sister, and she shoved me off. She said it was an accident, but I know she done it deliberately. I was screaming and everything and my Mum took me to hospital and then I got a plaster on my arm. I never, ever want to have anything broken again. It was worse than when I hit my head on a stone, or when I pulled my loose tooth out or when I got stung by a wasp, or when my sister staple-gunned my hand.' (Charlie Pinnock)

'My scariest experience was when I got lost in London. It was in a giant shop and we got split up. A nice lady found me, and they did a message on the loudspeaker. My Mum was really angry with my dad because she said it was his fault because he was looking at the football on his phone instead of watching me and we never went to London again.' (Adelle Clarke)

'I got stuck up a tree once, when I tried to get my cat, Womble, to come down. My sister said if we didn't get him, he might fall out of the tree and die. So, I climbed up, but then I couldn't get back down. The man from next door had to bring a ladder and climb up to get me. Womble came down when my Mum shook a box of biscuits.' (Barny Russell)

'My worst experience ever was when my Uncle Colin chopped down a tree in our garden, and it fell on the greenhouse and all the glass smashed everywhere. My Dad went ballistic and was going to kill Uncle Colin, but my Mum stopped him.' (Jane Farley)

'It was really scary when we went on a ferry last year and the waves were really big. Loads of people were being sick and it was the worst journey ever. I thought my stomach was going to come out of my mouth, it was THAT bad! And also, my Nan's hair went on fire once 'coz Grandad's cigarette fell on it when he went to sleep. It went up in big flames and my dad tipped a bottle of lemonade on it to put the flames

out. When Nan's hair fell on the floor, she was TOTALLY bald and that was REALLY scary.' (Jake Wilson)

Reading these made me think about frightening things from my own childhood that happened to me. Luckily, they were few and far between, mostly involving my sister, now I come to think about it. There were quite a few bicycle incidents when we were going too fast down the lane. I was always trying to catch up with Jenny and fell off more than once or twice into nettles, or onto stones, and once, into a ditch full of stagnant water. (My mother's face was a picture.) We tried to make a treehouse once using some of Dad's old wood – we borrowed his hammer and a load of nails. We were doing quite well until Jenny hammered a nail through my hand (accidentally, of course). I've still got the scar to prove it. And then, of course, there were things that happened to us as teenagers. Things that my parents never found out about. We had a pact that we would keep each other's secrets, although mine were pretty lame, compared to Jenny's. The boys we hung out with used to do the craziest things, though. I shudder now when I think about some of them. James Havers' collection of roadkill in formaldehyde particularly sticks in my mind, and Glenn Barclay's enthusiasm for home-made fireworks, Peter Gardner's fascinating ability to pick locks and miraculously open car doors, Gerry Hudson's obsession with breeding poisonous snakes, and possibly the most dangerous and death-defying of all - Richard West's amazing talent for free-climbing up buildings, or any other vertical structures he came across. Richard's incredible agility coupled with his audacious charm got him in and out of trouble fairly regularly. The police were not too impressed with the frequency of phone calls from the public reporting a 'burglar' attempting a break-in at various locations around town. He's gravitated to mountains now, where he's free to do whatever he wants. At least I think he's still doing it. I'd rather not know if he's fallen off one of them.

I jumped out of my skin when the front door opened, forgetting I had a lodger now. Otto rushed and jumped up to welcome William as if he'd always lived here. It did feel a bit odd having someone around again after such a long time being on my own.

'Did you win?' I asked him later, over dinner.

'Nah, we were a player down,' he said. 'But we still did OK.'

'And how were your new boots?'

'Yeah, great, thanks.'

'We've only got two weeks left of term, William,' I said, thinking I'd better find out if he was doing anything in the summer. 'What do you normally do in the school holidays?'

'Nothing much,' he said. 'Just go to the park and stuff.'

'So, you don't have a holiday or see any relatives?'

He looked at me as if I'd suggested something really outlandish. 'No.'

'Oh, right. Have you *ever* gone away on holiday?'

'Nah. My Mum does, sometimes.'

'Where does she go, then?'

'Well, she's been to Spain quite a lot. She went last year for a month, with a bloke called Wayne who she's known for ages.'

'Why doesn't she take you?' I asked.

'Dunno. She says she needs her own space.'

'So, who looks after you then?'

'No one. I can look after myself,' he said, tucking into his cottage pie with gusto. 'This is really good, by the way. I wish my Mum could cook.'

'I take it she doesn't, then?'

'No,' he said, - 'she sometimes gives me money for chips, but usually I just make a sandwich, if there's any food in the house. She doesn't go shopping much…'

'I see…' Since William was relaxing quite a bit, I was gleaning quite a lot of information, so I tried to extract more. 'Is that why you were in the school kitchens the day of the fire, William?' He went quiet. 'It's OK – I'm not going to say anything to your friends at school.' He looked at me and nodded. 'Has it always been this way?'

'She used to be better, but she just gets drunk all the time now and people are always coming round and taking drugs. The house is like a pigsty. It's always noisy and the dogs are always barking. I can't sleep and my Mum doesn't care – she just tells me to shut up.' He was becoming more upset by this point, so I changed the subject.

'What do you think you'd like to do when you leave school, William?'

'Not sure. My Dad's a lorry driver. I might do that. It's quite good money.'

'Well, OK, but you are quite a clever boy, and you could go to college, or even University if you carry on doing well at school.'

William shook his head and laughed. 'No way! Uni's for losers.'

'Well, you're only fourteen, at the moment, so we've got time to work on that attitude!'

'How did the rest of your weekend go?' said Fay, as we grabbed a cup of tea before lessons.

'Not quite as good as I'd hoped,' I said.

'Oh…'

'Well, I've suddenly acquired a child and it's not what it's cracked up to be…'

'You're right there!' said Fay, laughing. 'I used to have a very rosy idea of family life. You soon realise it's bloody hard work! But, Laura, he's only been with you for two days!'

'I know! I'm struggling already! Last night, I had to pick up his filthy kit off the bathroom floor before I could have a shower, and then I realised he'd used up all my shampoo…'

'Haha, that's nothing!' laughed Fay, - 'tip of the iceberg, my girl! Just wait till he's been there a month – you're going to need more than one yoga session a week with Morag to keep you sane. But what about Gabriel? I suppose having William staying put the kybosh on that…'

'Yes, of course it did! And Gabriel texted me yesterday to say he's going away for two whole weeks, without a proper explanation. He's asked his sister to walk Otto! I mean, that's just a bit odd, isn't it?'

'Oh dear. Sounds like that man is on thin ice.'

Noel came in and sat down opposite us. 'Do tell! How did Saturday night's extravaganza go? Evelyn is looking particularly po-faced this morning.'

'Ah, Noel – you missed all the fun!' I said.

'It depends on what you think constitutes 'fun', Laura.'

'Well, basically everyone drank way too much, and it descended into a bit of a drunken rabble,' I told him.

'So, no surprises there, then. I told you it was a bad idea.'

'Who are you talking about?' said Dan, joining us.

'The parents,' I said, - 'although Morag's looking a bit sheepish this morning…' we all looked over at where she usually sat.

'Where is she?' said Dan.

'She left when she saw us coming,' said Fay, - 'I think she's embarrassed.'

'So, let me guess,' said Noel, - 'she danced topless on the bar with a rose between her teeth? Or did she molest some poor unsuspecting man under the table? I told you – drink is the root of all evil…'

'I thought that was 'money'?' said Dan.

'Only if you spend it unwisely,' said Noel.

'It wasn't a total disaster,' said Dan. 'Some of the parents want us to do another one at Christmas.'

'I don't think Evelyn will agree to that. She said if we do another one, there'll only be soft drinks available,' said Fay.

'Well, as long as she doesn't mind a very small turn-out – say about 6 people…' I chipped in.

'The PTA said they made a shed-load of money, so it was actually a roaring success,' said Dan. 'Anyway, I thought it was a good night out. Beth and I had fun.'

On the way to class, Ray caught up with me to let me know the situation regarding his replacement. 'Just to let you know, Laura, Evelyn's told me it's someone called Valerie McPhearson. She's from Durham, apparently. Evelyn was very keen – no other contenders came close. She's coming next week to meet everyone.' My heart sank at the mention of her name. I'd known her at university.

'Right,' I said.

'Don't sound so enthusiastic!' said Ray.

'I know her,' I said, 'from Uni. We, um, didn't get on very well.'

'Oh, well. I'm sorry to hear that, Laura. Maybe she's changed - it was a long time ago.'

'Hmm, well, I suppose I'll find out soon enough, won't I! Oh, Ray, why do you have to go!'

'Sorry. Look, Laura, like I said, maybe it's time for you to have a change too. Think about it – could be the best thing for you…'

At lunchtime, I rang Orla and was lucky to catch her, by all accounts. I explained what had happened over the weekend and was met with a long pause before she spoke.

'Is William at school?' she finally said, - 'because I need to come in and talk to him. This isn't normally how we do things. It's most irregular.'

'Well, I'm sorry, but he obviously needed somewhere to go, and…' She cut me off mid-sentence.

'There are procedures – I'll get back to you,' she hung up.

'Well, that was rude!' I said out loud, putting my phone away. No sooner had I put it away when it rang again.

'Hello, Laura?'

'Yes, Mrs Wang - what's the matter?'

'Well, I think your Mum did something to washing machine. It's water everywhere…can you come soon?'

CHAPTER 14

Well, that was stressful! I don't know what possessed my mother to put a rock inside the washing machine. That duvet will never see another bed, that's for sure. Poor Mrs Wang must be seriously considering her employment options right now. Anyway, I now have a dilemma – if I get Mum a new washing machine, she could easily do the same thing again. I mean, rocks and washing machines are just not compatible. Neither are rocks and duvets. It took me an hour to clean up all the soggy feathers plus the tsunami of foam which had swept across the kitchen and into the lounge. My mother, seemingly oblivious whilst glued to *Countdown,* was up to her knees in feathery suds.

'What to do with machine?' said Mrs Wang, as we surveyed the smashed glass door swinging perilously from one broken hinge.

'I'll have to ring the council. I'll need to get some help to move it, though. It'll have to wait a few days. I'll do her washing from now on. We can't have another disaster like this.'

I gathered up the shredded duvet and crammed it into a binbag.

'Where are you taking it?' asked my mother.

'To the tip, Mum. It's completely wrecked.'

'You're not throwing it away, are you? I'm sure it can be mended. People these days just throw things away without a thought. When I was young, we always patched things up and breathed new life into them – it's much less wasteful, Laura.'

'OK, Mum. I'll take it home and sew it back together,' I lied. 'I'm going to take your washing home too, Mum.'

'Why aren't you calling the plumber out? It'll be an easy fix, Laura. It just needs a new door.'

'Mum, it's got a hole in the drum the size of the Grand Canyon. It's not fixable!'

'Well, things these days just aren't made to last, are they? What a waste of money *that* was. I'll be phoning that company up to complain. They should give me my money back.'

'Mum, it's twenty years old! And… I'm sure that nowhere in the instructions did it say it was a good idea to put a great big pointy rock inside it and set it going on full spin.'

'Well, I didn't have a tennis ball.'

After Mrs Wang and I had used up nearly every towel in the house to try and dry out the lounge carpet, I needed to get back to work.

I'm going to have to hurry up and sort out a place for Mum at Sunnyside. I can't see Mrs Wang putting up with her for much longer and, in any case, it's too much of a worry when I know she's on her own. I'm sure she'll be quite happy at Sunnyside – it seems very nice and friendly. At least she won't have easy access to many domestic appliances there. Thank goodness I'd already removed most of these from Mum's house. Of course, she has noticed some of the things are missing – like the food mixer, the liquidiser, the toaster, the microwave…basically anything that chops, burns, or has the potential to explode. 'I can't even find a decent knife, Laura,' she complained the other day, - 'I don't know what's happened to them all.'

'Orla's been looking for you,' said Evelyn, as I scooted past her office.

'Is she still here?'

'Yes – waiting in Ray's office for you. I haven't changed my opinion, Laura…'

'No, I didn't expect you to,' I said, holding my ground.

'It'll end in tears.' Evelyn turned and went back to her desk.

I found Orla looking slightly agitated, sitting in Ray's swivel chair.

'Sorry,' I said, - 'I didn't know you wanted to see me. I've had a family emergency – my mother…'

'I've spoken to William and explained that he can't just live wherever he wants,' she butted in, - 'not without proper consultation, anyway. We can put him into emergency accommodation until we find him somewhere suitable.'

'Where will that be?'

'I'm not at liberty to tell you that at the moment, I'm afraid.'

'Oh. Well, what does William think?'

'He will have to comply whether he likes it or not.'

'Has Evelyn Ferrier got anything to do with this?'

'What do you mean?'

'Well, I know she doesn't agree with William staying with me.'

'We've had a discussion, but rules are rules, Laura. William's parents haven't agreed to it anyway.'

'Can't you get their permission? They don't want him there anyway.'

'It's a complicated process, Laura. Look, I understand you want to help but we will do our best for him. He can stay with you until we sort something out.' She looked weary. 'We've got 380 kids in care in this borough alone,' she said, 'and I am trying to find fifteen places right now. The problem is, we need more verified foster carers.'

'So, let him stay with me, then!'

'I wish it was that simple,' she said.

When I got home later, there was a message from Isla to say everything was fine and Otto had enjoyed a long walk by the river.

'Did you enjoy yourself, then?' I said to Otto, who was still damp. 'I think you went for a swim, didn't you?' I'm sure he almost nodded and he was definitely smiling when I said that. Dogs really are amazing creatures. I'm sure they're not as dumb as they look. When William came in, he went straight to his room. Otto followed him and scratched at his door to be let in.

I rang Jenny to tell her that I'm booking Mum in for a week's respite.

'How did your weekend go?' I asked her.

'Hmm, well, on a scale of one to ten, it was maybe a two…'

'Oh, why?'

'Jack didn't tell me we were camping. I was completely unprepared for roughing it. Honestly, I was so cross with him. His friends thought it was hilarious. I tried to make the best of it, but you can't really go abseiling wearing sling-backs and a tea dress, can you!'

'Oh, no!' I laughed. 'What did you do?'

'Well, I did what any self-respecting person would do – I went and booked into the nearest hotel.'

'Well, at least you didn't go home.'

'I don't know if Jack is going to work out, Laura – he actually had the cheek to call me a 'party pooper'! I think he may be a bit too young for me. He's plainly quite immature.'

'How old is he, Jenny?'

'Twenty-seven,' she said, quickly.

'What? He's ten years younger than you!'

'I know. It was fine to start with. Anyway, what about you? How was the Ball?' she said, not wishing to engage with this subject any further.

'Awful.'

'Did you go on your own?'

'Yes, I did,' I lied.

'I don't mean to speak out of turn, Laura, but isn't it time you got back on your horse? It's been six years…'

'Yes, I know. I am thinking about it.'

'Well, you shouldn't wait around too long. Look at me, on the shelf at 37.'

'Nonsense,' I said, - 'the right man will come along soon…'

I don't believe he will, to be honest. Jenny goes through men like a knife through butter. I don't know how she does it, but they don't last five minutes. If I was very brave, I would give her some advice, such as - don't be so critical, don't be so selfish, don't be so bossy, don't be so dismissive, have a sense of humour...The list is quite long, so I think I'll just leave it. I do want to stay friends with her after all. Of course, I don't tell her much about my boyfriends because I don't want to hear her 'advice' either.

'I'm going to try and book Mum into *Sunnyside* for a couple of weeks, while I'm away.'

'Where are you going?'

'Hebridean islands.'

'On your own?'

'Yes. It'll be a lovely rest for me.'

'Well, my advice is to take your thermals and buckets of midge-repellent.'

'Really?'

'Yes, it's freezing cold up there and covered in biting insects.'

'Thanks.'

'You're welcome. Right, I need to go. Let me know if you get Mum in and I'll try to visit her while she's in there.'

Trust my sister to take the shine off my holiday plan. I bet she's just jealous, especially after her disappointing weekend, and even more disappointing boyfriend. Perhaps I should invite her to come with me...on second thoughts, that would be a terrible idea. I can't believe I entertained that possibility for even a nanosecond. I'm going to stick to my guns and be totally alone and enjoy the peace and quiet. Mind you, if I don't hurry up, I'll have to take my mother with me, which would be even worse.

I rang *Sunnyside* immediately. The last thing I wanted was to be forced to take my mother away with me. We haven't been on holiday together since 2003, and that was when Mum was perfectly compos mentis *(well, mostly)*. She'd decided in her wisdom, that a walking holiday in the Alps would be an ideal choice for a recalcitrant, lazy and miserable teenager. I swore at the time that I'd never go on holiday with my parents EVER again. It was possibly the most boring and depressing week imaginable. There was no one there under 50 and we had to walk miles every day – it was just like that film with Ingrid Bergman and all those hundreds of children tramping interminably over hill and dale with no end in sight. Suburbia seemed like heaven when we got home. I don't know what my mother was thinking of – apart from possibly forcing me to appreciate that what I had at home wasn't so bad after all. It worked, if that was her intention. Anyway, now that she's definitely a bit unhinged, I can't possibly have a holiday with her. It would be unthinkable.

'Hello, is that the Manager?'

'Yes, Mr Pilkington here…'

'We visited you on Saturday – my mother is Rose Blewitt.'

'Oh, Yes…'

'I know it's a bit short notice, but do you have a two-week vacancy in three weeks' time?'

'Well, it's a bit unusual for us to take someone as soon as that – we would have to do some checks first. We have to make sure she's safe to stay with us - does she have a criminal record, for instance?'

'Um, no, not that I know of,' I laughed.

'You can never be too careful, Miss Blewitt. We get all sorts…'

'Oh, I hadn't thought about that. Do you have residents like that there, then?'

'Certainly not,' he said, affronted.

'Well, one can't be too careful,' I said back. 'Look, Mr Pilkington, the only thing wrong with my mother is that she's old, and as I'm sure you noticed, she has dementia. She's not aggressive, or dangerous,' *(I crossed my fingers)* - 'not knowingly, anyway. Please feel free to do as many of your checks as you need to. I really would like to book her in – you will be doing me a huge favour. I can pay you up front,' I added, hoping to clinch the deal. He promised he'd call back by the end of the week.

I knocked on William's door and told him I had to go to my yoga class.

'William - don't worry about what Orla said, - we'll work something out between us. OK?'

'OK.'

'I'll get fish and chips on my way back around 7.30pm. Is that OK?'

'Yes, thanks. Can I have a steak pie?'

'Sure,' I said.

Morag was not her usual energetic self this evening. I suspect she must still be suffering from the after-effects of over-indulgence on Saturday. She did mention she could see a change in my body-shape, though. Apparently, I have 'more of a waist now'. Well, I'm glad someone noticed, because at the moment, I don't feel I'm benefitting as I should from all this vigorous exercise.

'You have to give it time,' she said. 'Rome wasn't built in a day.'

Of course, I could try harder on the diet front. Pie and chips for tea probably isn't the best thing to do. I'm probably undoing all the hard work in one fell swoop. I'm not feeling motivated enough – that's the problem. Morag's patchouli oil and incense sticks don't seem to do anything for my stress levels except stink the flat out. Poor Otto hides under the table whenever I light one up, and William is none too keen either. He hasn't said anything, but his face says it all. He probably thinks I'm a bit weird. He's going to think I'm even more weird when I follow Morag's instruction to move the furniture into the correct Feng Shui positions for positive energy flow.

After William and I had scoffed our dinner – him with gusto, me with guilt, I told him I was going to the park with Otto for an evening walk. I reckoned if I marched round the park for one hour, at a brisk pace, and did about 7,400 steps, that would burn off the unwanted calories. I was half way round when I heard someone shouting my name.

'Hey, Laura, how's it going?' said a sweaty, red-faced Elliott, as he came running up from behind.

'Oh, hello Elliott. I'm fine thanks. And you?'

'Yeah, good! I'm training for the half marathon next month,' he said, running on the spot while he chatted.

'I see. Well, don't let me hold you up…'

'You're looking great!' he said, - 'we should have a drink some time, for old time's sake. What do you think?'

Otto ran up to me from across the park, barking.

'You've still got the dog, then?'

'Yes.' Otto gave him a hard stare.

'Right, OK, catch you later, then.' He smiled, waved, and jogged off.

'Good boy,' I told Otto. 'You tell him.'

It was a bit unnerving, meeting Elliott unexpectedly like that. I felt irritated by him all over again. When I got home, I poured myself a big glass of wine and watched *For the Love of Dogs* on the telly, to console myself.

CHAPTER 15

'You're not going to believe this,' said Dan, on our way to the staffroom on Wednesday morning.

'Go on then…'

'The porno doll has made another appearance.'

'You're kidding! I thought it had been disposed of.'

'That's what we all thought. Someone must have got it back out of the rubbish bin.'

'OK, so where is it, then?'

'I'll show you,' sniggered Dan. We walked back along the corridor and outside to the courtyard behind the kitchen. 'Look over there…'

Across the grass and straddling an overhanging branch was the doll, newly inflated, moustache re-drawn and wearing a witch's hat.

'Cripes, how did they get it way up there?' I said, staring at it. 'It's more than thirty feet off the ground!'

'They must've climbed up there,' he said.

'Well, I don't have time for this, I'm afraid,' I said. 'My Year 11s have their English GCSE this morning. You'll have to deal with it. Maybe you could throw one of your javelins at it to knock it off its perch…'

'That'll make great viewing on social media, won't it!' said Dan, looking round at the kids who'd already gathered to gawp at it.

'I'm going to need backup,' he said.

Once my Year 11s were safely ensconced in their exam, I quickly went to teach my Year 8s. Unfortunately, the view from their window was perfect for the comedy show that was Gareth and Bryce attempting to clamber up a ladder that was too short. Watching them failing to retrieve the offending item was pretty funny. Whoever put it up there must have tied it on well, because they still hadn't managed to remove it by the end of the lesson.

'They've started early with their nonsense this year, haven't they?' said Fay, when we sat down for coffee break.

'Hmm?'

'The kids – the last exam isn't until Friday.'

'Oh, yes, God knows what they used to attach that doll to the tree. Gareth and Bryce are really struggling to get it down.'

'That's assuming it *is* the kids,' said Fay.

'Well, who else would it be?'

'Someone with a grudge against Evelyn, possibly.'

'Well, whoever it is, they've got a wicked sense of humour. By the way, what are we going to do about the raffle prizes we couldn't give out on Saturday?'

'Well, we've got all the Ball invitations, so we could put them into a hat and draw the winners tomorrow lunchtime. Most of the staff will be here…'

'Sounds like a good idea.'

'Good morning, ladies,' said Noel, plonking himself down opposite us.

'Noel, would you do us a favour tomorrow lunchtime and draw a few raffle tickets to pick some winners? We weren't able to do it on Saturday.'

'Oh, yes – Belinda told me about the unfortunate, most unedifying occurrence,' he said imperiously.

'Haven't you ever been drunk, Noel?' asked Dan, sitting down with us.

'Never.'

'I don't believe you,' said Dan. 'You'd have us believe you were some sort of holier-than-thou character from the dark ages! I reckon you've got a secret past of reckless youth you're not telling us about…'

'Well, I hate to disappoint you, Dan, but I'm afraid my life has been as uneventful and unexciting as it is possible to be.' He opened his *New Scientist* magazine and started to read an article about the life cycles of arthropods.

'I wish I'd travelled more and done more things before settling down to teaching,' said Dan. 'Don't you sometimes think you might have missed out a bit?' Noel pretended not to hear him.

'I certainly wished I'd waited a bit longer to have a family,' said Fay.

'I wish I'd had a better idea about what I wanted to do with my life,' I said, in a rare moment of candour. 'I've always wondered about whether I should have been a journalist – you know, going to exciting destinations, traveling the world…'

'Well, looks like we're all going to end up like Noel!' said Dan.

'Oh,' said Noel, nonchalantly flicking the pages over, - 'I forgot to mention the time I spent a year travelling with the Tuareg tribe in the Sahara…' We all looked at him. 'And, I'd forgotten all about my trips around Indonesia, Thailand, Cambodia, Vietnam, the Philippines, and Australia…' He said all this with a completely straight face.

'I knew it,' said Dan, - 'you old goat!'

Noel laughed. 'You lot are so easy to hoodwink.'

At lunchtime, I stood and waited for my Year 11s to emerge from their exam. Some of them looked happy, at least. Quite a lot of them didn't. I watched them all troop out and wondered what the future had in store for them. At their age I had no clue what I wanted from life. I can barely remember what I thought about at sixteen, apart from which CD to buy, or which crop top looked good with cargo pants. After chatting with them and discovering some of their answers to the questions, I decided to take the afternoon off and work from home.

I opened the door to my flat and realised straight away that Otto wasn't there and must be out with Isla. There was a lingering smell of stale food, cheesy trainers and damp dog, so I thought I'd better do some housework for a bit. Having an extra person and a dog seems to make quite a bit of difference to the usual workload, especially when neither of them does anything to help. I'd forgotten how annoying it can be. Henry was a past master at doing as little as possible on the domestic front. It wasn't much different to living with William, except Henry was a grown man who should've known better. I wandered round the flat tidying and cleaning and then went into William's room, which was already a tip. He'd left his cast-off underwear everywhere, including a solitary sock dangling from the lampshade. I noticed a pile of schoolbooks by his bed and sat down to have a quick look through them. From what I could see, the work he was managing to do was getting reasonably good marks, apart from maths, which he was obviously struggling with, judging by the amount of red ink.

Suddenly, the front door opened, and Otto came rushing in.

A tall dark-haired, woman with soft grey eyes just like Gabriel's, stood in my kitchen, smiling and patting Otto.

'Thank you very much for stepping in to help,' I said.

'Oh, it was fine. I work from home, so it's not a problem. In fact, I enjoy taking a dog out. My dog, Bertie, died last year, and I haven't got round to getting another one yet.'

'I'm sorry to hear that. Otto is actually my mother's dog, but she can't look after him any more. My goodness, you and Gabriel are very alike, aren't you!'

'We're twins actually. Didn't he tell you?'

'No, I didn't even know he had a sister until he told me you were coming. To be fair, though, we've only been out twice together, and the last date couldn't really be described as a proper date, so I haven't had a chance to give him the third degree yet!'

She laughed, - 'he's not the most open of people, I'm afraid. He can be a bit of an enigma. He doesn't deliberately withhold information - he just doesn't see the point in telling people things they don't need to know.'

'Mm – like not telling me he was going away. Do you know where he's gone for two weeks, Isla?'

She looked a bit uncomfortable. 'Well, yes, I do, but it's …'

'Confidential?'

'Yes, you could say that.'

'Can you give me a hint?'

'Look, Laura, I think he should tell you himself, but I do know that he really likes you, if that helps. He never stops talking about you.'

'Oh, well, that's nice to know…would you like a cup of tea, or coffee?' I asked her, realising I wasn't being very hospitable. 'We can sit outside in my very small but sunny garden.' I opened the back door.

'It's nice out here,' said Isla, - 'nice and secluded.'

'I think the correct term is 'confined',' I said, laughing.

'Have you seen Gabriel's place?'

'No, not yet.'

'It's pretty small. He doesn't even have an outside space, apart from his balcony.'

'Well, I suppose he's working – he won't have time for a garden.'

'Mm,' she said, - 'he's not really doing much at the moment.'

'Yes, he did mention something. He hasn't really said what work he usually does, to be honest. Apart from saying it's dull.'

Isla laughed. 'He's right there! It is, *deadly* dull! Honestly, Laura, I don't even bother asking him to explain it any more. He's an actuary – it's all about analysing screeds of data. I think I'd rather watch paint dry.'

'What do you do?' I asked her.

'It's almost as dull, but not nearly as well paid – I'm an accountant. Actually, I like the people I deal with, which makes it OK. You're a teacher, aren't you?'

'Yes, but not a very good one, it seems. They tell you it's the most rewarding thing you can do, but I'm living proof that it isn't! I've been thinking a lot recently about a career change.'

'To what?'

'That's the problem. I don't really know. I know what I'd like to do, but it wouldn't pay the bills, unfortunately.'

I found myself telling Isla all about my sister, my mother, my ex-boyfriends, and then felt embarrassed I'd rattled on. 'Sorry, Isla, you don't want to hear all that!'

'Oh, it's fine – it makes me feel like I've got nothing going on in my life compared to you, though!'

'What, no annoying ex's, no mad mothers or irritating sisters?'

'No, not yet anyway! I'd better go,' she said, finishing her coffee and getting up. 'It's been lovely to chat to you, Laura.'

'I've enjoyed it too. Hopefully, we'll meet again.'

'I really hope so.'

When William came in, I had a chat with him about making an effort to keep things a bit tidier, put his washing in the basket, and to try *not* to leave crumbs and empty packets everywhere. I'm not sure if he really took it on board, but when I showed him a glass from his room with mouldy milk in it, I think he got the picture.

'It's all blue and furry,' he said, amazed.

'Yes, and it would make you very ill if you drank it, William.'

'Why would I drink *that*, though?'

'If I got fed up cleaning up after you, maybe…'

It took him a while to realise I was teasing him. 'Oh, yeah…very funny!'

'Now,' I said, - 'I need a strong lad to help me move some furniture…'

Thursday morning was overcast and threatening rain. I tried to persuade William he should wear a raincoat. He looked at me as if I were two sandwiches short of a picnic.

'No one wears those,' he said, shocked I would even suggest it.

'A brolly, then?' He practically ran away from me and was out of the door before you could say 'knife'.

As I walked to school, it began to rain heavily, and I was very glad I had mine with me. I watched all the soggy kids traipsing along the road, their dripping wet hoodies hanging off them, looking like a mob of crows huddled together. What a strange mentality these teenagers have - a collective aversion to self-preservation, a complete and utter determination to be as foolhardy as it is possible to be. It's a wonder any of them survive into adulthood.

Before I went into the staffroom for a quick cuppa, I had to go and see Evelyn about the new replacement for the Head of Department, Valerie Mc Phearson.

'Try not to drip everywhere,' she said, as I took my coat off.

'Good morning, Evelyn,' I said.

She did have the humility to look a bit sheepish. 'Oh, yes, good morning Laura. I expect Ray has told you that Valerie McPhearson is going to be our new Head of Department. She's coming on Tuesday afternoon to meet everyone. Ray will show her around. I just wanted to check with you if there's anything you wanted to ask?'

'Well, I was wondering why she's moved down here from Durham, to work. Do you know?'

'She said she wanted a challenge – something to get her 'teeth into'. I think that's very commendable and I'm looking forward to working with her. I hope you will find her to be a hard-working and inspiring colleague. I'd like to think that you'll both enjoy a collaborative and supportive, mutually satisfying relationship.'

'Thanks, Evelyn, I'm sure we will, as long as it doesn't involve whips and chains,' I said, flippantly.

'Really, Laura, can't you take anything seriously!'

'Sorry, Evelyn, of course I'm hoping she works out well for us…'

'On a separate note,' she said, frowning, - 'I had another conversation with Orla yesterday. She's asked me for a character reference, regarding William.'

'Oh.'

'Don't worry, I haven't said anything detrimental about you personally, although I was tempted. Some of your teaching methods are somewhat eccentric, and as you know, I don't share your enthusiasm for them. I did, however, express my grave concern about the position you have put yourself and the school in, by housing a troubled and disaffected young man.'

'Right, well thank you for your concern, Evelyn, but we are doing fine.'

I had to leave before I said something I regretted and went to the staffroom to let off steam.

'You don't look happy,' said Dan. 'I'll get you a cup of coffee.'

'Thanks, Dan. I've just had a meeting about William, with the Führer. Honestly, I could punch her in the face. She's so interfering.'

'What did she say?'

'She thinks I'm taking a risk by giving William a home. She also thinks that, somehow, it's going to affect the school's reputation! I mean, that's ridiculous, isn't it?'

'It's because you're single, Laura. She thinks you'd be open to suspicion. It's just how people think. Imagine if it was a young girl staying with a single male teacher…'

'Well, that's different, isn't it?'

'Depends on your viewpoint, but all I'm saying is she thinks you've put yourself in a vulnerable position. I personally wouldn't be able to take in a young lad – it would be far too risky for me.'

'I know, Dan, but it's not as if Social Services aren't aware – it's all been registered properly. Anyway, I can't worry about what people think. This is about William's welfare. She's not going to bully me into submission.'

'You'll have to grow a pair, then,' said Dan, smirking.

'Do you know what else she said?'

'No…'

'That I'm eccentric! Just because of some of my alternative teaching methods.'

'You're just different in your approach, Laura. She doesn't have a creative bone in her body. Don't let it bother you. You get good results, don't you?'

'Not as many as I'd like.'

'Well, you can't make a silk purse out of a sow's ear. You do as well as you can in the circumstances. We all do.'

'Thanks Dan – you are a good friend. I'm really worried about Valerie McPhearson coming here in September as well. I know her from college. We're not very compatible. She's 'old school', for a start....'

'You're going to be a lone star in a sky full of rocks,' said Noel, as he sat down with his paper.

'Haha, that's very funny, Noel.'

'Just my humble observation.'

'He's right, Laura,' said Dan, - 'you stick to your guns. Have some more coffee – that'll put hairs on your chest.'

I had a sickening feeling in the pit of my stomach after my confrontation with Evelyn. I don't know if I want this kind of pressure in my life. Like people say, we've only got one stab at it, so we shouldn't waste it being miserable. Oh, well, there's only one more week left after this one, and I can forget about school for the rest of the summer. Bliss.

At lunchtime, Belinda brought all the invitations in a box and Noel picked out Larry's lucky winners.

'Well, there's a couple of people who will be pleased. I would have loved to win the meal for two,' said Fay. 'I can't think when it was that Scott and I last went out anywhere smart with lovely food.'

'You should tell him to take you out,' I said.

'I know. It's too easy to fall into a routine of work and domesticity,' said Fay. 'Once you're married with kids, it's just so exhausting to even think about making an effort to get dressed up to go out.'

'Well, you are an exception with five kids under twelve, Fay. I don't know how you hold down a job as well.'

'It's called a 'military operation,' she said, - 'plus Scott is fantastic. But my secret weapon is my mother – I really couldn't do it without her help.'

'You're so lucky. My mother couldn't wait for us to be independent. She actually told me once, that she didn't like children! Can you believe it?'

'Really?'

'Yes. And she also told my sister and me that if we ever had kids and needed a babysitter, we'd have to hire one.'

'Oh, no! Well, where my Mum's concerned, the more the merrier! Truly! You'll have to give them to her when you have yours.'

'I can't see that happening now, Fay.'

'Never say 'never', Laura. My friend Brie is forty-five and she just had her first baby.'

'Good grief, that's practically one foot in the grave!'

'You crack me up!' laughed Fay.

Later, at the flat with William, I got a phone call from Mr Pilkington.

'You'll be pleased to know, Miss Blewitt, that we have a room available for your mother to stay with us.'

'For the dates I requested?'

'Yes.'

'Oh, thank goodness! That's fantastic.'

'You did say you'd be able to pre-pay…'

'Yes, of course.'

'Thank you. I am sending you an email with the invoice attached, plus our banking details. Once the funds are in place, I'll send you confirmation.'

'William, we are going out to celebrate,' I said, literally jumping for joy. 'I just need to look at an email and then we can go to get a take-away or something.' I scrolled down and realised I'd missed quite a few relatively important emails which I should have responded to in the last week. There were a few from disgruntled parents. One was from Sanjay's dad, asking what the school was going to do about Ryan throwing his bag into the river. Another one was from Harry Beamer's mum asking where he got a giant bar of chocolate from, because she didn't believe what he'd told her about winning it. There was one from the care home that smelt of wee, asking if we were still interested, and one from the holiday cottage in the Isle of Lewis asking me to confirm my booking. Then Mr Pilkington's email popped into my inbox, and I nearly had an apoplectic fit.

'What's wrong?' said William, alarmed.

'Um, nothing…well, just …good grief… it's £2,000!!'

'What is?'

'For my mother to stay in a care home for a couple of weeks.'

'Wow! That's a LOT of money,' said William.

I rang Jenny.

'I told you it was expensive,' she said.

'I can't afford £2,000, Jenny!'

'Well, ask Mum to cough up, then.'

'You are kidding, aren't you? She won't want to go, so I'm pretty sure she won't agree to it.'

'Well, it's not me going on holiday, is it!' It was all I could do not to scream down the phone at her.

'If we share the cost, that's fair, isn't it – because you want to go away at some point and the reason you can do that is because I'm here, keeping an eye on Mum, aren't I?'

There was a long silence. 'OK,' she finally said. 'I'm going to have to go now – Jack's waiting in the car.'

'Going somewhere nice?'

'Just up to Claridge's.'

'Still with him, then, Jenny?'

'For the time being. He's promised to make up for the camping fiasco, and he does like to spoil me.'

Stay calm, I told myself. My sister is never going to change, so there's no point in trying to point out how utterly selfish and thoughtless she is. She definitely takes after our mother.

'Right, William, where shall we go?'

'I'll just stay here…'

'Oh, don't you want to get something out?'

'Er, yes, but…'

'Oh, I get it – can't be seen out in public with your teacher, I suppose. That's fair enough. I should have thought of that. I'll go and get something and bring it back.'

I suppose it's bad enough being seen out with your parents, but to be seen with your teacher would be a fate worse than death. The kids would make mincemeat of him. Oh, dear! Every day seems to bring up a new problem. Maybe Orla is right about this situation not being suitable for William. On the other hand, anything's got to be better than where he was before, surely?

'So,' I asked William over our takeaway pizza, - 'tell me about your dad - you haven't really mentioned him.'

'He's a tealeaf,' said William.

'Oh – what did he steal, then?'

'All sorts. Our house was always full of stolen stuff. My Mum used to go mad at him 'cos he filled every room with it all. And then he'd have these massive bonfires in the garden to burn all the boxes and stuff. The neighbours used to complain, and Dad got into loads of fights. It was proper scary. My Mum's not scared of him, though – she hit him with a frying pan once. She said he was waking the baby up.'

'Baby?'

'Yeah, my sister's. She doesn't live there anymore.'

'Where is she, then?'

'Don't know. She went off with some dude.'

'How long is your dad in prison for, William?'

'Ten years. Well, he's done two, so he's got eight more to go.'

'That's a long sentence. What did he do to get that?'

'They called it 'aggravated' or something. Basically, he had a gun, and it went off.'

'Good grief! Was anyone hurt?'

'Just my dad's finger. It got shot off. The man in the shop tried to get the gun and it went off.'

'Oh, that's horrible…'

'My Dad's a f***ing idiot. I don't want to end up like him.'

'Well, there's no reason to think you will, William.'

'My Mum says I will.'

'She's not in control of who you decide to be, *you* are. Anyway, she can't say things like that to you if you're not there anymore. This is the start of a new chapter for you, William.'

CHAPTER 16

'Can I go swimming?' asked William, on Saturday morning.

'Yes. But you don't need to ask. You're free to do what you want, you know.'

'I need money to get in.'

'Oh, of course. Here's £10 – is that enough?'

'Yes thanks. I might need money for food as well…'

It's beginning to get expensive, having to fork out for a teenager. He seems to have acquired a voracious appetite since moving in here, and I noticed the other day that his trousers are getting a bit short. I suppose I'll have to hurry up and get used to this new Mum role - I just haven't had time to adjust, and it's a bit of a steep learning curve, to be honest. Should I be giving him pocket money? And how much? At this rate, I won't be able to pay for my holiday. And that's the next problem to address – what to do about William while I'm away? I need help.

'Cath?' It's me.'

'Hi! How's it going? Regretting it already?'

'Well, I am a bit. He's costing me a fortune in food, never mind everything else he needs.'

'They should help you with all that, Laura – you should ask Orla.'

'Yes, I will, but it feels a bit wrong to ask, somehow.'

'Well, his own mother gets paid to look after him, so don't be shy. They can't expect you to pay for everything.'

'OK. I will.'

'Is it going OK apart from you being eaten out of house and home?'

'Yes, I think so. He seems happy here. We've chatted quite a bit – he's opening up, which is a good sign. He tells me some shocking things, though, Cath. Honestly, it would make your hair stand on end! But listen, I'm in a bit of a pickle over what to do when I go away. I don't know what to do with him.'

'Well, you can't leave him on his own.'

'No.'

'Is there anyone you could ask to look after him? What about your sister?'

I nearly choked on my coffee when Cath suggested that. 'Um, that's a NO. There really isn't anyone.'

'Well, you'll have to take him with you, then.'

'I thought you might say that.'

'There isn't an alternative, is there!'

'I was hoping you might come up with a magical solution, Cath.'

'Sorry, but I can't think of anything. It's not going to be the holiday you'd planned, I'm afraid.'

'No. Well, at least I've managed to get Mum into *Sunnyside* for respite.'

'Phew, that's a relief.'

'It definitely is. Mind you, it's costing an enormous amount of money – I could have another holiday for that amount.'

'My mother has decided to go on a Caribbean Cruise this summer,' said Cath, - 'she's going with a friend. I nearly fell over when she told me how much it was. It's her money, though, so she's entitled to spend it how she likes. Maybe when we're old and decrepit, you and I will be doing the same thing. What do you think?'

'Haha, well, if you're paying…'

'And dare I ask – how is your love-life going?'

'Hm, not as expected.'

'Oh…'

'Well, what would you think if your new boyfriend suddenly went away for two weeks without saying where or why?'

'That's a bit odd.'

'Exactly.'

'Maybe he had a family emergency?'

'I don't think so.'

'Or a work deadline?'

'No. He's not working at the moment. I can't help thinking that…'

'He's married,' said Cath, finishing my sentence for me.

'Well, yes…When I asked his sister why he'd gone away, she was evasive.'

'You met his sister?'

'Yes, she's walking Otto for me.'

'Oooooh, brilliant chance to pump her for information, Laura!'

'Well, I tried. It's difficult, because Gabriel and I have only just started going out together. I don't want to come across like some jealous possessive woman.'

'In that case, just chill a bit and see how things pan out,' said Cath.

This conversation didn't help one bit. All it did was make me feel even more suspicious. Watching an adaption of *Jane Eyre* on the TV after lunch, only served to make me even more paranoid. Gabriel does bear an uncanny resemblance to Mr Rochester, and my mind is now working overtime.

When William came home, he went straight to his room again. I suppose it's what fourteen-year-olds do, but I did detect the unmistakable whiff of a herbal product, which hung in the air for quite some time. I have my suspicions, but I don't want to make assumptions just yet. I mean, the skate park is full of teenagers smoking weed – it probably just drifted onto his clothing. Anyway, I don't want to be one of those judgmental adults who think the worst of young people.

I woke bright and early on Saturday morning and took Otto out. Thank goodness there's only a week to go at school. I'm on the home run now – just have to survive this last week and hope that Evelyn doesn't find an excuse to sack me. I'm probably being over-sensitive, but I get the feeling she would if she could. This teaching malarky is pretty lacking in job-satisfaction, I must say. But who do I know who can say they enjoy their job? My sister certainly doesn't appear to be happy in hers as a PR Manager, but then I suppose she's not a happy person in general. Noel is just counting down the months until he retires, Bryce can't wait to leave, Evelyn is miserable too. Fay is the only one who likes being a teacher, and I suppose Dan does, come to think of it. Maybe I'm just not cut out for teaching. That's probably why I'm finding it so draining. I really hope this holiday gives me a chance to re-charge my batteries, because my enthusiasm for this job is at rock bottom right now.

We went to the bakery for some bread on the way home and I found myself standing next to one of my Year 7 parents.

'It's Miss Blewitt, isn't it?' she said. 'You teach my boy, Callum.'

'Oh, yes. He's a good worker,' I said, not really knowing which one he was.

'Really?' she said, - 'because he's a lazy bugger at home!' She let out a loud, cackling laugh.

'Oh, well, I think he's got potential to do quite well.'

'I'm glad you think so,' she said, not convinced. After she'd gone away, I was racking my brains trying to think which boy it was. Then as I walked home, I remembered. He *is* a very lazy boy and terrible at English. Oh, well, there are so many kids at St. Jude's, it's impossible to remember all of them.

Once I'd fed Otto, I put four chocolate croissants in the oven to warm them up and went to have a quick shower. William was up and sitting in the kitchen when I came back. I went to the oven to get the tray out and discovered they'd gone. In front of William was an empty plate with chocolaty crumbs on it.

'Did you eat them?' I said, a bit taken aback.

'Yeah. They were banging.'

'What, all four of them?'

'Yep.'

'Well, they weren't *all* for you, William.'

'Sorry. I was starving. Can I have some toast now?'

'Oh, well, OK…' I got the loaf out and cut some slices. 'How many?'

'Four, please.'

'Good grief, you'll explode! By the way, how did swimming go?'

'Oh…yeah, it was great.'

'What did you do with your swimming trunks? They'll need washing…'

'Oh, no it's fine – they dried out already.'

'Well, they still need washing.'

'Nah, it's fine.'

'Where are they, William?'

'I left them at my mate's house.'

Hm...something tells me he didn't actually go swimming. This Mum role really is proving to be as challenging as teaching.

'I've got to go to my mother's house now,' I told him. 'What do you plan to do today?'

'I'm meeting some mates at the park,' he said. 'I've got to go now too, 'cos I said I'd see them at half ten.'

'OK, see you later,' I said. 'And try not to spend all your pocket money on junk food.' He disappeared, grabbing a couple of packets of crisps and three biscuits on his way out.

There was no answer when I rang my Mum's doorbell. I looked in through the kitchen window, but there was no sign of her. After some rummaging, I found her spare key under a stone and went inside. The place was empty. I rang Mrs Wang.

'Do you know where Mum might be this morning, Mrs Wang? She's not at home...'

'No, Laura. She not say she going somewhere. Maybe gone walkabout again?'

'Oh. I hope not.'

I went next door and tried to speak to her neighbours. The ones on the left were quite rude when I rang their bell. They said they hadn't seen her this morning because they'd only just got up on account of being disturbed at 4am by an 'infernal racket' coming from my mother's house. They said it sounded like someone banging saucepans. The neighbours on the other side said they hadn't seen her since she nearly set the whole street on fire. They didn't seem too happy either.

'She's a bit of a liability, isn't she! You really ought to do something about it,' said Mrs Bright. 'She could be anywhere by now, or she might have got herself run over on the road or kidnapped, even.'

'I knew an old woman who disappeared, and they didn't find her body for three years,' said Mr Bright. 'I think it was in a ditch by some fields, miles away…'

'No, Roger, it wasn't – it was in a scrap metal yard, she was in a pile of crushed cars.'

'No, that was that other one. I know what it was, she'd fallen down an old mine shaft – that's what it was. Someone's dog found her – 'cos of the smell.'

I had no idea my mother's neighbours were so awful. They had no idea I was being ironic when I said they'd been 'most helpful' and I would be sure to ask their advice if ever my mother went missing again.

I rang the police and told them about Mum. Who knew they had a special Missing Person's unit to deal with old people like Mum? Apparently, around 40,000 of the poor old things get lost every year. That department must be very busy.

I rang Jenny. 'Jenny, Mum's disappeared.'

'Oh, not again! When?'

'It must have been this morning, because apparently she was making enough noise to wake the dead at 4am this morning.'

'What do you mean?'

'I don't know, exactly, but it involved most of the kitchen pans and a rolling pin. Anyway, I'm just letting you know. I'll call you later if there's any news.'

While I was in the house, I took the opportunity to have a good look round and check for any problems. Mrs Wang is obviously doing a great job, because there weren't too many strange discoveries, although upstairs in Mum's bedroom, the carpet was rolled back as far as it would go. She must have given up because she would have had to lift furniture to finish the job. Odd thing to do, though. Anyway, apart from a few misplaced items, like cups in drawers, several onions under her pillow and a spider plant under the duvet, there were no more horrors to discover. There was a funny squeaky noise I couldn't work out, which was a bit odd. I probably should get the plumber to check her boiler. I also noticed her dressing gown and slippers were missing from the bathroom, so I rang the police back to tell them what she might be wearing. That should make her easier to spot.

I drove round town for an hour hoping to catch a glimpse of my mother but to no avail. I'll just have to let the police do their job I suppose. The Brights have really upset me, though, with their doom-ridden scenarios. Some people have no manners. Now I can't get rid of all these awful images in my head, of my mother lying abandoned in the middle of a field somewhere, or worse – prostrate and unconscious at the bottom of a deep, dark well. I went home, disheartened by my fruitless search, and did some marking to try and keep my mind off it.

Last week I'd set some homework for the Year 10s which was to imagine they were the Prime Minister and what they would do if they were in charge of the Country. I noticed that William had actually handed something in this time. Their ideas ranged from ridiculous to almost sensible and thought-provoking. Unfortunately, the silly ones were in the majority. Denise said that she would make sweets and drinks free for all kids and that schools would all be closed, and kids could do whatever they wanted to. She would ban classical music and the news and anyone over sixty would have to go and live on an old peoples' island. Everyone would have a huge house and servants and as many dogs as they liked. Charlie Pinnock decided that everyone would live in Australia and eat steaks and ice-cream all day long. People wouldn't have to mow the grass because there wasn't any, and you could watch TV in your room without anyone telling you off. Money *would* grow on trees, despite what his mum says, and he would build the biggest skating arena in the *'WORLD'*. Adam's effort was a bit more down-to-earth and showed some empathy for people less fortunate than himself. He thought that he would give poor people free wood to burn and pay old ladies to knit scarves and socks for the homeless *"like during the war"*. He also thought that people should be given land to grow vegetables and have chickens. Chloe's was only two lines long: *"If I was the Prime Minister, I would put all the rich people in prison and then get all their money and cars and stuff and give it to all my mates."* Fergus's wasn't much better, saying that he would buy Wembley Stadium so all his family could go to every match and be in the Royal Box with the best views. William's contribution, on the other hand, was quite interesting. He said he would "*compulsory purchase land that wasn't being used for anything and build lots of houses for poor people, and only people with low incomes would be able to live in them*". He thought that school was quite a good thing, but you should be able to leave at fourteen and get a job if you wanted to and then you could get a flat of your own to live in and then you could be as untidy as you liked. He also said that instead of going to prison, people should be made to do gardening or cleaning because "*those jobs are the pits, and at least they would be doing something useful*". As Prime Minister, he would make every Friday a holiday and give everyone extra money to spend on leisure activities, or McDonald's.

Maybe that's what he spent his £10 on? Oh, well, it's only what most kids would do with their pocket money. I think I used to spend mine on sweets or the cinema. Then, at sixteen, I got my first Saturday job. I was over the moon, because I could suddenly afford to buy my own clothes, rather than suffer Jenny's hand-me-downs or my mother's bossy choice of 'sensible' attire, and I was able to make my own disastrous fashion choices with gay abandon. It was so exciting to earn my own money and spend it how I pleased.

Suddenly my phone rang.

'Good news,' said the policewoman, - 'we think we have found her.'

I got to the local wildlife park within ten minutes of their call and made my way down to the river. My mother was sitting on a bench with two policemen chatting away as if nothing had happened.

'We've just been explaining to your mother, that ducks have to stay in the park where they belong,' said one of them, smiling. My mother was clutching a covered basket on her knee, and I could see a little beak poking out.

'Mum, what are you doing with a duck?'

'I need it for the garden,' she said. 'They can eat 200 a day, you know.'

'200 what?'

'Those horrible locusts I told you about.'

'I tell you what, Mum, how about letting me carry the basket and we'll go home and get you dried out and have nice a hot drink.'

'It's a good job she was wearing that bright orange dressing gown,' said one of them, - 'otherwise we might not have found her so quickly. Luckily, a member of the public rang in and told us they'd seen a woman acting strangely, wading into the water and waving a loaf of bread.'

'Well, thank you very much for finding her,' I said. 'Come on Mum, let's get you home.'

'We'll leave you to return the duck, then,' they said, walking off. I was hoping that by the time we got home, Mum would have forgotten all about the duck.

'Laura, what did you do with that duck?'

'It's in the boot of the car Mum, having a sleep. I'll get it out later and put it in the garden for you.'

'Oh, good,' she said. 'Those pests won't know what's hit them.'

'By the way, I said, getting her to sit down while I made us some lunch, - 'why have you got onions and a plant in your bed?'

'I didn't have any garlic, Laura. It's supposed to help you sleep. I've been so worried about these locusts coming, so Doreen suggested garlic under my pillow to help me sleep, but I didn't have any, so I thought onions are almost the same thing, aren't they? Doreen said it would work wonders…'

'And the plant?'

'Oh, that…well, plants help to clear toxins from the air. I saw it on David Attenborough's programme about air pollution. You should try it, Laura.'

'I see. Well, the plant will work better on the windowsill, and I don't think you want all your sheets smelling of onions, do you? I've changed your bed, so it smells nice and fresh. And another thing, Mum – what were you doing banging pans at some ungodly hour this morning, waking the whole street up?'

'It's what you have to do, Laura – it scares the locusts off.'

'Please don't do that any more, Mum, or you'll have the noise-abatement people visiting from the Council.'

'Well, I've got my duck now, anyway.'

'And the carpet, Mum – why is your bedroom carpet rolled up?'

'Monty Don said that carpets are really good for keeping your weeds down. I've never liked that carpet anyway – your dad's mother bought it for us.'

'Right, well, the thing is, Mum, you could get someone to come and do the garden, then you wouldn't have to worry about weeds or ducks or locusts any more. Would that be a good idea?'

'Mm, I suppose so.' She got up and went into the kitchen to get a biscuit out of the cupboard. 'Where are all my pots and pans, Laura?'

'Oh… I've taken them …to, um, give them a polish so they're nice and shiny for you…'

My mother looked puzzled and then annoyed. 'What am I going to use now, to scare those disgusting creatures away?'

'They're not coming to England, Mum. They LIVE in Africa. Have your tea.'

When I left, I decided to lock my mother in the house. I reckoned she was more in danger outside it than inside, even if only slightly.

By the time I got home, William was back in the flat, splayed out on the sofa, watching a very loud programme about police catching criminals.

'Please could you turn that down, William?'

'Oh, yeah, OK…' He said, only turning it down a bit.

'I mean, right down!' He did as I asked but looked huffy about it. I almost said '***whose house is this!***' but refrained. Instead, I asked him if he'd like pasta for tea.

'Is there any pizza?'

'No.'

'Have you got nuggets and fries, then?'

'No.'

'I'll just have crisps, then.'

'Um, right, William, you can't just eat crisps. I'll make us some nice pasta with tomato and basil sauce and parmesan cheese. You'll like it!'

He looked unimpressed and sneakily turned the TV up when I wasn't looking.

This is going to be quite challenging, and he's only been here a short time. I think I need to rewind back to the beginning and start all over again, I'm going to have to put some rules in place. He's not going to like it, but I can't go on like this. I've got enough to worry about already, with my mother doing strange things with ducks and onions and God knows what else.

I suddenly remembered there was a duck in my boot. What if it suffocates in there? I ran outside to fetch it in. I hadn't meant to bring it home, but there just hadn't been an opportunity to put it back without my mother seeing what I was up to.

Otto went berserk when he saw the duck and wouldn't calm down until I gave him a chicken stick to eat (I know that's a bit inappropriate, but I was desperate to stop him barking). I put the duck in the sink in some water and gave it some crackers to eat.

'Why is there a duck in the sink?' asked William, coming through.

'It's a long story,' I said. 'When we've had tea, I need to take it back to where it came from.'

'Can I come?'

'I suppose so – but you have to agree to have the pasta and stop eating crisps.'

'OK.'

Suffice to say, the duck did not stay where it was put, and after it had caused puddles of dirty water everywhere and jumped all over the kitchen tops, with Otto barking his head off again, I gave up trying to cook.

'Right. Come on William. We're going out. Looks like you're going to have nuggets and fries after all.'

I put the duck back in the basket, firmly put the cover back on, and we went out.

It was a good job no one saw us putting the duck back at the park. It probably looked a bit dodgy, particularly as the duck had made itself very cosy inside the basket and refused to get out. I had to turn it upside down and shake it. William thought the whole thing was hilarious, of course.

'Why don't we keep it?' he said. 'We could get eggs from it. That'd be really cool.'

'Well, two reasons, William: (A) – we don't have either a pond or any space, and (B) – it's a boy.'

He gave me a funny look.

'Boy ducks don't lay eggs, William.'

CHAPTER 17

I got up this morning, showered quickly, and slipped out with Otto for a walk in the early morning sun. It won't be quite as nice in the winter, but I'm committed now. Otto has brought me so much happiness these last few weeks, it's quite a revelation. Part of me wonders if things don't go too well with Gabriel, it won't really matter, because I've still got my dog! I am thinking of him as *my* dog now – there's no way Mum can have him back, even if the medication she's on makes an improvement in her, she's really too elderly to give him the exercise he needs. He's got so much energy.

When I got back to the flat, I remembered I hadn't rung Jenny to tell her about Mum. On the other hand, Jenny hadn't rung to find out, either. I think she's on another planet sometimes. I gave her a quick ring anyway.

'Mum's back home. The police found her in a park not far from her house.'

'Oh, good, Is she OK?'

'Yes, but she was trying to steal a duck.'

'What?'

'A duck, Jenny – you know, they're grey and brown with feathers…'

'I know that! I mean, why?'

'It's the locust thing – she's obsessed. I was tempted to leave it in the garden just to shut her up.'

'It would have escaped.'

'I know. It wasn't a well thought out plan. I had to lock Mum in the house though.'

'Oh, was that a good idea?'

'Not really, but I didn't know what else to do.'

'I've ordered a personal alarm for her, Laura. She can press it if she gets into trouble or has a fall. I've put your name down as the emergency contact.'

'Oh, right…thanks a bunch!'

'Well, it can't be me, can it! If you don't answer, the call goes through to the paramedics. Anyway, look, I've got to go. Sorry, but my taxi's here.'

Noel was in such a good mood this morning, he was actually smiling.

'What's got into you, Noel? You don't seem yourself today,' joked Dan.

'What do you mean by that?'

'Your demeanour is obviously more cheerful than we have come to expect from you, so it's a bit of a surprise. Have you won the lottery, Noel? Or had a pay rise? Or maybe your wife has gone away?'

'None of the above, Dan. Apart from this being the final week of term, which is always worth getting a bit excited about, I have just been informed that I've won a publishing deal with a well-respected and well-known textbook publisher in America.'

'Congratulations, Noel! That's fantastic news,' said Fay. 'What's it called?'

'*The Evolutionary Wonder of a Cockroach.*' Fay pulled a face. 'They're fascinating creatures, Fay. You'd be surprised.'

'Really?' I said, - 'no one likes them, though.'

'Except Noel and a few other mad people,' said Dan.

'That's because us scientists look beyond the common reaction to these amazing animals and have spent years researching their importance to bio-diversity, which is actually central to our human existence.'

'I'm going to miss you, Noel,' said Dan, - 'seven weeks is a long time without access to the font of all knowledge.'

'Where ignorance is bliss, 'tis folly to be wise,' I said, pleased with myself.

'Ah, Thomas Gray,' said Noel.

'So, Noel, what are you doing this summer?' asked Fay.

'Apart from dissecting various insects for my personal research at home, Muriel and I will be caravanning in North Wales and Anglesey.'

'Oooh, I'd love to do that,' said Fay.

'What! With five kids all cooped up in a metal box, in the wettest part of the British Isles?' said Dan. 'It's not floating my boat I can tell you!'

'Ahh,' said Noel, - 'you don't know what you're missing.' He got up and went off to his class with a distinct jaunt in his step.

Our conversation was brought to an abrupt halt when Evelyn entered the room, and everyone went quiet.

'Good morning, everyone,' she said. 'I just want to advise you all that the culprits who were responsible for placing that lewd and preposterous doll thing in my office, have been caught on camera doing it again in the school grounds. It appears that they were attaching the thing to a tree opposite the school kitchens, where there is a CCTV camera which I surreptitiously installed after the first incident. I have here a facsimile of a still photograph from the footage captured.' She pinned it up on the wall. 'I know it's rather blurry, but I'm hoping someone might recognise one of them. That's all. Thank you.'

We gathered round the photograph and peered at it. 'If that's the best she's got,' said Dan, - 'then there's no chance of catching the little blighters.'

'It's a very dark image, isn't it?' I said, - 'they must have done it at night. Looks like two people but it's hard to tell. You can't see their faces – it looks like they've got hoodies on. She's never going to find out who they are. She should just drop it. Anyway, what's she going to do if she does manage to find out?'

'Give them 100 lines, maybe,' said Dan, - '*I must not make indecent representations of my Headmistress in uncompromising positions…*'

'She could expel them,' said Fay.

'Not if they're Year 11s – they're leaving. Anyway, I don't know why she's expending so much energy on this,' said Dan. 'There are more important things to do. By the way, girls, where are we going on Friday for our end-of-term knees-up?'

'Now, that is a much more important question!' said Fay.

At lunchtime, I rang Mrs Wang quickly to check if Mum was OK.

'Yes, she is fine,' she said, 'but do you know why she talking about ducks in garden? I not see no ducks, and she keep saying you have put one in there…'

'Just tell her it flew away, Mrs Wang. By the way, when you leave, could you lock her in again, please?'

'OK. We will stop her getting lost, right?'

'Yes, hopefully.'

'My dog, Betty, is lost yesterday too,' she said. 'I so worried! I can't find her nowhere…'

'Oh, no! Where could she be?'

'I found her. She at your Mum's house. You never guess where! Poor dog was rolled in carpet!'

'Oh dear! Is she OK?' I said, with the sudden awful realisation that the funny noise in Mum's bedroom was probably Betty's woeful whimper.

'Yes, she fine thanks.'

Phew! Thank goodness for that. Imagine if she'd found that Betty had expired from suffocation by the rolled-up carpet, or death by Axminster, as it suddenly came into my head! How my mother managed to do it in the first place beggars belief. I think she's becoming very unaware of her surroundings. We were very lucky she didn't come a cropper herself when she was wading around in the lake – its probably got all sorts of death traps lurking beneath the surface; like old bicycles, shopping trollies, and probably even the odd car. Of course, being at home isn't safe either. Any number of things could happen to her – it's such a worry.

'Laura, I'm glad I've caught you,' said Bryce as I was walking past his office. 'William has had an accident.'

'Oh, Crikey! What's happened to him?'

'We think he's broken his arm – he fell off the trampoline. Dan's been looking for you.'

'OK. Thanks. Are they in the gym?'

'Yes. It happened about fifteen minutes ago.'

I could hear William crying out as I got nearer, and Dan trying to calm him down. Some of the other kids were still hanging around to see what would happen next. I shooed them away and told them to go and get changed.

'We've tried calling his mother, but she said it was up to us to deal with it,' said Dan, rolling his eyes.

'OK. I'll take him down to A&E in my car. Are you able to come too, Dan?'

'Yes, I'll sit with him in the back. Let me just put it into this sling.'

Poor William looked as white as a sheet as we made our way to the car. At the hospital, we had an excruciatingly long wait. I told Dan to go back to school as there was no point in us both waiting around.

'Did anyone call Orla?' I asked him as he got up to go.

'No, I don't think so.'

'OK, I'll do that now. See you later.'

I moved away from William for privacy and called Orla. 'I'll call his mother and let her know,' said Orla.

'Dan tried,' I told her, - 'she refused to come.'

'Well, I'll explain to her that there will be serious consequences if she doesn't.'

'Like what?'

'Like her behaviour towards William gives us grounds to go to court. I won't go into it now, though. Thank you for being there for him, Laura.'

'It really hurts,' complained William, when I went back to my seat.

'They'll give you something for the pain soon, I expect,' I said, trying to comfort him. 'I'm sure they'll fix you up in no time.'

'Will I get a cast on it?'

'Probably. I'm afraid you won't be doing any sports for a while.'

'That sucks!' said William, kicking the chair next to us with his foot.

'Let's just see what they say, shall we?'

'This is going to ruin my summer,' he said, miserably.

We were stuck at the hospital for four hours until William re-appeared with a bright orange cast on his right arm. He'd cheered up a bit now he could show it off to his mates, plus he'd been given a load of strong pain killers. On the way home I stopped at McDonald's drive-through to keep him happy, and he discovered that he was going to have to use his left hand to do everything. As we drove home, I realised that allowing him to order a large Cola was probably not the best idea…

Once I'd spent half an hour cleaning the sticky mess off the car seats with several buckets of hot, soapy water and a scrubber, I took poor Otto out, who'd been waiting patiently all afternoon for an outing. I left William playing one-armed computer games in his room, and escaped to the park for some therapeutic me time. There was no way I'd make Morag's yoga class – it was already 6:30pm.

'I had no idea how exhausting having a child could be!' I moaned down the phone to Cath, as I sat on my favourite bench in the park and watched Otto run round.

'Is everything OK?' she said.

'Yes, I suppose so. Apart from William's broken arm, my half-drowned mother, my absent sister, and an impending massive career fail…'

'Oh my God, Laura!'

'It's OK. I'm just very tired. I'm ready for a break now. How about you?'

'Well, I've only just started my new job, so it's not the same as it is for you. I can remember, though – by the time the last two weeks of the summer term came, I was desperate to finish. Everyone was, especially the kids. Have you heard anything from Gabriel?'

'No. Not a dickie bird.'

'Well, maybe he *is* a dud, then.'

'I really wanted him not to be…'

'I know. Listen, Laura, why don't you come over this Sunday. Bring William if you want – we'll have a BBQ and some drinks. The weather's going to be nice, and Matt would love to see you. My sister's boys will be here as well – they're nine and eleven. Matt's good with teenagers as well. What do you think?'

'Yes – thank you, Cath. That would be lovely.'

Tuesday morning's Year 7s were very lively, so I decided to give them a pop star wordsearch to do to keep them quiet. The last week of term is always like this. It's as if they've decided they're already on holiday. It's a job to keep them all focussed on anything.

'Whoever finishes first gets a bag of strawberry sherbets,' I said, waving the object of desire in the air. When Bryce came into the class, shortly after, it was a picture of serenity.

'Goodness, Laura, I'm impressed,' he said.

'Don't be,' I told him, showing him the sweets.

'Hahaha, a woman after my own heart. Just letting you know I'm arranging a leaving do for Ray on Thursday evening at the Royal Oak. Morag's collecting at lunchtime for a present.'

'What's she getting him?'

'I think it's a fancy pen, engraved – in a nice box.'

'Do you think he'll use it?'

'I doubt it! He can admire it from time to time and think of us still stuck here at the sharp end, while he swans about enjoying the comforts of a well-funded school in deepest Oxfordshire.'

'Could I have a quick word outside,' I said, indicating the door.

'Yes, of course…'

'I just wanted to say I'm a bit worried about my position here. Evelyn has a rather critical opinion of my approach to teaching, and she has been quite vocal about it recently.'

'Well, Laura, Evelyn and I have had quite a few discussions about teaching methods over the years. My feeling is, that a school needs diversity and teachers need to feel free to use methods that work for them. As long as they are not detrimental to the school ethos, of course…'

'And what does Evelyn say?'

'Well, let's just say she doesn't particularly agree with me, but she is willing to be flexible.'

'That's not a word I would normally associate with her, Bryce.'

'No, well I've got your back, Laura. I know you and Ray have had good results in the past, and the kids really like you, so don't get downhearted. OK?'

'OK. Thanks, Bryce. Let's hope my Year 11 GCSE results are good enough to persuade her.'

'That's the spirit! By the way, it's a plus-one on Thursday if you want to bring anyone.'

I wasn't looking forward to the afternoon at all. It's been ten years since I last saw Valerie. I'm not sure how she'll react when she sees me. It was all very awkward at the time and really, it was all Henry's fault. He should have been honest with her and told her about me. I didn't even know he had a girlfriend when we got together. No wonder she was upset when she found out. Actually, 'upset' doesn't cover it – 'furious' is more like it. The night she stormed into my room during my last year at University was something I'll never forget, however hard I try. It took me weeks to get the red dye out of the carpet. My duvet cover had to be binned, and Henry and I couldn't go anywhere for two days until we'd managed to wash it off our skin. I can still see Henry's bright red bum as he ran for cover. After that we always referred to her as the 'Red Dragon'. Now, ten years later, I wish that I'd never met Henry. He turned out to be a feckless drifter who charmed his way through life and sponged off most of his friends and family to get by. He was also a cheating scumbag. The trouble is, I fell for him, hook, line and sinker and he broke my heart when he left me for someone else. I haven't told many people about the dye-chucking incident. I imagine Valerie regrets what she did. It took all year for people to stop mentioning it. She must have been quite embarrassed about the whole thing. Maybe she and I will be able to bond over the fact that we both ended up being unceremoniously dumped by Henry the Horrible, and that we lived to tell the tale.

'I've brought you some lunch from the canteen,' said Fay, handing me a chicken salad.

'Oh, thanks.'

'They were running out, so I grabbed two.'

'Oh, that's great. I'm starving. I forgot to eat any breakfast this morning, after yesterday's shenanigans with William's broken arm. Of course, he needed lots of help to get ready this morning, so I was running late.'

'That's such bad luck just before the summer holidays.'

'I know. I don't know what I'm going to do with him.'

'I'm guessing you will have to take him with you to Scotland?'

'I don't think I've got any choice, Fay. I can't leave him by himself, and his mother seems to have washed her hands of him. So much for a quiet rest!'

'Well, we did try and warn you…'

'I know. I'm my own worst enemy. It looks as if my love-life has come to a grinding halt too – well, it never really got off the ground, so there's no loss there!'

'What's happening with your mother?'

'I've got her booked into a very good nursing home where she's already made friends with one of the inmates, so at least that's one problem sorted. Are you going anywhere with the kids?'

'Just the usual – to my mother's house in Bournemouth. It's just so easy with her to help and it gives Scott and me a break. She loves looking after them.'

'I'm actually envious of you right now!'

'You have to look at it this way, Laura – you've managed to avoid the responsibility of children for over ten years.'

'Hm, well, if my current experience is anything to go by, I think I'll stay that way!'

'Haha, Laura, it's just that you haven't had the chance to build up slowly to having a teenager. Most people have the option to gradually get used to the terrible teens, not be suddenly hit by the sledgehammer from hell!'

'Well, I wouldn't describe it quite like that…'

'Just wait, it'll get worse before it gets better!' Fay laughed.

'You're enjoying this, aren't you!'

'Only because you've said to me in the past that kids just need a happy home life to behave well and respect their parents.'

'OK. I am being forced to revise that completely naïve and simplistic point of view now. Don't forget, though, that he's not my child, so it's even harder.'

'OMG, Laura! I've just had a terrible realisation…'

'What?'

'In six years' time, I'll have *five* teenagers in the house at once!'

'Good grief, you'd better start planning your escape now!'

'What are you girls finding so funny?' said Noel, unwrapping his home-made cheese and tomato sandwiches.

'Ah, just life, Noel, and the struggles of being a mother. You wouldn't know about such things, I'm afraid.'

'Well, I'm obviously not a mother, but I do have a son, so I'm not completely oblivious to the trials and tribulations of family life.' He bit into his sandwich.

Fay and I looked at each other, amazed at this new and interesting piece of information.

'You've never mentioned him before, Noel. What does he do?'

'As little as possible as far as I know.'

'Oh, don't you see him, then?'

'Not really. He lives with his mother in Sweden.'

'So, Muriel isn't your first wife?'

'Yes, she is. I didn't marry Elsa. She was a perfectly nice girl, but it wasn't practical.'

'Why not?' said Fay, fascinated by this revelation that neither of us had any idea about.

'Her father didn't approve of me. He thought I was a *slöfock.*'

We burst out laughing. 'A what?' I said.

'It means a 'bum', basically.'

'God, Noel, you really are a dark horse, aren't you!'

'Never judge a book by its cover,' he said, smiling.

'Right, well, I'm off to meet my new boss, so wish me luck!' I said.

Ray was waiting by my classroom with Valerie. As I walked towards them, I could see she hadn't changed much. She still wore her hair in a sleek dark brown bob, her figure was still slender, and her face was the same round shape as before. She smiled and held out her hand for a firm handshake.

'Such a pleasure to see you again,' she said. 'It's been a while!'

'Um, yes. Ten years…' There was no hint of awkwardness on her part. I was trying very hard to be normal, but I kept seeing Henry's red bum.

'Shall we proceed?' said Ray. I allowed him to do most of the talking and took a back seat until we reached the staffroom, and Ray went off to make us some coffee. Now Valerie and I were alone, she took the opportunity to say something.

'So, Laura, I just wanted to say, before we go any further, that what happened in the past is water under the bridge as far as I'm concerned, and this is a new start. I hope you will be willing to feel the same way… After all, we were young and stupid, and it was a long time ago.'

'Yes, you're absolutely right, Valerie. We were just kids then. We've all moved on from those crazy days! Mind you, it doesn't change the fact that Henry was a two-timing chancing bastard and a professional sponger', I said, feeling relieved that we could finally laugh about it. 'So, we're both better off without him, aren't we! I mean, I can't think what we saw in him – can you? He wasn't even particularly good-looking, and that STUPID beard he grew! Wasn't it just AWFUL!!'

Valerie cleared her throat and looked suddenly flustered.

'I was just about to tell you, Laura, that Henry and I are back together again.'

'Oh, shit! Sorry! I had no idea…'

'That's the main reason I came south, actually. Henry's back working down here. He's got a proper job these days…'

By the time Ray came back, the atmosphere was so frosty, you could skate on it.

'I expect you two have had lots to catch up on,' he said, pretending not to notice. Would you like to come and chat to Bryce and Evelyn, now, Valerie?'

'Yes, I think that would be a very good idea,' she said.

'It was a complete car crash!' I wailed when Dan asked me how our meeting went. I was feeling tired and emotional at the end of a long day.

'You need a drink,' said Dan. 'Come on, I'll take you down to my local.'

When Dan dropped me home around 7pm, William had already got through five packets of crisps, half a bag of popcorn, and three bowls of cornflakes.

'I need to show you how to cook,' I said, clearing up all the discarded packets from the sofa.

'I can't, though, can I?' he said, waving his orange arm.

'No, I suppose not. It's a great excuse to do even less, isn't it!'

William grinned. 'The doctor said I had to rest my arm and be careful not to strain it...'

CHAPTER 18

On Thursday, I decided to make up for not going to yoga this week by turning up to Morag's Lunchtime session.

'Since this is our last one,' said Morag, - 'I'd like to thank you all for coming along and I wanted to let you know, before you find out from anyone else, that I'm going to be leaving. Tomorrow will be my last day at St Jude's.'

We all stared at her.

'I asked Evelyn to keep it quiet, but you've all been very loyal yogis, and I felt you should hear it from me.'

'Where are you going?' said Fay, - 'we'll miss you, Morag!'

'Well, you're going to hear this soon as well, so I might as well tell you. Ray and I are making a new life for ourselves. It was important to have a clean break, as I'm sure you will appreciate.'

'Ray Fletcher?' said Fay, eyes like saucers.

'Yes. Now, let's stretch those arms up as high as you can, and breathe…one. two, three, and out, two, three…'

'Did you know?' said Fay, afterwards.

'No! I would have told you. I'm absolutely gobsmacked. How on earth did they keep that quiet?'

'So, Ray is leaving his wife of 17 years…wow!'

'And he never said anything to you, either?'

'No, not a thing. I had no clue – I mean, I just can't believe it! I'd never have guessed in a million years.'

'Just goes to show, Fay, you never know what's going on in people's lives, do you!'

When school finished, I walked home in a kind of daze. The truth is, this piece of news has shaken me more than anything else in recent times. I thought I knew both of them pretty well, and to discover that they've been leading a double life all this time has made me seriously question my observational skills. I always thought I had a sixth sense about such things. I suppose they wanted to avoid gossip and scandalous talk. They've certainly done that. And, of course, they'll be long gone by the time the news gets round school next term.

Isla had left a note for me when I got in:

Hi Laura! Tomorrow is the last day I'm walking Otto as G is back. It's been lovely to take him out. I would take him home with me in an instant, if you ever need a break! Love, Isla x

William appeared shortly after me and threw his jacket and bag down on the hall floor, as usual.

'William, please can you hang your stuff up!' I said, telling him off.

'God, it's worse than being at my Mum's house,' he moaned. 'I might as well go back there.'

'Really?' I said, - 'I thought you liked it here?'

'Well, it was OK before you started having a go.'

'William, you can't just do whatever you want. Anyway, you can go back there any time you like,' I said, - 'but I was planning on getting Chinese food this evening as I'm going out. Of course, it's fine if you'd rather go back home…'

'Well, maybe I'll go back some other time,' he said.

'OK, good. I've got to go to a farewell party this evening for one of the teachers. I don't think I'm going to be very late. You'll be OK until I get back, won't you? It'll be around 11pm. You can always call me if you need to.'

'Is it for Mr Fletcher?'

'Yes, it is.'

'He's shagging Miss Turner, isn't he?'

'I beg your pardon! Really, William!'

'Everyone knows. Chloe Stevens saw them in the *Dog & Duck* three weeks ago.'

'What was Chloe doing in a pub on a school day, or any other day for that matter?'

'It's 2 for 1 on Tuesday and Thursday afternoons...'

'Good grief, William! Do their parents know they're going into the pub?'

'Yeah, they don't care.'

'That's terrible.'

William shrugged. 'It's no big deal…'

'And what about Mr Fletcher and Miss Turner – do all the kids know about them?'

'Yeah,' he said, smugly. 'We know everything.'

'So, who put that doll in Mrs Ferrier's office, then?'

'Can't tell you.'

'Can't, or won't?'

'That'd be snitching.'

'I see. Well, William, today has been a real eye-opener. If I need the low-down on anything else, I'll be sure to come to you first, next time.'

The Royal Oak was busy and hot inside. I made my way through to the back and into the function room, where I found Bryce and his wife, Jo, chatting to Evelyn and Tim. A waiter came round with a tray of glasses of wine.

'This is very civilised,' I said, - 'not having to queue at the bar, I mean.'

'Well, it's our end of term social, as well as Ray's leaving do, so I thought it would be nice to change up from plastic cups of Buck's Fizz in the school hall, to something a bit more sophisticated,' said Evelyn. 'I think we all deserve it, don't you?' She wasn't looking at me when she said this. Tim smiled weakly at her and nodded, dutifully.

'I just wanted to tell you how much we enjoyed the Ball, Laura,' said Jo. 'I haven't had so much fun for ages!'

'Thank you, Jo, we all put a lot of effort into it, didn't we Bryce?'

'We certainly did! Shame it went south at the end!'

'I think that's an understatement, Bryce,' said Evelyn, giving him a disapproving look.

Bryce changed the subject. 'By the way, I hope no one minds, but I thought it would be a nice gesture to invite Valerie and her partner Henry along this evening. It's an opportunity for them to get to know a few of the staff. In fact, I think I can see them just making their way over…'

I made a quick getaway by saying I needed the loo, and went to find Dan.

'Ah, Laura, thank God you're here. I'm dying of boredom. Fay's not here yet and there's no sign of Ray, even though this party's for him as well.'

'Dan, did you know about Ray and Morag?'

'What are you talking about?'

'Ray and Morag have been having an affair – they're both leaving!'

'You're kidding!'

''We're not,' said Fay, joining us.

'Not only that,' I said, - 'but all the kids at school have known for ages!'

'Well, that doesn't surprise me. They've got superpowers when it comes to sniffing out a scandal. Wow, Morag and Ray! Who'd have thought… Well, good luck to them, I guess…'

'I feel sorry for his wife, though,' said Fay.

'How come everyone's having a more exciting life than me?' said Dan, - 'it's not fair!'

'Dan, there's more to life than sex,' I said.

'Who says?'

'Anyone who isn't having any,' said Fay, hooting with laughter.

'Isn't that your new boss?' said Dan, pointing at Valerie.

'Yes, but you're not going to believe this…the man she's with is Henry, my ex from six years ago.'

They both looked at me with astonishment. 'You mean Henry the Horrible!' they both said, in unison.

'Ssshh,' I said, - 'not so loud!' I noticed, happily, that he'd lost his hair and put on even more weight. He still had the same smug expression on his face, though.

'Oh my God, Laura, how did that happen?'

'I don't know, but could my life get any worse? I mean, what did I do to deserve this?'

'Have another drink,' said Dan. 'It's the only thing to do.'

I'm NEVER listening to Dan again. I don't know how I got through the morning, except that six cups of coffee seemed the only answer. By lunchtime I knew I had to go home and sleep it off. Thank God I didn't have any more lessons. I also managed to avoid Evelyn, who was apparently trying to see me urgently, all morning. I crawled into bed and slept all afternoon. I didn't even hear Isla bringing Otto back, except I was vaguely aware of a furry companion softly snoring next to me on my bed. I woke up three hours later when Orla rang me around 4pm.

'Laura, I've been busy trying to get some things in place for you. I just wanted to let you know that from Monday, you'll start to get some financial support for having William.'

'Oh, good…thank you…'

'I tried to speak to his mother today, but she was too drunk to discuss anything. It's so sad for these kids when the parents are incapable of looking after them. William has been lucky to find a nice, safe and healthy environment with you where he'll be looked after properly for the first time in his life.'

'Um, yes, thanks Orla.' *Crikey, I don't think I've ever felt so guilty – I made a resolution there and then to never drink that much again.*

'Is he there?' she asked. 'I'd like to speak to him if possible…'

'I don't know,' I said, without thinking. 'I'll just check…No, sorry, he's not home yet.'

'Oh, OK. Out with his mates I suppose.'

'Yes, I'm sure he'll be back soon.'

After she rang off, I suddenly felt my inadequacies as a substitute parent quite acutely. I wasn't exactly being very reliable or responsible, getting drunk, having a massive hangover all day and not knowing where he was. I'm not much better than his own mother. I blame Dan for this – it's all his fault. He has no idea what it's like to have these kinds of adult responsibilities.

By 8pm, William still hadn't turned up, and I began to wonder if he was all right. Usually, the need for food meant that he'd appear pretty soon after school finished. As far as I knew, he didn't have any money on him. He wasn't answering his phone, either. I waited until 8.30pm and then took Otto to go and look for him.

I found him at the skate park with loads of other kids. When I saw him, I realised I couldn't just go up to him – he'd be mortified. I just had to go back home again and hope that he would come home before it got too late. I will have to negotiate with William a time to be home by, or I'm going to spend the whole of the summer holidays worrying. I suppose he's used to staying out as long as he wants – no one cared where he was before. This is going to be another big challenge for me and my sanity.

I realised I hadn't eaten much, myself, all day, so I rummaged in the cupboard for something easy. There was a tin of spaghetti hoops I'd bought for William, so I put some toast on and heated them up. My phone pinged suddenly, and I realised I had lots of messages from earlier in the day.

'Oooh, I'm popular,' I said to Otto, jokingly. When I started reading them, my mood changed dramatically.

From Dan at 1:30am last night: *Just checking you're OK? I'll call you tomorrow. X*

From Dan at 8:30am this morning: *Won't see you this morning. Hope you are feeling better than I am! (Hangover from hell.)*

From Fay at 8:45am this morning: *Ooooooh err! You went for it, didn't you! Sorry I had to leave early – can't stay up late these days! Dan says you're in trouble…call me when you can face the world!!*

From Dan at 1:00pm: *Evelyn is wondering where you are? Hope you haven't jumped off a bridge or anything! I'm sure it will all be forgotten about by September… x*

From Evelyn at 2:00pm: *I need to speak to you urgently, Laura. Please give me a ring when you get this message. E.F.*

From Evelyn at 3:00pm: *Please call me as soon as you can. We need to discuss what happened last night. E.F.*

'Oh cripes, Otto! What on earth are they talking about? It sounds serious.'

I rang Dan.

'I was about to come round,' he said, - 'I was getting worried.'

'Sorry, I hadn't looked at my messages until just now.'

'Are you OK?' said Dan. 'You were *so* drunk last night! Everyone was asking about you at school this afternoon.'

'Um, well, I've got a terrible hangover if that's what you mean…'

'I'm talking about what happened, Laura…'

'I don't know what you're referring to, Dan.'

'So, you don't remember throwing a plate of vol-au-vents at Henry's head, then? Or calling him a double-crossing snake? Or telling everyone that Valerie's pet name for him was 'Stud Muffin' at Uni?'

'Oh God! No, I don't!'

'Not any of it?'

'No, seriously, I don't.'

'You were funny, though…it was great entertainment!'

'I can't imagine everyone thought it was funny,'

'No, obviously…'

'What else?'

'You told Evelyn she was an old boot with a face like a cat's bum.'

'Aaaarggh! No! I didn't!'

'Yep, you did.'

'Oh, God, Dan, what am I going to do? No wonder Evelyn's been trying to speak to me.'

'She'll probably just tell you to apologise.'

'I don't know, Dan, it's really serious this time - she could sack me. Why did I throw the food tray at Henry?'

'I think it was because he said he was looking forward to settling down now he had a serious relationship after so many superficial past girlfriends. He said he'd finally found a girl who was loyal and honest…'

'What an utter creep! No wonder I threw something at him.'

'I think the fact that Valerie was looking at him all doe-eyed and saying that he'd had some 'regrettable relationships', didn't help your mood either.'

'And why was I rude to Evelyn as well?'

'She tried to tell you to go home before you made it worse for yourself. I stepped in then and took you outside.'

'This is the worst thing I've ever done, Dan. I don't think I can come back from it.'

'Oh, I don't know. Everyone will calm down – it's not as if you actually maimed anyone, is it? And you were extremely drunk, so, you know, we've all been there…'

I just wanted to crawl back under the duvet and stay there until Doomsday. How can I possibly go back to school after this? Some of what happened is starting to come back to me now: Henry's grinning, supercilious face, Valerie's doting, childlike admiration for him, the pent-up fury I felt, the irresistible appeal of chucking something at his bumptious baldy head, and an overwhelming desire to beat him to a fine pulp. I'm normally a very unconfrontational sort of person. I can't believe I behaved so outrageously. Maybe I had a sort of fit or something, or someone spiked my drinks? I mean, it can happen anywhere, can't it? Anyway, whatever it was, I am SCREWED. There's no way Evelyn will forgive my behaviour and Valerie will refuse point blank to work with me. My life is FINISHED with a capital F.

CHAPTER 19

When Cath knocked on my door at 10:00am on Saturday morning, I was still in my dressing gown.

'Am I glad to see you,' I said.

'You look terrible,' she responded. 'Was it a good party, then?'

'It was two nights ago, and, no, it wasn't…'

'Oh, dear…'

'Let's go outside with our coffee, where William can't hear us.'

'Where is he?'

'Asleep, probably. He came in around midnight last night.'

We sat in the morning sun, and I regaled her with my sorry tale of woe.

'Cripes!' she said, when I'd finished. 'I'm lost for words…'

'That's a first,' I said, smiling.

'What will you do?'

'I have no idea. Wait to be told to go on gardening leave, probably. At least it'll give me plenty of time to sort my mother out.'

'Has she improved at all, with the medication, I mean?'

I guffawed with laughter when Cath asked that. 'Sorry,' I said, - 'but you won't believe the latest thing. She's written off her washing machine by putting a bloody great rock in it to fluff up her duvet.'

'Oh, my God! She didn't!'

'And she thinks a plague of locusts is about to descend on 21 Marigold Close and strip her garden of all plant life. She's been making her neighbour's lives miserable, and then, the other day, she stole a duck form the park and almost spiflicated her housekeeper's pet Chihuahua trying to roll up her bedroom carpet. I'm having to lock her in her own house. She keeps escaping and getting lost. It's a nightmare, honestly. I think the stress of coping with my mother probably contributed to my meltdown the other night. Everything's getting on top of me.' I suddenly felt tearful. Cath put her arm round me and tried to tell me everything would be OK. She went and made us another cup of tea.

'I think having William is the last thing you need right now, Laura,' she said, sitting down again. 'Why don't you tell Orla you made a mistake. She'll understand. You've had so much to cope with recently.'

'Oh, I don't know, Cath… in some ways I quite like having him around. He's annoying and ungrateful, but compared to my job, I'm not sure it's any worse. In fact, I'd say he's got the edge!'

'Well, I think you should tell Evelyn about your mother. She might be more sympathetic than you'd expect. She was actually quite kind to me, you know.'

'OK, I'll think about it. Thanks, Cath. I'm sure you're right. I don't know what I'd do without you!'

'Vice versa!' she said, giving me a hug. 'I tell you what, let's take Otto out and get some lunch. Go and get ready. I'll wait for you. Shall we take William with us?'

'No, he won't want to be seen with me, but I'll leave him some money. He'll be perfectly happy.'

By the time I came home in the late afternoon, I'd resolved to email Evelyn and apologise, explaining my situation with my mother. I also bit the bullet and told her about my history with Henry. It was the most humiliating thing I've ever had to write. Especially as my relationship with Evelyn has never been good at the best of times. Oh, well, it's done now. I'll have to find a way to apologise to Henry and Valerie as well, but I don't know quite how.

It was getting near to teatime, so I went to find William. He was in his room, so I knocked and waited for a response.

'Just a minute,' he said. Then I heard a girl, giggling and some noises that sounded like stuff being moved around.

I opened the door tentatively and immediately recognised it was Denise Channing. 'Hello, Miss,' she said, pulling on her hoodie. 'I'm just off now. See you later, Will.' She grabbed her bag on the way out and legged it out of the door.

I looked at William with the raised eyebrow/bulging eyeball face that all mothers use in these situations.

'We're just mates,' he said.

'I thought you didn't want anyone to know you lived with me, William?'

'I'm not bothered any more.'

'OK, well, that's good, but on this, more pressing topic, having girls in your room is definitely not allowed. Plus, if you want to have friends over, you have to ask first. OK?'

'Uurrgg,' he said. 'That's so boring.'

'Well, I haven't said you can't have any friends round, have I?'

'Ollie Pinnock's allowed girls in his room.'

'Well, I don't care what other people allow their kids to do. If you're staying with me, we need to come to an agreement about these things, William. I don't want to be unfair, but I have to consider your welfare as well as my responsibilities.'

He was yawning already, - 'Yeah, OK...'

'And,' I carried on, - 'I know you've had sex education lessons in school...' He covered his ears and started making Lalalalala noises. 'So,' I said, loudly, over the noise, - 'you're NOT practicing in my house, OK? You're too young anyway, to be thinking about girlfriends. You should be playing in the park and riding on your bike at your age.' *God, I sounded just like my mother...* 'And, while I've got you vaguely listening to me, please can we have a sensible time when you are home in the evening, so I don't have to phone the police to go looking for you?'

Oh, my goodness, it didn't even occur to me that I'd have to deal with this! I don't feel remotely equipped. I need help! I can't even rely on my own experience of how my parents dealt with it. Their attitude was to allow NO ONE *into the house, male or female, apart from their own small handful of friends. Their contribution to informing us about anything to do with the opposite sex was to leave an ancient book lying around about reproduction, next to the toilet in the bathroom. It had very simple illustrations which were basically line drawings with arrows. Jenny and I thought it was hilarious. 'This is out of the ark,' she said, as we flicked through the pages of stick men and women in rigid, unrealistic positions. It makes me laugh, now, when I think about it. My parents avoided anything unsavoury – even when they talked about someone having a baby, it was always 'she's in the family way', or 'she's eating for two now'. If someone had died, it was 'he's with the angels', or 'she's in a better place'. It's a bit confusing for a child when grown-ups say such odd things. It was ages before I realised my Uncle Geoff had actually died because Dad just said, 'he'd kicked the bucket'. Once, I heard my mother say that Jeanie's daughter down the road, 'had a bun in the oven'. I couldn't understand what the fuss was about - surely everyone baked cakes?*

I decided to cook a proper meal for tea and went out to get a chicken and some vegetables to make a curry. We've been having too much fast food recently. I've got an obligation to feed William on something wholesome and filling. Back at the house, I started preparing it, and then realised that he'd gone out again. 'I'm going to make it anyway,' I said to Otto. 'It can always be heated up. Curries are good for at least three days.' I gave him a piece of chicken for being such a good and loyal companion. I was just pouring myself a small glass of wine, when a message from Gabriel finally popped up on my phone. I hesitated before looking at it, not really wanting any more dismal news.

'OK, Gabriel, what have you got to say for yourself, then?' I opened it.

Hi, Laura! Sorry I haven't been in touch. Would really like to see you. Are you free tonight? Sorry for short notice. Gx

'Well, Gabriel, my furtive friend, I'm not just going to jump when you click your fingers. You can wait, Mr Secret Squirrel.' Otto barked when he heard the word 'squirrel'. 'No, Otto, not that kind of squirrel. This one is playing even harder to get. But two can play at that game.' I turned my phone off and sat down to watch the news. I was only half listening and thumbing through a magazine at the same time, when a familiar voice caught my attention. I looked up and saw Elliott being interviewed by our local reporter.

'Thanks,' Elliott was saying, - 'it was a bit of a struggle towards the end there, but I made it! Thanks to all my mates who supported me – *"Teamwork Makes the Dream*

Work" is my motto. Y'know, you have to have devotion and perseverance to keep going. I've always believed that…'

'Well, thank you Elliott. We'll let you go and enjoy your victory. Well done and many congratulations!' Elliott ran off punching the air.

'For goodness' sake!' I said out loud. 'I don't need to listen to you spouting nonsense and being all *look at me, I'm so ultra-fit and successful!'* I switched it off. I went and checked my emails, but there was nothing from Evelyn, so I picked up a book and read for a bit until the food was ready. By the time I went to bed, I was quite proud of myself that I'd resisted answering Gabriel's text message.

'I'm coming round in half an hour,' I said to my Mum on the phone. And I'm bringing William to help me.

'Well, you'd better hurry up, they'll be here any minute…'

'No, Mum, it's Sunday today. The Council will collect your washing machine tomorrow.' I put the phone down and turned to speak to William. 'We don't have to be there very long,' I said to William's grumpy face. 'You'll get to meet my mother.'

'Is she very old?'

'Well, yes, a bit, but the main thing is that she's got Dementia, which means her brain doesn't work very well. She forgets things a lot and has funny ideas about some things.'

'I've got a granny,' said William.

'Oh, that's nice, William. Where does she live, then?'

'HMP Bronzefield.'

'Oh, right. Why is she in there?'

'She was helping my dad.'

Mum was sporting her new wrist alarm when we went into the house. Mrs Wang must have put it on for her.

'I've brought this strong young man to help me move the washing machine, Mum. He's called William.'

'Can't your father help?' she said to me.

'No, Mum, he's gone to a 'better place', remember?' Her eyes glazed over while she thought about it.

'Right, William, let's get that thing out onto the street.'

It took us forty-five minutes of manoeuvring it out of the kitchen, down three steps and down the garden path.

'William, would you make us all a cup of tea, please?'

'Who's that?' said my Mum, pointing at him.

'I told you – it's William.'

'I used to have a boyfriend called William,' she suddenly piped up. 'He was a very handsome boy. We used to go dancing at the Lambeth Town Hall. Ah, he was a cheeky one, though. He used to try and put his hand down your blouse…'

'Mum! Not in front of children, please!'

'What children? That's William! He's no child, I can tell you…'

'Mum don't say anything else. Let's have a nice cup of tea.' I could see William sniggering in the kitchen.

'Ah, I used to love going dancing there. When I met your father, we used to go dancing every week.' Mum then started singing, or rather, murdering Doris Day's *Secret Love* to herself.

William brought the tea in and some chocolate digestives.

'Help yourself, dear,' Mum said to him, - 'you need feeding up.'

'That's what my nan always says.'

'Does your nan like dancing?'

'Oh, yeah, she does. She likes Elvis.'

'I saw him once.'

'Did you?' I said. 'You've never mentioned it before.'

'He performed at the Lyceum. I went with my best friend Dianne. It was very exciting. He had those huge glasses on and a cowboy hat. He played the piano so beautifully…'

'Mum, that was Elton…'

On the way home, William actually said he'd enjoyed himself. 'Your mum is really funny,' he said, laughing. As soon as we got back, William made to leave, saying he was meeting his mates.

'You need to be back in time to go to my friend Cath's, OK?'

'Yeah, OK.'

'Don't be late.'

While I was at Mum's, I had noticed two more messages from Gabriel. One was from late last night, and the other one came in while my mother was warbling away. Mum's terrible singing made William cry with laughter. Maybe I should take him more often.

'Laura, did you get my message? Sorry it's late. Just wanted to be sure…G x'

Then this morning:

'Hi, Laura. Call me if you get this message. Need to talk.' Gx

I called him back. His phone rang once, and he answered straight away.

'Laura, thanks for calling back. Are you free now? We could take the dogs up to the common. It'd be a chance for me to explain things a bit…'

So, I agreed to meet him in the hope that his story was a half-decent one.

'I'm not going to be taken for a fool, Otto,' I said, as we left the flat. Just because my record isn't great in that department doesn't mean I'll be taken in by more of the same. I admit it, I'm a sucker for a hard luck tale, but I think I've learned my lesson now. Right, off we go. Best foot forward…'

I wonder if other people talk to their dog as much as I do? William says he thinks I'm a bit bonkers, because they don't have a clue what you're saying to them. But how do we know? They might understand more than they let on. Anyway, Otto likes me chatting to him, I can tell. He smiles and wags his tail, and that's good enough for me.

Gabriel was waving at me from the big oak tree where Otto chased the squirrel that first evening.

'I missed you,' he said, as soon as I got near enough.

'Really?'

'Yes, I did. I've got to tell you something important though, Laura. It might change everything. I've been putting it off because we've only just met. To be honest, Laura, I'm quite worried about telling you.'

'Let's take the dogs off the lead and let them run, and then we can talk.'

My mind was racing. What could it be? Was he married, like Cath said? Is he dying of a fatal disease and only has months to live? Maybe he's a convicted felon… or a drug addict? Could it be that he's about to be arrested for some terrible offence? Has he got a gambling habit, or a weird fetish? Maybe he likes licking shoes or something…

We sat down by the river on a bench. 'The thing is…' he said.

'Please just spit it out, Gabriel! I can't stand the suspense.'

'OK, right, well… how do you feel about spiders?'

'Um, as long as they aren't near me and I can't see them, I suppose they have a right to exist, unfortunately. I mean, I could quite happily live without them in my life. Why?'

'I'm an amateur arachnologist…'

'A what?'

'I collect and study spiders, in my spare time.'

'Are you serious?'

'Totally. I have quite a large collection. I wanted to tell you before now, but I didn't know how you'd take it, so I put it off.'

'I'm not sure what to think… I mean, it is a bit, well, unusual…'

'My last girlfriend left me because of the spiders. It's not something I can give up. It's more of a vocation than a hobby – it's why I'm giving up my day job. I want to create a specialist centre for the study of insects and spiders.' He was looking at me with a searching expression, waiting for my response. 'It's a bit of an obsession for me, you see. I have a particularly fine collection of tarantulas…'

My head is spinning now. When Gabriel and I parted company, I promised to contact him the next day and let him know what I thought about it all. I'd never have guessed this was his 'dark secret'! I'm not sure what to think about it, really. If he collected frogs or snakes, I probably wouldn't mind so much, but insects and spiders of any kind just make my skin crawl. And, worse than that, those tarantulas are great big hairy things with horrible staring eyes (8, to be precise, according to Gabriel). They don't exactly make great pets, do they? They don't do anything except crawl around eating bugs and sleeping all day. I can't see the fascination for them at all. Maybe I should introduce Gabriel to Noel – they'd get on like a house on fire.

William wasn't too happy about going to Cath and Matt's BBQ, but the promise of burgers and steak sandwiches encouraged him to reluctantly agree to it. 'There'll be some other children there,' I said.

'But I won't know anyone.'

'You'll be fine, William. You're not shy are you!' He pulled a face. 'Come on, you'll enjoy it when you get there. Cath's nephews, Billy and Peter, will be there.'

Cath and Matt have a big house with a large lawn at the back and a patio with plenty of room for kids and ball games.

'You're so lucky,' I said to them, when we got there. 'I wish I had more space in my garden.'

'Well, you could always consider moving.' said Matt.

'I might have to, now,' I said, - 'especially with a teenager in the flat.'

'How are you getting on, William?' said Cath.

'OK,' was his monosyllabic response.

'She hasn't got you scrubbing floors, then, or cleaning out chimneys?' said Matt.

William smiled. 'She makes me tidy up…'

'That's appalling,' said Matt, - 'slave labour!' He handed William a burger. 'When we've eaten, I reckon we should have a game of football – you and me against Billy and Peter. What do you think?'

'Yeah, OK.'

'What happened to your arm?' said Billy.

'I was doing a flip on the trampoline, and I fell off.'

'Wow!'

'Can you do keepie-uppies?' Peter asked William.

'Yes…'

'Will you show us?' asked Billy.

It wasn't long before all the boys were kicking a ball around with Matt trying to keep up with them.

'He would have loved to have kids, you know,' said Cath, sadly. 'He's really good with my sister's boys.'

'Have you considered fostering or adopting, Cath?' I asked her.

'We've talked about it. I want to make sure I'm going to be well enough first.'

'Yes, of course. Well, you can borrow William any time!'

'He seems OK,' said Cath, watching him having fun with the boys.

'It depends,' I said. 'He can be a grumpy pain in the neck, and it's going to be difficult to keep him out of trouble.'

'You could do with a male influence around…'

'That's what Orla said. I can't just magic one out of nowhere, though!'

'What about Gabriel?'

'I haven't even told him about William. Anyway, I'm not sure it's going anywhere… I saw him this morning, actually.'

'So, what did he say? Where has he been for two weeks?'

'You're not going to believe this…'

'Go on…'

'He's been in Bolivia, on a spider hunting trip.'

'No!'

'Yes. It's true. He's an arachnologist.'

'A what?'

'Someone who loves spiders…He's got loads, apparently. His favourites are those massive Tarantulas.'

'So, where does he keep them all?'

'I don't know. I didn't ask.'

'What if he keeps them in his bedroom? Oh my God! Laura, that's awful!'

'He said his last girlfriend left him because of them.'

'What did you say, when he told you?'

'I was a bit lost for words, to tell you the truth. I said I wasn't keen on them.'

'But you HATE spiders, Laura! You run a mile if you see one,' Cath laughed. 'How on earth are you going to cope with ones the size of a house?'

'I don't know.'

'It sounds to me like this relationship isn't going to work.'

'Maybe I could get used to them – you know, people with phobias can be trained to not be scared of things, can't they?'

CHAPTER 20

There's nothing so heart-warmingly marvellous as a lie-in on a Monday morning when everyone else is at work. It's just so decadent and satisfying. I was about to go and make myself a cup of coffee to have in bed while I read my new book '*Resuscitate Your Life*', when I got a text saying my mother's alarm had gone off. I sprang out of bed and got dressed as quickly as possible, left a note for William, and drove at break-neck speed to her house.

Once I got there, I found her sitting quite happily eating a toasted muffin and pouring a cup of tea.

'Mum, I got a message to say your alarm had gone off…'

'Oh, yes, it's wonderful, isn't it! I thought you'd like to have breakfast with me…'

'But, Mum, it's for emergencies. Like if you fall down and hurt yourself or something.'

'Well, this *is* an emergency, Laura. I've run out of marmalade. You didn't bring any, did you? I always have marmalade on my muffins. And another thing – can you do my washing? Someone has put my washing machine outside on the pavement. I asked Mr Bright if he could put it back, but he said it was only fit for the tip! That man is very rude, don't you think?'

'Mum, please don't press it again, unless you actually need help!'

I stayed and had a cup of tea with her until Mrs Wang came.

'Ah. Laura! Nice to see you,' she said.

'How are you, Mrs Wang?'

'Not too bad,' she said, putting Betty down. 'I got some news, though. I can't look after your Mum no more. I finish on Friday.'

'Oh, that's such a shame! Why not? Where are you going?'

'I have to look after my Mum now.'

'Oh, is she ill, then?'

'No, not ill. She just crazy like your Mum!'

'Oh, I'm sorry to hear that, Mrs Wang.'

'It OK. She not as bad as your Mum. She can't run away – she only got one leg.'

'Ah…poor old lady!'

'She not poor,' said Mrs Wang, - 'she rich lady.'

'Mum, I've got to go home now. I need to go and walk the dog.'

'I used to have a dog…now, what was he called - I've forgotten.'

'Otto, Mum. It's Otto.'

'Oh, yes, that's right. Someone took him, you know. One minute he was there, the next, he was gone - just like that! Do you think they'll ever bring him back?'

'Who knows....'

'I was thinking I could get a cat, Laura. Cats don't need to be walked – your dad could put a cat flap in the back door…'

'Well, I'm not sure if you'd remember to feed it, Mum.'

'Of course I would, Laura. I wouldn't forget something like that!' She tutted at me.

'I not like cats,' said Mrs Wang. 'They poop in tray. Smell really bad, and bring dead mouse in house…'

Oh dear! This is not good news. Mum won't have anyone to look after her when she comes out of respite if I don't sort something else out. It's a disaster. I don't know how I'm going to find someone as good as Mrs Wang again – she's been a treasure. This is all I need, just before I'm about to go away.

When I got home, I put Mum's washing in the washing machine and told Otto we were going out for a walk. I needed to think about Gabriel's disconcerting disclosure. I suppose there are far worse things that he could have told me. Some people find out terrible things about their partners – things which would be truly unforgivable. I mean, it's not as if Gabriel has done anything bad, or has any weird fantasies or even plans to do anything unacceptable. Keeping spiders as pets is perfectly fine, isn't it? I mean, it's not a crime to like ugly, scary, grotesque creatures that should never have been invented in the first place, is it? The main thing is, does he keep them far, far away from his house?

The man whose shoe Otto Peed on was in the park. He gave us a wide birth. I smiled and waved at him, but he didn't smile back. 'Some people are miserable buggers, aren't they, Otto?' I said to him. 'There's just no pleasing some of them.' As I watched Otto playing, I realised that if Gabriel and I broke up, I'd have to find another dog-walker next term as well. *And*, I'd have to pay them. Since our first date, Gabriel refused to let me pay him, saying he was no longer the hired help, and it wasn't necessary. He said he wanted to carry on walking Otto, if I didn't mind. So that was a win-win! Gabriel's the only good thing in my life at the moment, so I think, on balance, I'd be pretty foolish to give him up for the sake of his strange but tolerable passion for spiders, which I can probably overlook if I try hard enough.

I went home with a renewed sense of purpose. William had gone out again. He's like the phantom lodger at the moment. I'm going to have to tell him about going away to Scotland soon. I don't think he's going to be very impressed with the idea – I'll have to try and make it sound like an exciting adventure rather than what it actually is – a desolate, remote escape from civilisation.

I decided to bite the bullet and ring Gabriel. There's no time like the present…

'I've got something to tell you, as well,' I said.

'Oh…'

'It's going to sound a bit mad.'

'What, even more mad than me?'

'Possibly. There's this boy called William – he's in my class at school…'

After I explained everything to Gabriel, there was a bit of a silence.

'So, let me get this straight; you're basically fostering a teenage boy for the foreseeable future, having had no experience whatsoever in looking after children?'

'Well, yes. But I do teach these kids, so I'm not a complete novice…'

'You've turned yourself into a single mother with a teenage son, overnight…'

'Um, well, yes, I have.'

'I see. Was that wise?'

'Possibly not. No, not really. But, anyway, it's done now, so, you know, there's no going back.'

'I think I need some time to digest this news, Laura. It's a bit of a surprise…'

'Don't you want to know what I've been thinking about your infatuation with spiders?'

'OK, well, go on then…'

'If I didn't have to look at them, or have them anywhere near me, I think it might be OK.'

'Maybe we should take some time to think about things, Laura. Would that be all right?'

I'm determined not to be down in the doldrums. I went shopping for some holiday clothes on Tuesday afternoon. I looked up what I'm going to need for a trip to the islands in July, and basically you have to imagine it's Autumn. The woman in the outdoor pursuits shop was very helpful, so I think I shall be prepared for all weathers. I even got Otto a waterproof trouser suit.

Orla rang me when I got back and asked if she could come and visit in the afternoon.

'I need to speak to William, Laura. Can you make sure he's there?'

'I'll try,' I said, - 'but he's difficult to pin down.'

'Tell him I've got a present for him – that should do it.'

When Orla turned up mid-afternoon, William wasn't home yet.

'He's on his way,' I told her. 'He forgot…'

'Typical boy, I suppose! Oh well, it gives us a chance to chat. I should have visited sooner – I have to check where the child is living and make sure it's suitable accommodation. I've just been so busy these last two weeks. I knew it would probably be fine, anyway.'

'I'll show you his room,' I said. We went in and Otto had made himself very comfortable on William's bed.

'You let the dog sleep on the beds, then?'

'Um, well, yes… William likes his company.'

'I see. Well, it's not very hygienic, but I'm not a dog person, so I suppose I can't see the appeal…'

When I showed her the bathroom, she was quite unimpressed to see my mother's underwear hanging up to dry. 'Do you always hang your knickers up in the bathroom?' she said.

'Those *aren't* mine,' I said, embarrassed by the inordinately large and voluminous bloomers dangling from the rail. 'They're my mother's. Her washing machine broke down.'

In the kitchen, she noticed the fruit bowl with a lonely, mouldy satsuma languishing at the bottom, the large stack of pot noodles in the corner, and the fact that my windows needed cleaning. She also took a keen interest in the number of empty wine bottles in the recycling box.

'As I'm sure you know, it's important for young boys to have a healthy, balanced diet,' she said, eying up the basket full of crisps. 'It's not easy being a single, working mother. I'm one myself. It can be stressful and lonely,' she said, looking at the empty bottle of Chardonnay on the windowsill. 'Do you think you can manage William? He's a bit of a handful, I imagine.'

'Well, so far it's been OK. He stays out quite late, which is a bit of a worry.'

'How late?'

'He came in at midnight the other night.'

'I'll speak to him. That's unacceptable, Laura. He's too young to be out that late. Anything else?'

'I think he's smoking weed.'

'I don't doubt it. They're all doing it.'

When William came in, I was relieved that Orla's focus shifted from me to him.

'I've got something for you,' said Orla, getting a package out from her bag. 'From your Granny.'

'Can I open it?'

'Of course!'

William ripped open the paper, and his face fell. 'It's a puzzle…' He looked mightily disappointed and threw it down on the kitchen side.

'I expect she's forgotten how old you are,' said Orla.

'My birthday was three months ago anyway,' he said.

'I know, but it was nice of her to think about you, wasn't it?' William shrugged, - 's'pose so.'

'She's been asking if she can see you. What do you think? We could go next month. I can arrange it if you like.'

'Yes, OK, I don't mind.'

'And what about your dad? Do you want me to arrange a visit to see him as well?'

'No, I don't want to see him. He's a prick.'

'Well, the thing is, William, he's still your dad, despite the fact that he's made some bad choices in his life. He didn't have many opportunities when he was growing up, you know. The life he had was all he knew. It's easy to fall in with the wrong people in those circumstances.'

'He's still a prick.'

'OK, well if you change your mind, just let me know.'

'I won't.'

'I didn't know he'd be allowed to see his family in prison?' I said to Orla when William had gone to his room.

'Oh, yes. It's encouraged - supervised, of course. At the moment, he's obviously not interested, but he may change his mind. Has he been back to see his mother?'

'I don't know…'

'Keep an eye on that – it's not a good environment for him. It's better if he doesn't turn up there.'

When Orla had gone, I realised that taking William on was the easy bit. It hadn't occurred to me that I was taking on his whole family as well. Gabriel's words '*was that wise?*' would very likely come back to haunt me, over and over again…

After Orla's comments, I made an effort to make a nice salad for tea.

'What's that?' said William.

'It's a salad.'

'What else is there?'

'Well, I suppose you could have left-over curry…'

'Nah, I'll have one of these,' he said, grabbing a pot noodle.

'Orla says you should be eating more healthily,' I said. William had already disappeared into his room while he waited for the boiled water to work its magic on the shrivelled contents. When he came back for it, I made him sit down at the table.

'I've got something to tell you, William. We're going away on Saturday for two weeks.'

'Where?'

'Scotland.'

'That's a long way…'

'It is, quite far – especially where we are going. We're going to the Hebrides – Lewis to be precise. We will be taking the train to Inverness and then I'm hiring a car to drive to the cottage. I'm really looking forward to it. What do you think?'

William looked it up on Google. 'There's nothing there!'

'Well, there aren't many people, but it's got amazing scenery…'

'It's DEAD!' exclaimed William.

'I've looked at some things we could do, William. There's fishing, boat trips, surfing, and there's a karting centre, and kayaking…'

'Will there be a Mc Donald's?'

'I don't know, but I bet there's some good places to eat.'

He wasn't happy. 'I can't do anything with one arm, though. It'll be the pits.'

'I'm sure it won't be as bad as you think. What about going on the train? Have you been on a train before?'

'No.'

'Well, you'll love it! We need to go out and get you some new things for the holiday, though.'

At the shops, William proved to be a tricky customer.

'I'm not wearing a coat,' he said.

'What are you going to do if it rains, then?'

'Stay in the house.'

'William, that's ridiculous. You'll miss all the fun if you do that. Everyone in Scotland has a raincoat. It rains a LOT there!'

'Why are we going, then? Why can't we go somewhere where it's hot?'

'Well, I wasn't planning on you coming with me until recently.'

'I'll just stay behind, then.'

'No, William, you can't. There's no one to look after you.'

'I don't need anyone.'

The next day, I took him to the shops to get what he needed. Eventually, I persuaded him to agree to waterproofs and walking boots. He swore he wouldn't wear them, but I bought them anyway. It may not have been the sensible thing to do, but I hoped he would see sense when he saw all the other young people wearing practical clothing. I noticed in the shop that they were selling full mosquito net outfits as well, so I bought two of them, much to William's horror.

'Why do we need those?'

'In case of midges.'

'What do they do, then?'

The woman in the shop, who happened to be Scottish, felt obliged to join in our conversation at this point, to expound on the terrors of midge-season in the Western Isles, and how huge clouds the size of elephants would engulf whole areas, to the point where you could barely see your way.

'I'm not going,' said William, when we came out of the shop.

'She was exaggerating, William. It won't be as bad as that. In fact, sometimes there aren't any at all.'

William instantly Googled 'midges in Scotland' and insisted on showing me pictures of midge-infestations and people who'd been bitten all over and covered head to toe in big red lumps. I went straight to the chemist and bought a bag-full of creams and repellents.

Maybe my sister was right after all. I hope not, though. It'll ruin our holiday. Mind you, I don't know how William and I will get on together – he won't be able to disappear off to see his mates. We might drive each other mad, cooped up in a cottage. Oh well, in for a penny…

By Friday I still hadn't heard anything from Gabriel. I decided to send him a message to let him know I was taking William away on holiday with me. I'm not expecting much to happen. I think Gabriel's got cold feet. I can't blame him, really. It's a lot to consider, potentially taking on a woman with a teenager in tow. When he asked me out, he thought I was an unencumbered singleton with no dependants. I suppose I should have told him about William sooner. The truth is, I didn't because I suspected this would be the outcome.

I rang Mrs Wang to check Mum's things were packed.

'Oh, yes, she ready now.'

'OK, I'm coming to pick her up. Does she understand where she's going?'

'Well, I tell her it's holiday in nice place,' said Mrs Wang. 'Like luxury hotel.'

Mum seemed quite happy about going, which was such a relief. We had a bit of a wobble when we got there, but Mr Pilkington was very helpful.

'This room doesn't have a very good view,' said my mother when we went in. 'I'd like to upgrade, please.'

'I'm afraid we don't have another room available, madam. However, this room has the best room service, and the comfiest bed.'

'Oh well then,' said my mother, - 'I suppose it'll do.'

After we'd unpacked her things and put them away, we went into the lounge for tea, where Grace was sitting in anticipation of a reunion with her long lost friend. 'There you are!' she said.

'Oh, look, Margery's staying here too! Isn't that a coincidence,' said my mother.

Phew, that went more smoothly than expected, thank goodness! I don't know what I'd have done if she'd decided she wasn't going to stay there. I can rest easy now. I'm sure she'll be fine once she settles in. They'll look after her very well.

Back at the flat, I got William to take Otto out while I carried on packing and sorting everything out. 'We're going out for tea,' I said to him when he came back, - 'I can't be bothered to make anything now, I'm too tired and we've got an early start tomorrow.'

CHAPTER 21

We made the train by a whisker. Honestly, what part of 'hurry up' does a child not understand? Of course, William only having one good arm was extremely unhelpful. I had to wrestle two wheeled suitcases, plus a rucksack and an over-excited dog all by myself on to the train. Where are all the guards these days? I could have broken my own arm trying to cope with it all. With hindsight, I should have got one of those big trollies, but there weren't any lying around in our vicinity. Anyway, we managed it just in time. Once we'd settled into our seats, I was so exhausted I went to sleep. My last instruction to William, before I drifted off, was to 'watch Otto doesn't wander off'. An hour later, I woke up when the drinks trolly came along.

'Do you want anything, William?' I asked him.

'Diet coke, please.'

'We ought to get Otto some water for later,' I said, looking down at the floor where he should have been.

'Where's Otto?' I said.

'He was here a minute ago,' said William.

An announcement came over the Tannoy System at this point: *Could the owner of a brown Cockerpoo please make their way to the front of the train and claim their dog, which is currently causing a nuisance in the buffet car…'*

'For Goodness' sake! William, please go and retrieve him.'

After what felt like an eon, William finally came back. 'He ate someone's breakfast off their plate,' said William, laughing, - 'the man was going mental!'

'Oh, God! That's awful!'

'He said I had to pay for it.'

'So, what did you say?'

'I told him to get lost…'

'Oh, good grief!'

'He's coming to look for you, now,' said William.

'Thanks a bunch!' I said to him.

Well, that was embarrassing. I think it's definitely the last time I take Otto on public transport.

'You owe me another breakfast – it's £25,' said the red-faced man, scowling down at us.

'I'm sorry, but I don't seem to have any cash on me,' I said, rummaging in my purse.

'Well, you'll have to come with me and use your card, then.'

I told William to stay put, and more importantly not to let Otto out of his sight.

'Your son could do with learning some manners,' said the man, as we walked down the carriage. 'Do you know, he was very rude to me just now.'

'I'm sorry,' I said. 'He's not my son, though.'

'Well, whoever he belongs to hasn't done a very good job.'

'That was the longest journey EVER!' said William when we got off at Inverness.

'Yes, it certainly was. I'm glad I booked a sleeper coming back.'

The flight from Inverness to Stornoway was, thankfully, only an hour long. I picked up the hire car and we drove to a supermarket to get some provisions. I don't think I was buying rationally, though, as I was so tired by then.

When our cottage came into view, it almost took my breath away. It was the most idyllic little white croft cottage, nestled at the base of a hill. We trundled down a rough track, where it was just a few yards from an inlet, not far from the open sea, with white sandy beaches stretching for miles.

'Oh, William, look at this! Isn't it just like heaven?'

'Not really… there's no other houses…'

'I know, isn't it great!'

William looked sullenly out at the huge expanse of heather, rocks and sky.

'Let's get our stuff into the house and I'll sort out some food. I'm starving!'

I woke in the morning to the sound of distant seagulls and water gently moving across the stones in the bay. The sun was bright and sparkled on the blue, blue sea. I suddenly thought of that lovely line from one of Lord Byron's poems: "*O'er the glad waters of the dark blue sea, our thoughts as boundless, and our souls are free…*"

There was no sound from William's room. He probably wouldn't wake up for some time. It was a very long journey for him – I mean, he's never been further north than Enfield. Otto stirred from the bottom of my bed and scratched at the door to be let out. Downstairs the view was just as lovely. I let Otto out through the back door in the safe knowledge that he couldn't get into any trouble here. He could run wild and free, and hopefully come back when he wanted. I'd find out soon enough. The air was so clean and fresh it was almost intoxicating. I threw on a jumper and some pumps and walked out along the grassy path by the water. I could see Otto running about further down by a little jetty. There was a small blue boat bobbing on the water, tied up to a post, and I could see a man moving some lobster pots around on the deck. Otto was making friends with him.

'I hope he's not bothering you,' I said, as I got closer.

'No, lass, not at all. I like dogs – got one of my own somewhere about – he'll be back in a while.'

'My name's Laura. I'm staying in the croft cottage with my foster child, William.'

The man smiled and told me his name was Dougal. 'I fish here from time to time. My cottage is over that little hill, just there,' he said, pointing. 'It's not far. Do you like fishing?'

'I've never tried it,' I said. 'I think William would enjoy it. I was going to take him out on a fishing trip while we're here.'

'I don't mind taking you – if you'd like…'

Dougal looked about seventy-five with a jolly face and a friendly, easy way about him. I thought it would probably be safe enough to accept his invitation.

'That's very kind of you, Dougal. We just got here yesterday, actually. William is still asleep – it was rather a long journey.'

'Where from?'

'Just outside London. This place is so peaceful! Such a contrast to the city.'

'Ay, well, it doesn't suit everybody, but I like it. Been here all my life. I wouldn't live anywhere else. You should come over to my house for supper while you're here and bring your boy along. My wife makes a cracking fish pie. I'll ask her which day she'd prefer.'

'Oh, you can't do that, I mean that's putting your wife out…'

'We don't get many visitors round here, Laura. I'm telling you she'd be delighted.'

'Well, OK! Thank you!'

'I'll take you both out tomorrow if you like. The best local fishing ground is up by Shearman's point. Shall we say here, for 9am?'

In the kitchen, I dug out the loaf we bought and some eggs. I heard some movement from William's room, so I thought I'd make something for us both to eat. 'Is scrambled eggs on toast OK?' I shouted up the stairs. I heard a grunt so assumed that would do. 'What shall we do today, William?' I said, when he appeared bleary-eyed at the table.

'Nothing,' he said. 'I'm too tired.'

'Well, once you've woken up, I think we should go and explore. Tomorrow we're going fishing. A nice man called Dougal is taking us out. Won't that be fun!'

'Fishing's for old people.'

'No, it isn't, William. Lots of people go fishing. In fact, you have to be young and strong to work full time in the fishing industry - it's a very hard, physical job, you know. You might catch a really big fish, William. As big as Otto, maybe!'

'Or I might catch a shark,' he said, his mood improving, - 'like Jaws – that'd be awesome!'

'Well, I don't think there'll be any Great Whites swimming about round here, William. We might see some seals, though.'

We spent the day driving around and getting to know the place. So far, William was tolerating the holiday quite well.

On our first proper evening, I made a fire on the beach and showed him how to put marshmallows on sticks and roast them in the flames. We found some old wooden pallets to sit on round the fire and I let him try some cider. 'Don't tell Orla,' I said, half-joking. 'You'll get me in trouble.'

The next day I was pretty excited about the prospect of going out with an experienced fisherman onto the high seas, and hopefully catching our own fish for supper. 'Come on William, hurry up,' I said. 'You'll have to take waterproofs to protect your arm, and it'll be cold out at sea. You'll need a warm jumper.'

Dougal was waiting for us by the jetty. 'I'm looking forward to taking old *Maisie* out. It's the first time I've taken her out to sea for quite a while.'

'Oh, I thought you said you fished round here…'

'I do, but normally I stay in the bay here. It's probably about a year since I took her out properly.'

I looked at Maisie's hull and noticed quite a lot of bumps and patchy paintwork. 'She is seaworthy, isn't she Dougal?' I asked, suddenly feeling a bit nervous.

'Oh, yes, she's a great little boat. I've had to patch her up a bit over the years, but she's as good as new now.'

'OK…have you got life-jackets for us?'

'Oh, yes, somewhere…' Dougal wandered about on the deck looking under various boxes until he found some very old, smelly ones that looked as if they were as old as the boat.

'Right, let's get her started up,' he said, climbing into the cabin. It took a few goes before she stuttered into life. 'There we are! I knew she'd do it!' he said, slapping the steering wheel. Maisie wasn't the speediest of crafts – in fact I thought she was going to give up the ghost on several occasions as we chugged over the waves to Dougal's chosen fishing ground. 'I've made us some tea,' Dougal said, once we got there. He handed me a stained, chipped mug with a substance inside it which bore no resemblance to any tea I'd ever tasted. I threw it over the side when he wasn't looking. Dougal sorted William out with a chair and a rod and showed him what to do. After an hour, William and Dougal had caught a few little mackerel, but nothing much else. William was getting restless. 'Let's try this other bait I brought. It might do the trick,' said Dougal, getting out a bucket with some rotting sardines in it. After another hour of not catching anything at all, I was beginning to realise that fishing was probably the most boring pastime known to man, and I had no means of escape.

'What time do you think we should be getting back?' I asked him, hoping he'd say, 'in about half an hour'.'

'Well, it's a good day for it with the wind in the West,' he said, - 'so I reckon in another couple of hours, give or take…'

'Oh, really? But what about lunch. I didn't bring anything.'

'Oh, don't worry about that. My wife made us some jellied eel sandwiches.'

After another interminable hour, I noticed the sky darkening and the sea began to feel quite choppy. 'The weather seems to be turning, Dougal. Do you think we should head back now?'

'Oh, it's all right for a bit, I'd say…'

William suddenly shouted that he'd caught something. 'Hold firm,' said Dougal, running over to help him. 'Slacken it off a bit…that's right…now reel it in,' he instructed William, excitedly. The game of one-armed fish tug-of-war went on for about ten minutes, until William finally landed his fish – a magnificent skate the size of a table.

'That's a whopper,' said Dougal. 'Well done lad!" I reckon that's about 40 pounds!' William was grinning from ear to ear. I got my phone out and took some photos of him holding up his prize.

'Now we need to put him back in,' said Dougal.

'What?' said William. 'Why can't we keep him?'

'These fish are endangered. We have to put him back in. The weather is turning. I think we should get going.'

'Is there a storm coming in?' I asked, getting worried.

'Oh, no, I don't think so. Just a wee squall.' He stood at the helm and turned the boat round. Very slowly, we made our way back. Not before the horizontal rain began to pelt down like rods beating against the slippery deck. Our little boat began to rock violently from side to side. William and I sat huddled behind Dougal in the cabin, watching him wrestling with the steering wheel and listening to the waves crashing all around us, the sky completely disappearing as we plummeted downwards.

When we finally got to shore, William and I were utterly exhausted and very shaken up. We stepped off the boat onto the jetty and William was instantly violently sick. Dougal had recovered his composure and was smiling again.

'Ah that was a wee bit of a rough ride home. Sorry about that, but the weather can change suddenly up here. No harm done, eh! Right, I'll be off. Let me know if you'd like to do it again.'

William and I staggered back up to the cottage in the pouring rain, clutching our little bucket of fish.

'Let's go to that pub we saw on the way here – what was it called?' I said to William the next day.

'The *Bonnie Bally*.'

'Let's go there for lunch. It looked nice from the road.'

'I still feel ill.'

'Well, maybe in an hour or so, you'll perk up.'

I have to say, I wasn't all that great myself. I honestly thought we were done for out there. These fishermen must have stomachs of steel and the nerves to go with it. Neither of us could face gutting and eating our catch last night. This morning the sea looked as calm as a mill pond again. Just goes to show, you never know what's going to happen – you have to be prepared for anything in these parts.

I went out with Otto along the shoreline for some fresh air. He ran round chasing seagulls and splashing in the water. I thought about my book, and how I haven't even started it yet. A pipe dream, most likely. Maybe I'm being too ambitious to think of writing a novel. Maybe I should just keep a journal instead. After all, who's going to read it anyway…except me? I wonder if I could interest William in reading a book while we're out here. There were some quite interesting ones on the bookshelves. I laughed to myself, when I thought about that. He'd say it was a load of rot, or his favourite expression, 'dead'. Maybe he's right about that. Most kids don't read anything any more. It's a sad fact.

The *Bonnie Bally* was quiet with just a few old men in there, and a young couple sitting outside in the sun. The woman behind the bar was a cheerful and chatty person who introduced herself as Davina. She showed us the menu and William chose scampi and chips with a coke. 'I think I'll have the same, William - good choice.'

'So, have you been here long?' Davina asked.

'Only a couple of days. We went out in a boat to go fishing yesterday afternoon. That was quite an experience!'

'Oh, I bet it was! That storm was bad. I'm surprised there was a boat going out in that. The forecast was for severe weather – the Met Office issued a gale warning yesterday morning. Which boat was it?'

'*Maisie* – Dougal's boat.'

Davina suddenly burst out laughing, and shouted to the group of old men at a nearby table to listen in. 'Tam, did you hear that? Guess who took their boat out yesterday afternoon?' she said, barely able to contain herself. 'That boat of Dougal's is a rust-bucket. It's so full of holes it could double as a sieve! You must have been well drookit!'

The men were all in stitches. 'Ay, lass, it's true,' said Tam. 'That boat was classed unseaworthy aboot ten year ago. It's no much better than an auld skiff, hahahah!'

'He's a big glaikit eejit,' said Davina. 'You're lucky to be alive, and that's the truth.'

'I caught a massive fish, though,' said William. 'Laura, show them on your phone.'

'Fair play,' said one of the men, - 'that's a braw fish. You did well, lad.'

Then, inevitably, they all started comparing fish-catching stories and who got the biggest catch. William was all ears as we ate our food.

'I tell you what, son, you could come out with us on a proper boat. What d'you think of that? See if you can catch a bigger one, eh?' William was wide-eyed. 'Oh, yeah. I'd like that. Can I go, Laura?'

'Well, I don't see why not. I think that's a splendid idea.'

I arranged with the men to bring him to the pub the next day. He could hardly disguise his excitement about the prospect of another fishing trip that evening. He helped me gut the mackerel and we roasted them on sticks over our campfire on the beach.

'This is the life, William,' I said.

'Yeah. Can I go fishing every day?'

'I'm not sure about that. I think it depends on weather conditions. And they can't go out all the time – they have lots of other things to do, like mending nets and painting things…' (*I really have no idea what fishermen do when they're not out at sea, but it sounded knowledgeable.)*

'I could do that,' said William.

'OK, well, we'll see. You've only got one good arm, don't forget. You might get bored.'

I was looking forward to a day on my own after I dropped William off with the fishermen. It was a perfect day for sitting outside the cottage and attempting a bit of writing or reading, or just sleeping for that matter. I was still coming down from the adrenalin rush of yesterday's experience of being tossed about like a cork on those terrifyingly humungous waves. I made myself a big mug of tea and took it outside on the little patch of warm grass in front of the cottage, with Otto curled up next to me and the glittering waters stretching out for miles to meet the hot, summer sky. I opened my book and started reading…

Something scrunched lightly on the gravel path near the house, and I stirred from my nap. My book had fallen out of my hands onto the ground, and the bright light blinded me when I opened my eyes. I shielded them from the sun and looked up.

'Hello, Laura…'

'Gabriel!' I said, sitting up. 'What are you doing here?'

'I thought you might like a visitor.'

'But we're miles away from home!'

'I know.' He smiled. 'I flew. It's the best way. Any spare coffee, by any chance? I've been up since 5am...'

'I can't believe you've come all this way!' I said.

'Well, I've been giving things a lot of thought, and, while I think you're obviously a bit bonkers, I thought I'd like to carry on seeing you, if you don't mind, that is… By the way, where is your new son? What have you done with him? Did you get fed up with him and toss him into the sea?'

'That's not very far from what nearly happened yesterday!' I said, smiling at him. I told him all about our near-death trip out on the high seas, and William's new-found delight in going fishing.

'When's he back?' said Gabriel.

'I imagine around teatime…'

'Great! We've got all day. I'd like to start by taking you for lunch somewhere delightfully twee and very Scottish, followed by a romantic walk along the cliff path, and then we'll take it from there, shall we?'

CHAPTER 22

William had the time of his life yesterday. He brought back a lobster and told me they've said he can go with them tomorrow as well, if he wants to. I couldn't believe my luck! After all the worry about William hating it here, and now he's having a ball. I must say I thought his first trip out with Dougal would have put him off, but it seems that he actually thought it was fun! Anyway, I'll have to buy those fishermen a few pints to thank them – they've saved my life! And, as for Gabriel, well, I'm still reeling from his unexpected arrival yesterday. We had a lovely day together. He opened up completely and told me all about his dream of creating a wildlife centre and place for studying and learning about insects and spiders and how he wants to educate people about the importance of them for the survival of our planet. He also told me about his failed relationships with women who didn't understand his obsession and how he needs to be sure that I can accept his plans for the future. We talked for hours about shared experiences, hopes and dreams, family and friends. He wants to go and visit a man in North Uist tomorrow, who's discovered a fly in his back garden that was believed to be extinct. Then I started to worry that maybe he's only here to visit another insect enthusiast, and not really here to see me. I'm not entirely sure. It was still nice to be wined and dined, though, and I did enjoy his company, so I decided I should just go with the flow for now. He's staying somewhere in Stornaway. I invited him for supper tomorrow evening and to meet William. I might try and cook the lobster, which is still alive in a bucket, poor thing. I feel a bit sorry for it, but lobster is quite delicious, so I'll have to get over that. I'm hoping Gabriel knows how to dispatch it quickly and painlessly, being an expert in all things zoological.

'What are you going to catch today?' I asked William, on the way to *Bonnie Bally.*

'Salmon, I think.' Then he added, knowledgably, - 'It's the new season, you know.'

'I see. You're getting into this fishing business in a big way, aren't you!'

'I've learned quite a lot. Tam said, if I lived here, he'd give me a job on his boat.'

'Did he indeed!'

Well, that's a turn up for the books. William's enthusiasm would, of course, wain in the winter months no doubt, when he'd have to be out in all weathers getting cold and wet and stinking of fish. I have noticed he's stopped saying he won't wear a coat, though, so that's something. There's hope for him yet.

I had a day free today, and I knew Gabriel would be busy with his insect man. The weather wasn't quite so nice for just sitting around outside. I thought I'd go for a really long walk round the coast with Otto. I packed some lunch, and we took off. I don't think I've ever been anywhere where I literally saw not a single soul. It felt like I was completely alone on the planet, except for the animals and birds. I took lots of photos of things that were too far away (that's what Jenny will say when she sees them) and a few really good ones of Otto. When I went to pick up William at the end of the day, he remarked on my complexion, saying it was a bit on the red side. What he actually said, was; '*your face looks like a big tomato'*. Back at the cottage, I looked in the mirror and realised that I did, indeed, resemble a 'big tomato'. *Damn it, just when I'm attempting to look alluring.*

'Someone's here,' said William, as I was trying to cover up the worst burnt bits with foundation.

'Just coming,' I said. 'Get the wine out of the fridge.'

'She's burnt her face,' I heard William saying to Gabriel.

'You've caught the sun, then?' said Gabriel, smiling.

'Yes, I burn easily, being pale-skinned. I forgot to put any sunscreen on.'

'It matches your hair,' he said, making William laugh.

'This is William,' I said, - 'and, William, this is Gabriel.'

'I know. You're Laura's boyfriend.'

'How do you know that?' I said.

'Because my friend's big brother's wife works at school in the kitchen, and she said you had a boyfriend at the Ball.'

'It's impossible to keep a secret at that place,' I said. 'Everyone seems to know everyone else.'

'But I know anyway.'

'How?'

'Because I've heard you talking to your friend Cath.'

'All right, Big Ears! Go and get our dinner – he's still in the bucket under the table.'

Gabriel knew what to do with the lobster, even though I don't think he liked having to kill it.

'That was a good catch, William,' said Gabriel.

'I got some salmon today as well.'

'So, are you going to be a fisherman when you leave school?'

'Dunno.'

'Tam on the boats offered him a job today, so he must be good,' I said.

'Or you could carry on at school and go to college - would you consider doing that?'

'Nah. I'm not staying at school. That's for nerds.'

'I see. Well, what if I told you that nerds can earn quite a bit of money?'

'I don't care.'

'Hm…what are your favourite trainers, William?'

'Um, *Air Max* or *Yeezy*, maybe…'

'OK, well, don't you want to be able to buy your favourite trainers when you start earning money?'

'I can just get a job.'

'You can, of course, but usually people with qualifications can get better paid jobs.'

'My Dad just goes an' nicks stuff he wants…'

'Right…' Gabriel raised his eyebrows at me.

'That didn't work out well for him, though, did it, William?'

'No, not really.'

'He's in prison,' I said.

'Well, anyway, all I'm saying, William, is that you could think about it. School's much easier than working, by the way. Imagine going to a job every day that you hate but you're trapped in it because you didn't think really hard about what you actually wanted to do in life.' William didn't respond.

'When we've finished eating, shall we go down to the pub for a drink?' I suggested, - 'they've got a dart board and a pool table.'

'Oh, yes! Good plan,' said Gabriel. 'If you're as good at pool as you are at fishing, you'll beat me easily, eh William?'

The sun had finally gone down at 11pm, when we emerged from the pub.

'I had a great time,' said Gabriel. 'I've got to go back tomorrow morning, unfortunately.'

Out of William's earshot, I whispered, - 'stay tonight, if you want to...'

'Are you sure?'

'I'm never entirely sure about anything, but 'almost' is pretty good, isn't it?'

'Are you going to get married?' asked William, after breakfast, when Gabriel had gone.

'That's not something people discuss early on in a relationship, William.'

'Well, I think you should.'

'Oh, right. Why do you think that, then?'

'Because he's quite cool, and he's got pet tarantulas. I mean, that's sick! I can't wait to tell Charlie Pinnock about that!'

'OK, well, I don't think I'll be basing my life choices on what you and your mates think. To be honest, I'm not too keen on anything with more than two legs that crawls, particularly if it's hairy.'

'You can get different coloured ones, Laura. Even blue! Do you think he'd let me have one to keep?'

'No. Absolutely NOT. I expect you can go and visit them at his place, but there's no way we're getting one. NO WAY! OK?'

The rest of our holiday went by quite quickly with William going out every other day on the boats. I managed to read three whole books and write some ideas down for my book, plus I've lost at least 6lbs walking everywhere with Otto. On the last night, I invited Dougal and his wife, plus Tam and the fishermen, round to the cottage for a BBQ on the beach. I decided that this was not going to be our last visit to the Isle of Lewis.

'We've had such a lovely time,' I said to all the guests, - 'we're definitely coming back, isn't that right, William?'

'Yeah. Thanks everyone,' said William. I felt quite emotional when they all left at the end of the evening.

'So, William,' I said as we cleared up, - 'you're glad you came now, aren't you?' He nodded. 'Sometimes you have to give things a chance.'

'Yeah.'

'OK, let's get to bed, we've got a long day tomorrow.'

Ah, home at last! At least coming back on the sleeper meant we got back in the morning feeling nice and refreshed. It's always so good to come home, even if it means suddenly remembering things you've got to deal with that you quite happily ignored for two whole weeks, like my mother, and my emails, and my life…well, not all of my life, obviously, just the bit where I lost the plot. It was a sort of delayed reaction, I suppose. I should have thrown something at Henry six years ago when he announced he was leaving to go and live with someone else. I heard later it was someone he'd known for a while.

After walking Otto, my first job was to ring *Sunnyside* and find out when they wanted me to fetch my mother.

'Ah, Miss Blewitt…'

'Please call me, Laura, Mr Pilkington.'

'OK, Laura…we tried to get hold of you last week, but we were unsuccessful, so we rang your sister.'

'Jenny.'

'Yes. Well, it's been a bit of a funny old couple of weeks with your mother.'

'Oh, don't tell me, she escaped again?'

'No, she's been here the whole time.' He sounded tired. 'We had to take her personal alarm off her in the end. As you know, it was diverted to the staff here while you were away. She was constantly pressing it and our staff are quite busy, as I'm sure you will understand. We do our best to make our clients comfortable, but we can't be running errands left right and centre. Anyway, your sister gave us permission to remove it.'

'Oh, dear, I'm sorry…'

'Don't worry. Once we took it away, everything was fine, although she did try and 'borrow' the buzzer from the receptionist's desk in the foyer. Anyway, now we have a different problem.'

'Oh…'

'She doesn't want to leave. We tried everything, but unless we knock her out with a tranquilizer, we're not sure she's going to budge.'

'Well, couldn't she stay, Mr Pilkington?'

'Please call me James.'

'Can she stay, James, please?'

'I'll need to check, and of course we'll need to discuss suitability, etc.'

'Of course. Let me know what you need us to do.'

I rang Jenny straight away and told her about the possibility of Mum staying permanently.

'It's perfect, Jenny,' I said. 'It's a no-brainer!'

'Let's do it, then,' said Jenny.

'What did you say?' I said, not sure I'd heard her right.

'She was driving me mad while you were away! I don't know how you and Mrs Wang put up with it for so long. Why weren't you answering your phone, by the way?'

'Oh, the signal was very bad where we were.'

'Did you have a nice time?'

'Yes, we did. It was incredibly relaxing. William enjoyed himself more than he thought he would. What about you Jenny? How are things with Jack?'

'Oh, I've decided to break up with him. He's never going to grow up. He just wants to have fun all the time – I just don't see the appeal, frankly. I mean, there's more to life than joking around and partying, isn't there? Anyway, I've met someone else, through work. He seems more my type. He likes early nights and an organised timetable.'

'Oh, good…'

'He's called Carl. I'll bring him over next week. Any news on your love-life?'

'Um, well…*(should I tell her?)*… there's someone…'

'Ah, can you elaborate?'

'Well, OK, he's my age, he's handsome, intelligent, funny, and thoughtful – he's perfect, actually.'

'There's got to be something wrong with him! Is he solvent, Laura?'

'Oh yes, but he may not be quite so much, in the future…'

'That doesn't sound perfect at all.'

I laughed, - 'Jenny, you're so predictable.'

'Well, you can't be complacent about these things, Laura. Look at Henry!'

'He's got a job now, apparently.'

'Really? Well, miracles do happen.'

It will be such a relief to get Mum into *Sunnyside*. No more panicking, no more phoning the police, no more apologising to neighbours, no more worrying about her being on her own.

William came out of his room and announced he was going to meet his mates. He couldn't wait to meet up with them again. I suppose two weeks is a long time in a teenager's life.

'You'd better take some money for food,' I said, handing him a tenner.

I scrolled down through my emails and deleted most of them. Then I saw one from Evelyn. I took a deep breath and read it:

Dear Laura,

Thank you for your email and your apology therein. I do understand how difficult it is to care for a parent when you are working full time and the responsibilities are sometimes overwhelming, as I have personally experienced. However, throwing a missile at someone in full view of the Board of Governors, the PTA, and the whole of the staff of St Jude's is very difficult to overlook, as I'm sure you will appreciate. Therefore, I have no choice but to ask you to take some time off while you recover from this unfortunate and reckless conduct, and the consequences thereof, which will hopefully give you some much-needed time to think about your situation. I will re-evaluate your position in the Autumn term, and hopefully you will be able to return after Christmas.

I hope this will help you to get back on track.

Best wishes,

Evelyn D. Ferrier (Ms)

BSc (Hons) MA EdD

Goodness! Well, that's more than I'd hoped for. Evelyn has come up trumps, despite everything. I wonder if Cath had a hand in it, or, maybe Evelyn thinks more of me than I realised? The main thing is, I've still got a job, which is a huge weight off my shoulders. God knows what I'd have done if I hadn't – I don't have a plan B, apart from becoming one of those hermits who hide away in a hovel for the rest of their miserable lives.

I rang Cath to give her the good news.

'Thank goodness for that,' she said. 'I've been so worried about you. How was your holiday?'

'It was fabulous, Cath.'

'Did you get any writing done, then?'

'Not much, but I've got a plan for something, in my head. The holiday sort of inspired me.'

'And what about William – did you end up strangling him, or what?'

'Well, he actually enjoyed himself. He's taken to fishing in a big way. I couldn't keep him away from it!'

'Oh, that's such good news, Laura! I thought you were going to tell me how awful it was!'

'Something else happened…'

'I'm all ears…'

'Well, Gabriel turned up at the cottage, just like that, with no warning!'

'Wow, he must be keen then!'

'I hope so.'

'That is *so* romantic, Laura!'

'Isn't it!'

'So, it's all back on now?'

'Yes, I guess it is!'

'I'm sorry to have to mention this, but although Peter and Billy loved having William over, their parents are not so keen.'

'Oh, why is that?'

'Well, the boys were particularly enthralled by William's stories about his dad, which they regaled their parents with later on.'

'Oh, no – I'm sorry, Cath. What did he say?'

'Peter told them that William's Dad was always getting locked out of the house and had to sleep in the shed because he was 'pissed', and that his Mum has lots of boyfriends who give her money to 'have a nice time'…The thing is Matt's sister wasn't too happy about it. She's asked us not to have him over again.'

'OK. I understand.'

Oh dear. I suppose for William that life he had was normal. It's a good job there aren't any other kids in my family, if this is going to happen. I can't stop him talking about his own family, can I! There are times when I realise that I've bitten off more than I can chew, and this is, sadly, one of them. I'm going to have to have a conversation with him about when it's appropriate to speak about certain things, and when it isn't.

I realised I hadn't listened to my phone messages on the landline since I got home, so I switched it on while I made myself a coffee. There were several scam calls from abroad, six calls from my mother asking me to bring various things for her (including a shovel, a pair of wellingtons, and a balaclava), and one from Dan, saying he'd tried to ring me on my mobile, but couldn't get me, and could I call him as soon as I got back.

'Dan, it's me, calling you back…'

'Oh, great, you're back. Are you free for lunch? I'll come and get you. I've got something to tell you.'

'That sounds intriguing…'

We sat outside a local café and ordered pizza and two glasses of Prosecco.

'You're looking great,' said Dan.

'Thanks. Although, after this food, I'll put the weight back on that I managed to lose.'

'You've caught the sun a bit,' said Dan, looking at my peeling nose.

'Yeah, thanks, I know.'

'OK, so, guess who I had lunch with while you were away?'

'Kermit the Frog? The Dalai Lama? The Pope?'

'None of the above. It was Valerie! I had lunch with Valerie McPhearson.'

'Oh, my God! Why?'

'Well, she contacted me at the weekend after the party. She got my number from Evelyn.'

'Right…'

'So, she asked if I would mind meeting up – she said she wanted to talk about what happened at the party.'

'OK…'

'Anyway, she said she would be coming on her own, because she didn't want to involve Henry.'

'I see.'

'She said she was hoping you wouldn't lose your job over what happened, because in her opinion, Henry probably deserved it.'

'Did she?'

'Yes, she did. And - get this – she also said that Henry hadn't told her about living with you for all those years. She's only just found out that he was lying about that. He told her he was working abroad all that time.'

'Why, though? I don't understand?'

'He wanted her to think you were just a short-term girlfriend.'

'I still don't get it, really….'

'When you split up from him, Laura, did he tell you who he was leaving you for?'

'No. I didn't want to know. I was fed up with him in and out of work all the time. He was always needing money. He never paid me back, you know. We had a lot of arguments about it. He'd promise me that he would get a proper job, but he just couldn't stick with anything.'

'Well, he went back to Valerie…'

'Really?'

'Yes, and he told her a load of rubbish about his 'job abroad' and that he'd had to come back home because it was too dangerous to stay. He also told her that his bank account had been frozen there, and he had no access to any money.'

'Oh, my God! What a snake! But how did she find out?'

'Well, it seems that after you tried to brain him with that massive plate, she couldn't understand why. It didn't make any sense. He'd told her that you split up after graduating that year, and he'd gone off abroad. So, after the party she questioned him about it and he had to come clean, because he knew it would only be a matter of time before you told her, as you'd be working together. The cat was out of the bag!'

'Oh, wow! So, what's she going to do?'

'I don't know, but he's a first-class jackass, if you ask me. She's better off without him.'

'Gosh, I'm stunned, Dan. I can't believe it!'

'She actually told me she thought you'd done her a favour.'

'Poor girl, though. I mean, she's been with him for years. That's a long time to waste on a lying snake like him.'

'I think she knew that he was playing away a lot. You did too, didn't you?'

'Yes, I suppose did. I was stupid to put up with it.'

'Well, anyway, she's going to see Evelyn to try and explain everything. She's hoping to be able to work with you next term, Laura. She seemed genuine.'

'Evelyn's already emailed me. I'll show you…'

Dan looked at the message. 'Seems fair. Maybe once Valerie has spoken to her, she might ask you to come back in September.'

'I was kind of hoping for some time off…'

'To do what, may I ask?'

'Well, while I was on my paradise island, in the wilds of Scotland, I realised something. All this time, I've been planning to write a book about my favourite poets – a sort of anthology, but then I thought, I should be writing my own stuff. It was a kind of epiphany, Dan. I suddenly just knew it.'

'I'd better get you another drink to celebrate!'

'Just a soft one, please, Dan. I'm not going to have a repeat of the other night – you're such a bad influence!'

'I try my best.'

Well, well, what a revelation! I can't quite take it all in. I wonder what will happen to Henry, now? Not that I care. I hope Valerie will be OK. Starting a new job under these circumstances is 'the pits' as William would say, although I now feel so much better about working with her. And I'm hoping she'll be an improvement on Ray. I can't believe no one realised what he was doing. Of course, now, I know why he was always disappearing and needing me to cover for him. It never occurred to anyone that Morag was missing at the same time. Amazing how something can be happening right in front of you, and you can be completely blind to it.

CHAPTER 23

Orla rang on Wednesday morning and told me she'd managed to get a visiting time slot at the prison, for William to go and see his Granny. I'm in two minds about the wisdom of this plan. I can't imagine it being a good idea for a 14-year-old to be exposed to the grim reality of incarceration, but at the same time, maybe it would put him off any idealistic notions he might be harbouring about the attraction of a life of crime. I'm quite concerned about what he's up to during the day, since we came back from Scotland. He disappears at lunch time and doesn't come back until the evening, when he's hungry. I have no idea where he is all that time. When I question him, he's very vague – it seems that all these kids do is hang around in various locations in town. It's a mystery to me how anyone can spend hours and hours literally doing nothing.

'You need another hobby,' I said to him this evening. 'All this mindless loitering can't be good for you. We need to find something to occupy your brain.'

'Hughh?'

'Your brain is a muscle that needs to be exercised, William, or it will shrink to the size of a pea.'

'Rubbish,' he said. 'Anyway, there's nothing to do round here.'

'What about going with your scooter to the skate park?'

'It's broken.'

'OK, well, what about your bike? Actually, come to think of it, where *is* your bike, William?'

'Stolen.'

'When were you going to tell me about that, then?'

'Dunno.'

'We need to inform the police. I had that bike marked and registered. The police might be able to locate it.'

'No, you don't need to do that…'

'Why?'

'Because I know who took it.'

'Well, we should go there and get it back.'

'No, it's fine. I'll sort it.'

'Hmm – I smell a rat, William.'

William smirked and told me there was nothing to worry about.

'Did you sell your bike?' I asked him straight out.

'No!'

'I just wondered, because you're wearing new trainers and a new jacket that I don't recognise…'

'My mate gave them to me,' said William, getting annoyed with my questioning.

'Really?'

'Yeah. Anyway, I'm going out now…'

'But you've only just come in!'

'I'm meeting someone.' He left, banging the door on his way out.

This parenting business is REALLY hard. How am I supposed to know what he's up to? Whatever it is, it's not good – I know that much.

In the morning, I left William sleeping as usual, and went to visit my mother at *Sunnyside.* James Pilkington hasn't contacted me since our conversation the other day, and I was wondering if he'd forgotten me.

'Ah, Laura, how nice to see you again,' he said, when I got there. 'I was going to give you a ring today. Your mother has been settling in…'

'Oh good. No more dramas, then?'

'Not recently, but it's never a dull moment with your mother!' He forced a smile.

'And are you any further forward with offering Mum a permanent place here?'

'Well, we're still mulling over the finer details,' he said, - 'but we'll let you know as soon as possible.'

I wondered if they are worried about how disruptive she's going to be. That's not hard to understand. I mean, she doesn't just sit quietly watching the telly, or knitting, or something. She's wandering about, interfering with other people's affairs, encouraging them to join her in her latest enterprise. I suppose that makes it quite difficult for the staff. Jenny told me that while I was away, she tried to get everyone to go outside in their coats, woolly scarves, hats and gloves. She'd seen a news bulletin about freak snowstorms in Australia. The fact that it was 30 degrees outside obviously had no impact on her whatsoever. Mum's message requesting shovels and balaclavas makes sense now.

'Hello, Mum!' I said, going into her room.

'Ah, Laura! Thank goodness you're here. Someone's kidnapped Margery.'

'Oh, really?'

'Yes. Laura. She was here yesterday, and we were just chatting when some people came and took her away. I haven't seen her since – there's something very fishy going on.'

'Let me find out for you, Mum.'

'They're all in it together, Laura. I don't trust them. They won't tell you the truth.'

Oh, good grief. Now she's being paranoid, on top of everything else…

I went to find a member of staff. 'Oh, Grace went out with her family. She came back late yesterday evening. I expect she'll be up and about soon.'

I returned to my mother and told her. 'Mum, Grace…I mean Margery went out with her family. No one was kidnapped.'

'Don't you believe it, Laura. They were in disguise. I saw them with my own eyes – they were wearing strange pointy hats. I know when I see funny business going on.'

'Let's have a cup of tea, shall we,' I said, trying to distract her. 'How do you like it here, Mum? It seems very nice and comfortable.'

'Oh, it is, but it's not as good as the Dorchester where your father and I went last year. They gave you warm, fresh towels every day, and chocolates in a bowl, and you had your own minibar. Do you know, I asked them for a brandy cocktail after dinner the other night and they didn't seem to know what I was talking about.'

'Well, I think this hotel is a non-alcohol one. You know - it's for healthy people.'

'Well, I can tell you, there's plenty of unhealthy people here, Laura, so that's a myth. Have you seen all those poor old things in the lounge? They're asleep most of the day, and they look very pasty. And another thing – with all this snow coming, they should really wrap up properly – it's going to be freezing cold. They won't survive the night the way some of them go about in barely a nightshirt.'

'Mum, it's only snowing in Australia. We've got sunshine here. It's really hot outside at the moment…'

'Your Uncle Bob went to Australia once. He didn't like it. He said they didn't have Newcastle Brown anywhere and he had to drink lager instead.'

'I can think of worse reasons to dislike a place,' I laughed.

'Doreen came to see me the other day.'

'Oh, that's nice…'

'She brought her old mother along. I think that woman has a screw loose.'

'Why do you think that, Mum?'

'She was talking gibberish the whole time to Doreen.'

'She's Chinese, Mum. She probably can't speak English.'

At this point Mum saw her friend appearing in the corridor outside her room. 'Ah, Margery, you're all right!'

'Yes,' she said, - 'I'm perfectly fine.'

'Thank goodness,' said my mother, - 'I thought those terrible people were never going to bring you back!'

'Oh, they had to catch the 8:45 back to Worthing…'

'Did you have a nice time with YOUR FAMILY?' I asked, looking pointedly at my mother in an attempt to stop her saying anything else.

'I did – thank you for asking. It was my birthday. They came all dressed up, wearing party hats and all, and they had one of them big birthday balloons – it was so lovely of them! It cheered me up no end! By the way, why does your mother keeps calling me 'Margery'?'

On the way home, Gabriel rang me to see if I was free to go out for supper.

'That would be a very welcome diversion,' I said.

We sat outside the pub in the warm summer evening.

'You still look beautiful,' he said.

'You still look handsome,' I said, laughing.

'Thank goodness for that,' he said. 'I thought I might have lost my appeal after having to dispatch the lobster in that rather gruesome way…'

'Well, I did ask you to do it.'

'I know but I wondered if it was some kind of test – you know, to see how fainthearted I might be…'

'I wouldn't do that. However, I was impressed by your fearlessness in the face of a potentially savage assailant.'

'It had its claws tied together, Laura. It was completely defenceless!'

'Well, anyway, thank you for being such good company and for entertaining William too. I don't think he's ever really had anyone take much of an interest in him.'

'Talking about being brave, you are very courageous to take on a young lad like that. No one I know would do such a thing.'

'Brave, or foolhardy! I have to admit, I didn't really consider the consequences of doing it, but he's a clever boy and I'd like to see him succeed at something in his life.'

'I want to show you something…' Gabriel produced a couple of sheets of paper – one with a photograph of a house and one with a picture of a field on it.

'These,' he said, laying them on the table, - 'are details of some land and a house for sale.'

'They're quite far away,' I said, picking them up.

'Yes, I know. But I don't have anything tying me to this place anymore. Except you, of course…'

'Long distance relationships don't usually work very well.'

'True…'

'Can't you find anything nearer than Norfolk?'

'No, not really. I need land I can afford to buy.'

'I see…'

'I'd like you to come with me and look at this place. Would you?'

'Um, well…I don't know. How far is it from here?'

'About three hours.'

'Really?'

'I think William should come too.'

'But if it's just a day, he can stay here.'

'I think he'd like a road trip, don't you?'

'OK, I suppose so. I'll ask him, but if you buy this place, Gabriel, I won't see much of you, will I?'

'I'm sure we can work something out,' he said. 'Besides, I'm going to need your advice on things I'm not sure about.'

'Like what?'

'Like the right size of the enclosure for my Goliath Beetles, or how many species of moths I should exhibit, and what sort of toughened glass to buy. These things need a woman's touch, you know.'

'Very funny. You know I don't want anything to do with your bugs.'

'But you will help me with the house, won't you? My sister is too busy and, anyway, I'd really like your input. It's perfect timing, isn't it? I mean, you're not back at school until September, are you?'

'OK, you've twisted my arm. When do you want to go?'

'Is tomorrow OK? The vendor said I can go any time. No time like the present, is there!'

Well, that was a bit of a blow! I'm not sure what Gabriel is thinking. There doesn't seem much point in continuing with this relationship if he's going to move miles away. Just my luck, I finally find someone who I really like, and it all goes up in a puff of smoke. I knew I should have stayed away from men! They're nothing but trouble. Well, maybe it's for the best anyway. I mean, how many women want to be exposed to the world of creepie-crawlies day-in-day-out? It's not on my list of must-haves, I can tell you. Maybe Norfolk's got more bug-friendly women, happily waiting for Mr Right to come along and wow them with his venomous False Widows. I don't know what to think at the moment. It's all very perplexing and unsatisfactory. Why couldn't I just meet someone straightforward and normal who does normal things? At least Elliott was predictable, and although Henry was unpredictable, he was predictable in his unpredictability…

William came back late again. When questioned, he seemed vague about what he'd been doing.

'You're not getting into trouble, are you?' I asked him.

'No!'

'Well, I hope not, because it would be a shame to spoil your chance of doing something worthwhile in life.'

William looked at me and rolled his eyes. I tried to stay calm. 'I'm only thinking about your future, William. You want to stay here, don't you?' He shrugged and looked at his feet. 'I'd like you to stay, so I can help you to do as well as possible, William, which means staying out of trouble…'

'Yeah, OK.'

'Would you like to go on a trip tomorrow?'

'Where to?'

'Well, Gabriel has invited us to Norfolk to see a house, and we can have lunch out somewhere nice…'

'Sounds boring.'

'William! That's very rude! Maybe, Gabriel will show you his collection of giant spiders…' I said, knowing full well that this would be the only carrot I'd need.

'Oh, yeah! When can I see them?'

'We'll have to ask him tomorrow. Are you coming, then?'

'S'pose so…'

Otto lay fast asleep, stretched out on the sofa, taking up all the space. I gave him a pat and told him what a lazy boy he was. Then I suddenly realised that I couldn't really take him to Norfolk with me – it would be too much travelling for him. I rang Cath in desperation.

'This is so good of you at short notice, Cath,' I said, bringing Otto into her kitchen.

'It's fine. The boys are coming over again tomorrow – they'll love it!'

'Oh, well thank you, you're a star!'

'So, Norfolk's a bit of a long way to go for a day trip!'

'I know. It's a property he wants to look at – for his bug zoo.'

'Ah, I see…'

'I don't know why I'm going, really. He was very insistent.'

'He'd better not be enticing you away, Laura! I will miss you!'

'I don't think he's that serious, Cath.'

'How do you know?'

'He hasn't said anything – anyway, it's too soon. We've only just started seeing each other.'

'Mm, well, on the one hand, I hope he is serious about you, but on the other, I don't want to lose my best friend! Especially to a reclusive boffin type. I'll never see you!'

'Oh, don't worry, he's not like that, Cath! He's actually very sociable and funny. You'd like him, honestly.'

'I'll take your word for it! By the way, I've got some news,' she said, suddenly smiling a big beaming grin. I knew instantly what it was.

'Cath, you're not!'

'I am!'

'Oh, that's amazing news! How wonderful! I'm so happy for you. When?'

'April.'

'Oh, I'm so pleased for you both!'

Gabriel picked us up at 9am the next morning.

'Cool car!' exclaimed William, getting into the back seat. Almost immediately, he put his headphones on to listen to his music.

'We could say anything now,' I said. 'He'll be oblivious until we get there.'

'I won't risk it!' said Gabriel. 'In my experience, teenagers are wily creatures – tuned in with their super-antennae to detect anything they aren't supposed to hear or know about.'

'And what experience might that be, then?' I asked, intrigued.

'Well, you may be surprised to learn that I have had some experience dealing with teenagers. I sometimes take groups of kids away at weekends for outdoor activities – for a charity called A-Teens.'

'Really?'

'Yes! Don't look so surprised!'

'I just...well, I don't know – I can't imagine it.'

'Why? Don't I look like the outdoor type?'

'No! I suppose I have this image of you as an office bod leading a comfortable life in a plush, carpeted, centrally heated, sanitised cube, somewhere boringly urban.'

'Ah, well, you're mostly right, but when I escape from the hell that is a cosy desk-job, I go wild in the country! I could take William next time. I think he'd love it.'

'Well, you might be right.' I looked at William in the mirror who was now fast asleep.

'You're very kind to include him, you know, Gabriel. Lots of men would run a mile.'

'To be honest, Laura, I wasn't over the moon to discover you and William came as a ready-made family. It's not what I envisaged when I met you, but, you know, if William comes with a woman in tow, I've decided I'm willing to put up with you...' He was smirking now.

'Gabriel, be serious!'

'Ok, look – it's fine. I've accepted the situation. Anyway, I see it more as a challenge than a problem. I'm sure you will have your faults, but I can be strong and overlook them. I'm a stoical kind of guy.' I couldn't help but laugh, despite the fact that he was clearly avoiding a serious discussion on the subject.

The house was a run-down Edwardian villa set in about 10 acres of land, with a large but neglected mature garden surrounding it. The Estate Agent was already there to show Gabriel round.

'Wow! It's massive!' said William, looking up at the three-story redbrick building.

'It's got six bedrooms and three reception rooms,' said the agent. 'It's in good condition – just needs a bit of TLC.'

'I'd say!' I said, looking at the peeling paint and broken windows. Gabriel smiled. 'It's a project, certainly, but I think it'll be worth it. Come on, let's go inside.'

William rushed around looking in all the rooms, while Gabriel was more concerned with the outside space and how he might lay things out. The agent enthusiastically explained the likelihood of planning permission and costs involved while I vaguely listened. I watched Gabriel's expression light up when he talked about his plans and I realised that he was not just contemplating this move, he had already pretty much decided on it.

'Well, what did you think?' he asked me when we finally came away.

'The house is wonderful,' I said, - 'it'll be lovely when it's been renovated. It'll be a lot of work, though.'

'I think it'll be worth it. It'll be perfect for what I want to do.'

'The house is very big, Gabriel. You'll be rattling around in it. Unless you're planning to fill it with zoo attractions!'

'Oh, no – the house will be strictly private. We don't want the public coming in!' *(We?)*

William almost read my mind. 'Are we going to move here, then?' he said. 'Can I have the attic room if we do? It's way bigger than my room at the moment…'

'Oh, no, William – we are just here to help Gabriel decide,' I said, hastily.

'Oh,' he said, sounding disappointed. I noticed Gabriel was smiling to himself. I carried on, - 'I've got my job to go back to, anyway. We can visit perhaps, if Gabriel invites us. If he's not too busy of course.'

When we got back to my flat, Gabriel ordered an Indian takeaway as it was getting late, and we were tired from travelling. As soon as we'd finished, William disappeared to meet his friends.

'So, Laura,' said Gabriel, pouring us a glass of wine each, - 'do you think I'm mad to be thinking of this move?'

'I don't know if you really need my opinion, Gabriel!'

'Ah, well, I do care about what you think, you know.'

'But you're going to do it anyway…'

'Well, I'd like to, but I'd also like to think you could be excited about it as well.'

'But it's your plan, Gabriel. I'm just an onlooker!'

'What would you say if I told you I want you to come with me, Laura?'

CHAPTER 24

My head is spinning now! How can I go with him? I've got responsibilities. What would I do with my mother? And there's my job – I can't just leave – I mean, it's such a big risk. What if I say 'yes' and then find out Gabriel is not what he seems? He could be an obsessive fruitcake (I already have my suspicions). His true colours might suddenly emerge, and I'll discover that he's actually an utterly selfish arrogant cretin! Or what if I can't stand him after living with him for a while – he could turn out to be REALLY boring, or have terrible habits like chewing his toenails or wearing awful clothes, or whistling tuneless ditties around the house…In fact, now I think about it, there's a whole host of things that I might dislike intensely about him, that, as yet, lie undiscovered and unrevealed… oh, God it's such a dilemma. I can't possibly say 'yes'.

James Pilkington rang me to explain the current situation with my mother. 'I'm sorry to tell you, Laura, but we don't have a permanent vacancy for your mother at the moment. She can stay for two months, but then you'll need to find somewhere else for her. I'm sorry to disappoint, but we have a long waiting list, and I am not at liberty to make any exceptions. I did try.'

'Oh, well, thank you for letting me know, James.'

I secretly suspect that James probably thinks better of housing my mother long-term. Especially after corralling the inmates together and persuading them to don their winter garb on a roasting hot day. James probably thinks she's too much of a liability. Imagine if the families started suing *Sunnyside!* Anyway, it's all very stressful. I'm going to have to organise something else for her now.

'Come on,' I said to Otto, - 'I need to mull things over – let's go out to the park.' Otto wagged his tail furiously and smiled. He was definitely smiling – I don't care what my sister says. She thinks dogs can't show emotions, but what does she know? She's never had empathy for any animal, apart from stuffed ones. Funny how people can get so attached to inanimate objects. She definitely had an unhealthy obsession with a blue corduroy donkey when we were little, which meant more to her than any real human being. She hasn't changed much.

I took Otto over to the park and sat on my favourite bench. I was just thinking about ringing Jenny with the disappointing news about our mother, when I saw Fay over by the play area with her children. She saw me at the same time and came rushing over.

'Dan told me about what happened with your suspension from school…I couldn't believe it when you went crazy like that! Remind me never to get on the wrong side of you!' Fay said, wide-eyed. 'What's going to happen now, though?'

'Oh, it's all calmed down – Evelyn says I can go back after Christmas, once I've recovered my equilibrium! Valerie is OK about it all – apparently, she and Henry are splitting up. Dan reckons I might even be able to go back in September. Not sure I want to, though…'

'Oh?'

'Well, when I thought I'd get another four months off, it made me feel so happy!'

'You know I'm not going to let you leave without a fight! What will I do without my partner in crime!'

'I'm sorry, Fay! You know I'll miss you too if I go. Did you have a nice holiday?'

'It was so relaxing there. Scott and I reconnected and had some really nice quality time together, the kids loved it, and the weather was fab! What more could you ask for! What about you? Did you enjoy your self-imposed isolation up in the frozen north?'

'Well, it was better than expected,' I said, smiling.

'Did you get any writing done, then? I was hoping for a glimpse!'

'Um, no, not much – I had William…'

'Ah, well, it was a nice idea.'

'You knew I wouldn't!' I said, - 'it's impossible with kids around, isn't it?' Fay jumped up at this point to go and sort out a crying child with a grazed knee.

'I did think about what I want to do with my book, though,' I said, when she came back. 'The holiday kind of focussed my mind a bit.'

'And how is Gabriel? Any further developments I should know about?'

'Well, he invited me to view a property he wants to buy…'

'Oooh, that sounds like a BIG development,' said Fay, grinning. 'That is *very* interesting! That man is keen as mustard!'

'What makes you so sure about that, Fay?'

'He couldn't keep his eyes off you at the Ball. And he wouldn't have asked you to go and visit a house if he wasn't REALLY serious! I'm telling you, Laura, he's the genuine article! Just remember, I want a front row seat at your wedding!'

In the evening, I decided I'd better drive over to Mum's house and check everything was OK, just in case some awful catastrophe had befallen it. You never know what might happen when you go away. Once, when we all went to France on holiday, a squirrel got into the house through the bathroom air vent and chewed right through the door to the hallway. It got into the kitchen and found the food cupboard. The mess was indescribable. When my mother saw the damage, she nearly fainted. *"Rats with fancy tails"*, Dad used to call them. Luckily, this evening all was calm, and the only thing I needed to do was mow the lawn.

When I got back home again, I rang Jenny. 'We will have to put Mum's house on the market,' I said.

'Or let it out…' suggested Jenny, which sounded like yet another thing for me to have to look after.

'That sounds like more work for me,' I said.

'You just get an agent, Laura. It's easy.'

'Well maybe you could deal with it, then,' I said. 'There's quite a lot to do to make it lettable.'

'Like what?'

'Well, everything is very dated in there now, Jenny. It needs completely re-decorating, the kitchen and bathroom need updating, and the carpets all need replacing…' There was a long pause.

'Oh, well, maybe we should just sell it, then. We'll have to get Mum to agree to it.'

'That's going to be tricky. Any ideas, Jenny?'

'Not really…you could tell her the locusts are coming and she needs to sell quickly… I've got to go now, sorry…'

'I just wanted to tell you that Mum can't stay at Sunnyside – she's going to have to move out in two months.'

'Oh, no! Look, I'm sorry but I really have to go now. Let's catch up at the weekend, OK?'

It's so frustrating. We're going to have to start looking all over again. She's not going to like it. Not one bit.

At midnight, William appeared, and quickly disappeared into his room. I went and knocked on his door.

'I thought we had a deal, William. You were going to be home by 10pm, and in return I was going to start saving up for those football boots you wanted…'

'Well, my mates were still out.'

'Don't they have homes to go to?'

'S'pose so…'

'Look, William, midnight is too late for a boy your age to be out.'

'I always stayed out late before.'

'I know, but you have a nice home now, don't you? So, you don't need to do that any more. I can always take your TV out of your room…'

'Aw, no, that's not fair. You can't do that!'

'Watch me!'

'Please don't!'

'So, tell me, what are you going to do from now on?'

William scowled and mumbled, 'come back at 10…'

'Great! Well, I'm glad we sorted that out! By the way, we're going to see Gabriel's spiders tomorrow, so don't disappear in the morning.'

I went to bed feeling I'd achieved something. A small victory, but none the less, a step in the right direction.

I woke up this morning with mixed feelings about today. I'm going to hate every minute of it, but William will love it. I suppose this is what parenting is all about. Gabriel promised me that it won't be as bad as I think. I don't believe a word of it. I have resigned myself to the unavoidable certainty that it will be one of the worst experiences of my life. Being in the presence of Beelzebub himself would be preferable. I decided I needed to prepare myself both physically and mentally for this challenge of all challenges. Morag's meditation training has come in very useful - I practiced an hour before we left the house. Deep breathing exercises and plenty of electrolytes have made me feel a bit more geared up for it. William did wonder what the strange noises were, coming from behind my bedroom door.

'It's just some relaxation techniques, William,' I told him.

'It sounded like you were in labour…' said William, over breakfast.

'And how do you know what that sounds like?'

'I've seen it on the TV on *One Born Every Minute*. Anyway, we get shown in school. It's BRUTAL!'

'It's deep breathing for stress relief, William.'

'Why were you doing that?'

'Because I have a deep and profound fear of all things spider-related, and it helps me to stay calm.'

'You should smoke some weed, Laura. That'd be better than just doing weird breathing…'

'Well, thank you William, for your expert opinion, but I'll pass. Anyway, I hope you haven't got any weed...'

'Nah, but I can get some…'

'No, thank you!'

Gabriel turned up in his car just as this conversation came to a close.

'We're going to my sister's house,' he said. 'I can't keep them at my flat as I don't have the space.'

'Is it far?' asked William.

'About fifteen minutes in the car.' Gabriel gave me a sideways look and smiled. 'Don't look so worried!'

Isla's house was a Victorian semi with a large front garden, set back from the main road. There was a double garage attached.

'They're in there,' said Gabriel, pointing at the garage. 'Isla has kindly agreed to let me use her garage until I've got things sorted out.'

'That was lucky,' I said. 'Didn't her husband mind?'

'No. He's very easy-going.'

'Where is she?' I asked him as we got out of the car. There was no sign of anyone.

'She's out at the moment. She'll be back soon.' Gabriel opened the side door to the garage and switched the lights on, revealing at least twenty glass cases of different sizes and colours. It was warm and humid inside. I took my jacket off and laid it down.

'The temperature has to be around 24 degrees for these animals,' said Gabriel, taking his jacket off too. 'The cases on the left are all the tarantulas,' he said to William, who went straight over to look.

'Wow, they're mahoosive!' he said. 'Laura, look at this one – it's got yellow stripes and it's bigger than my hand! Which is the biggest?' asked William. Gabriel showed him a huge brown furry creature. 'It's got ten legs!' said William, mesmerised.

'This one is a Goliath Bird-Eating Tarantula. The two arms at the front are pedipalps – they're like hands - they can grab their prey with them. Underneath their heads, they've got fangs which they use to inject venom into their prey.'

'Can I see?'

Gabriel obliged and opened the case to get it out. 'She's called Morticia…'

'Why is she called that?' said William.

'Well, female tarantulas often kill the males.'

'I'm not sure we want to hear about that…' I said, feeling quite squeamish.

'I do!' said William, without drawing breath.

Gabriel went on to describe the horrific fate which befalls the poor enthusiastic suitors of these voracious and indiscriminate females.

'Eurgh, that's horrible!' said William, with morbid fascination.

'Morticia has eaten four of her boyfriends since I've had her,' said Gabriel, putting her back. Would you like to feed her?'

'With another spider?' said William, horrified.

'No! With her normal food.' He went to a small fridge and got out a big jar of mealworms. 'Just drop one in and she'll grab it,' said Gabriel.

William did as he was instructed. 'Look, Laura, it's eating it ALIVE!'

'I'd rather not look at that, thank you very much…' I flinched at the sound of it slurping and munching on its wriggling prey.

'Can I hold one?' asked William.

'You have to promise not to drop it, if I let you,' said Gabriel.

'I'll just stay over here,' I said, watching Gabriel scoop up another monster Tarantula and put it into William's eager hands.

'It's tickling me,' said William. 'It's all fuzzy! Do you want a go, Laura?'

'No. Thank you.' Gabriel put the spider back and then went over to the corner of the garage where there was a bigger case with a red sticker on it.

'What's in there?' said William.

'A very special and quite rare tarantula called Stanley. I've had him since I was your age.' Gabriel lifted up the lid. 'Oh!' he suddenly said.

'What's the matter?' I asked.

'He's not in here!'

'What do you mean?' I said, suddenly feeling queasy.

'He's not here!' repeated Gabriel, alarmed.

'But how could he have escaped?' I said, feeling the hairs on the back of my neck rising.

'The lid is loose,' said Gabriel, giving it a shake. 'He must have pushed it up.'

'So, he could be anywhere,' I said, looking nervously around the garage.

'We need to search for him,' said Gabriel.

'What does he look like?' asked William.

'Apart from being large and hairy with loads of legs!' I said, - 'I don't think he'll be hard to spot, will he?'

'He has blue legs,' said Gabriel, losing his sense of humour.

We looked everywhere in the garage but drew a blank. 'He could have got out under the door,' I said, looking at the gap. 'He could be in the garden…'

'I'll never find him if he's out there,' said Gabriel.

We searched the garden, and when Isla came back, she helped too, but it was hopeless. 'Put some food out and see if he comes,' said Isla.

'You'd better tell your neighbours about him,' said Gabriel.

'Oh, cripes! That's just what I need! That'll make me really popular!' she said, looking alarmed.

'I don't want anyone to hurt him. We need to tell them he's harmless.'

Isla rolled her eyes. 'I knew it was a bad idea to let you keep them here!'

'I'm sorry Isla,' said Gabriel, - 'but I don't know how he managed to escape…'

'Well, you'll have to let the police know about it as well. If anyone finds him, they'll freak out!'

'Do you think Stanley will be OK?' said William on the way home.

'He can't survive cold weather,' said Gabriel. 'That's why he needs to be found quickly. Luckily, it's the summer. You'll excuse me, if I go straight back to my sister's house,' he said, - 'but I can't rest until I've found him. I know you'll think it's a bit strange, but I'm very fond of Stanley – we go back a long way and I'm very attached to him.'

How can a grown man be fond of an ugly, horrid creature that would scare the hell out of any normal person? The whole time I was in that garage, my skin felt really clammy and the hairs on my arms were literally standing on end. I'd managed to hold it together until he discovered Stanley was missing, and then the thought of it running around freely was enough to turn my stomach. I still feel quite nauseous, even though it's nowhere near me now.

William couldn't stop talking about it when we got home. I took Otto out for a walk to calm my nerves and try to get things into perspective.

'Cath, it was awful,' I told her on the phone when I got back to my flat. 'They were terrifying!'

'Well, that was your first encounter, Laura. You need to give it time…'

'You *are* kidding, aren't you?'

'Well, maybe you just have to tell him that his work has to be completely separate. I mean, it can't be too difficult, surely. Loads of people leave their work behind when they go home.'

'I suppose so…'

'I'm sure you've got plenty of things in common. He doesn't need you to be involved in his work, does he?'

'You're right, Cath. I don't want to hold him back. He can have as many of the loathsome creatures as he likes. It doesn't have to affect me, does it! Thanks, Cath.'

'That's OK! Always happy to help!'

Later, when I was just settling down to watch a nice feel-good film with a glass of wine and a good supply of peanuts, Otto started behaving strangely.

'What on earth's got into you?' I said to him, as he was trotting round sniffing at the carpet and barking. 'You've had your walk, and your tea!' He wouldn't settle, so I put him in the kitchen and went back to watching my film. I must have fallen asleep at some point, because when I woke up, it was finished. I was half asleep and didn't quite register something moving in the corner of my eye, in the semi-darkness…then suddenly, I SAW IT! Above the TV - crawling along the picture rail. I swear I couldn't breathe for at least 30 seconds.

'WILLIAM!' I screamed. 'WILLIAM. HELP!' There was no reply. 'SHIT! He's gone out. OMG, where's my phone?' I scrambled in my bag for it. My hand was shaking so much I could barely call Gabriel's number.

When Gabriel arrived, I was hiding in the kitchen with Otto. The door to the lounge was firmly shut and I was on my second gin and tonic. It took him a while to find

Stanley, who had crept under the sofa and had unbelievably decided to choose this particular time to start moulting.

'I'll have to leave him there,' said Gabriel. 'It's not safe to move him. Their skin is very sensitive, you see. You can damage them if you move them.'

'But he can't stay here! I can't sleep knowing he's in my flat, Gabriel! You can't be serious!'

'Laura, I'm sorry, but it's true. I'm not making it up.'

'Well, how long for?'

'It takes about a week for their skin to harden up.'

'WHAT! No, Gabriel… Oh God, I think I'm going to be sick…'

William came home at this point and we both instantly reproached him.

'Why did you take Stanley?' I said.

'You shouldn't have taken him, William. That was very irresponsible.'

'What are you talking about?' said William, looking confused. 'I didn't take him!'

'Well, how did he get here, then?' I said.

'I don't know, but I didn't do it!' William angrily denied having anything to do with it and stomped off to his room.

'He must have done it, Laura. There's no other explanation.'

'I'm sorry, Gabriel. I thought he'd have more sense than to do something like this.'

'Look, why don't you and William come and stay at my flat tonight while I figure something out.'

CHAPTER 25

Apart from the obvious down-side of having to abandon my flat last night, it was very nice to spend more time with Gabriel. He was so happy about finding Stanley that he was positively glowing with excitement about the move to Norfolk, and very persistent about the idea of me going to join him.

'But we just don't know each other well enough, Gabriel,' I'd said, over our second bottle of wine.

'I know all I need to know,' said Gabriel, - 'you're perfect.'

'Now you're being absurd! How can you say that when you know I can't abide the main love of your life!'

'But I don't want to live with my spiders or share my bed with them!' he laughed. 'They don't exactly make good bed-fellows, do they! Also, their conversation is extremely limited and, although they're great listeners, they don't have much to say for themselves…I don't think they'd be any good at DIY either…'

'Hahahah,' I laughed, - 'how do you know I'm any good?'

'I'm betting you're better than me! I am the world's worst home-maker.'

'Well, your flat is OK, isn't it?' I said, looking round at the rather plain and unadorned interior.

'It's rented. I didn't have to do anything to it! When I sold my house in London, the agent said it would appeal to someone who wanted 'a doer-upper'. I thought it was fine how it was, but she shook her head sadly and showed me some pictures of recently sold homes in an effort to educate me. I did sort of see what she meant, but I was so busy with work, I couldn't be bothered. You've made your flat look very nice and comfortable – I don't really know how to do that. Anyway, I'm making it sound like I just want a live-in housekeeper! I think you'd be great at making the house look really wonderful, but really it's you I want, Laura! I don't really care whether you're any good at knowing the difference between sage green and taupe…'

'Hm, well, actually, I do… but I have no idea what I'd be getting into – I mean, you might be really annoying to live with. What if I discover you live like a student and never wash-up or that you play really loud rock music around the house all day, or that you have awful friends that I can't stand…'

'Well, I don't think I'm too annoying, apart from spending hours doing my hair and make-up in the morning, and I was a very tidy student when I was at Uni – better than the girls in fact, and as far as music goes, I only ever play Mozart or Bach to help me relax, and the odd Gregorian Chant… And, I have no friends, so you're safe on that score.'

'Very funny, Gabriel!'

'On a serious note, my last girlfriend wanted me to give up my interest in spiders completely. You would never expect that, would you?'

'No, of course not. Were you together for a long time?'

'About three years. She left me for the chef from our favourite restaurant.'

'Oh, no! That's terrible!'

'It was. It really rubbed salt into the wound…'

'I never know whether you're being serious, Gabriel!'

'Sorry. He was a chef, though.'

'The thing is, I've got two other people to think about. My mother whose dementia is getting worse, and William who is still at school here.'

'Well, maybe they won't mind going somewhere new?'

'And what about my job? I can't just give it up.'

'Couldn't you apply for another one in Norfolk? There must be plenty of vacancies for a talented, experienced English teacher like you…'

'You make it all sound so simple, Gabriel.'

He smiled and told me he wouldn't be giving up trying to persuade me 'any time soon'.

In the morning, William was still sulking.

'Let's take Otto and Cleo out for a bit,' I said, getting my jacket. As I put my hand into the pocket, I felt something long and squishy. I pulled it out and squealed, throwing it down. Otto immediately licked it up off the floor and ate it.

'It was a mealworm!' I said, - 'well, half of one. How did get into my pocket? And there's some bits of bark too…' I said, turning my coat pocket inside out.

'I think I know what's happened,' said Gabriel, – 'and we owe William a big apology. In fact, I'm going to take you both out for breakfast to make up for it.'

Now that I know Stanley was hiding in my coat pocket all that time, and that he was sitting right next to me all the way home in the car, I shudder to think about it. I mean, what if I'd sat on him! Urggh, it doesn't bear thinking about! Gabriel said he must have crawled in there when I put my jacket down in the garage. 'They like warm, dark places to hide in,' he told me. 'When we came into the garage and put the light on, he probably got scared and looked for somewhere to escape to.'

We had a Full English Breakfast at a café in town and then took the dogs for a run down by the river. Gabriel showed William how to skim stones across the water while Otto and Cleo had a lovely time getting in their way.

'What are we going to do about Stanley?' I asked Gabriel, on the way back to his flat.

'He'll have to stay at yours for a few days, I'm afraid, Laura. Sorry…'

'Well, we can't carry on staying with you,' I said.

'You could, but William might get fed up with being on the sofa.'

'There isn't enough room for all of us, Gabriel. I'll take William to my mother's house for a few days.'

William and I went back to my flat and collected some clothes and food. The door to the lounge remained firmly shut.

'Can't we just see if he's OK?' said William.

'No. He'll be fine. It's the lap of luxury in there, William. He's got soft furnishings, central heating, an endless supply of junk food crumbs to feast on, and over 250 TV channels to choose from…'

At my mother's house, it wasn't quite so great, according to William. 'I can't watch *Sky Sports*,' he moaned, flicking through the hundreds of other channels on Mum's TV. 'There's nothing to watch.'

'You're lucky, William. When I was your age there was a choice of only four channels and that was it.'

'FOUR?'

'Yes.'

'I'd have jumped off a bridge…'

'That's very dramatic, William, and complete nonsense of course. The thing is, we didn't know any different, so we just accepted it. We didn't have home computers or mobile phones or tablets then.'

'What did you do?' asked William, astonished.

'Read books, played outside, listened to music, did crafts – lots of things.'

'That sounds *SOOOOO* lame…'

'Well, it wasn't. It was what everyone did back then. Kids had hobbies. In fact, if I look round here, I could probably find some of the things I used to do. I think my mother kept quite a lot of stuff from my childhood.'

I left William watching old *Doctor Who* episodes and went searching in Mum's cupboards. It was quite a nostalgic trip back through time, unearthing games and toys from years ago, some of which I'd completely forgotten about. I laid some of them out on my mother's bed for William to see. I didn't really expect him to be interested – I think I did it for myself, to be honest.

'What's that?' said William, when I showed him the things.

'It's a Pogo Ball. Look, I'll show you. We spent hours doing this,' I said, bouncing on Mum's carpet.

'That's so pathetic!' laughed William.

'It was good exercise,' I said, getting off it.

'And what about these?' he said, holding up two sticky pads.

'Magic Mitts,' I said. 'They're brilliant. You need a tennis ball. You have to catch the ball with the mitt…but not in here,' I said, as William found the ball and was about to throw it against the wall.

'Oooh, there's a Game Boy!' he said, spotting something far more interesting.

'It probably still works, but it might need batteries.'

What a strange feeling it was, sleeping in this house again, after so many years. It took me quite a while to get to sleep. Apart from hearing William playing noisily on my old games, I was lying awake worrying about my mother and what to do about this house, and whether I can face going back to work again, and whether my relationship with Gabriel is doomed…

My sister must be telepathic: 'I've spoken to Mum about selling the house,' she said, when she rang me the next day. 'We can get it on the market ASAP. Can you ring some agents?'

'Oh, right…yes…OK. How on earth did you manage to persuade her, though?'

'Well, I just said that people from *Homes Under the Hammer* were very interested in it, and she leapt at the chance to be on TV…'

'That's a terrible thing to do!' I said, horrified.

'Well, you come up with a better idea, then,' said Jenny. 'Look, Laura, we don't have any choice. She won't be going back there, and we need to pay for her care. I told a little white lie to get things moving, that's all. She loves that programme. It's in her best interest, anyway.'

'But it's obtaining her permission under false pretences…'

'Laura, you're too purist about these things, she'll probably forget she even has a house soon.'

I decided to call Mrs Wang to see if she was free to come and help me sort Mum's things out and get the house ready to sell. I went out and bought a massive roll of binbags and some cleaning stuff. Jenny hadn't seemed too bothered about coming over to help me (no surprises there), but I knew Mrs Wang would be ideal. Thank goodness she said she would be free tomorrow to come and help. William disappeared as usual to go and meet up with his friends at the park, so I was alone with my thoughts, and a mountain of work to do.

'This feels a bit wrong, somehow,' I said to Cath on the phone in the evening. 'I mean, it's as if she's died…'

'I know – it's not easy to do it on your own, either. It's a lot of work as well. Would you like some help? I could come over… I'll bring a bottle.'

'She's kept so many things,' I said, when Cath turned up. 'I mean, who needs masses of curtain material any more? And just look at all these books! She never reads any of them.'

'We can bag it all up and take it to the charity shops, Laura. Here - have some wine to oil the wheels…'

'You can't join me though, can you!'

'I'll make myself a cup of tea.'

'Do you know, it's weird Cath, but I haven't given this house much consideration for years, and now I'm selling it, I suddenly feel attached to it for some reason. I feel really sad about getting rid of it.'

'Well, you've taken it for granted all these years and suddenly it's going –all your childhood memories are bound up in this house. It's because suddenly, everything's changing, and your security blanket is being whisked away.'

'You could definitely say that! I don't know whether I'm coming or going, particularly as I can't go back to my own flat at the moment.'

'Why can't you?'

'Oh, I didn't tell you, did I! Well, you're not going to believe this, Cath, but Stanley the humongously gigantic and very scary looking tarantula, is currently ensconced in my living room, recuperating from his latest moult, which apparently means he has to stay there for several days. Gabriel says we have to wait for his delicate skin to toughen up. Apparently, he could die if he's handled while he's in that condition. He isn't even meant to be there! The whole thing was an accident.'

'Are you serious?' said Cath, laughing.

'Yes. He hid in my coat pocket when I took William to see Gabriel's collection of spiders, and I had no idea he was there, and then he escaped into my lounge when we got back to the flat.'

Cath burst out laughing. 'Laura, that is the most ridiculous thing I've ever heard!'

'Well, it's true.'

'Maybe you should sell your flat instead and move in here!'

'That's very tempting. Anyway, Gabriel will take him away in a few days, but it has made me feel a bit nervous about going back, I must say. Every time I look at the TV, I'll be expecting to see his enormous legs sticking out from behind it…'

'Eurrghh! I think you're very brave to carry on seeing Gabriel after that experience, Laura! I would probably have knocked it on the head by now.'

'I have thought about it,' I said, - 'but apart from the spiders, there's nothing wrong with him – well, not that I've noticed anyway…'

'Well, every man has his faults, Laura. Matt isn't perfect, you know. He's always buying things we don't need, and he's very messy.'

'Ah, but you can forgive him!'

'Mostly – although right now he wants to buy things for the baby. I have to stop him – it's too soon, and well, you know…things can go wrong…it might not happen.'

'Oh, Cath! It will…of course it will! Look, maybe some of these old toys will be useful…'

Cath looked at the odd collection of things my mother had kept. 'Oh, I remember Furbies! And, oh, look! You had a Cabbage Patch Doll, Laura! Some of those are collectable now, you know.'

'Do you think there's any point in keeping this stuff?'

'Maybe you could give some of these things to your own kids?'

'Hm, well, judging by William's reaction, if I have any kids, they certainly won't be interested in ancient relics like this! To be honest, I'm beginning to feel like an old relic myself!'

'Oh, Laura – don't be daft! Mind you, I don't think you should waste too much precious time agonising over what to do about Gabriel - I think that if you like him, you should take the bull by the horns. Go on - take a risk and go with him.'

'But you told me not to!'

'I know, but I was being selfish. Anyway, don't listen to other people – you have to follow your heart, Laura.'

Over the next two days, Cath and I went through Mum's house like a whirlwind. Mrs Wang came and helped as well, with little Betty in tow, which was company for Otto.

'Your Mum, she have lot of stuff,' she said, when we'd finished bagging up all the unwanted items.

'Would you like any of it?' I asked her. 'You are welcome…'

'No thank you, I got plenty rubbish at home.' Mrs Wang sometimes has quite an unvarnished way of saying things.

'Oh, OK,' I said, feeling slightly put out.

When James Pilkington from *Sunnyside* called me around 6pm that day, I wasn't feeling in the best of moods. Six trips to the tip and four rejections from charity shops had exhausted my capacity to cope very well with negative information.

'Laura, I'm sorry to call you this late in the day, but we have a slight problem. Do you think you could come over?'

I whizzed round to *Sunnyside* to see what the matter was, and then wished I hadn't. The hallway was piled high with boxes, and there was only just enough room to make my way down the middle to the reception desk.

'What's going on?' I said to the woman at the desk.

'I think that's a question for your mother…' she said, rolling her eyes.

James appeared from behind a stack of boxes, looking flustered.

'What's she been up to now?' I asked, nervously.

'It appears that after watching several episodes of *Dog Rescuers,* your mother decided to order hundreds of dog beds and food items to donate to Battersea Dog's Home.'

'Oh no! How did she manage to do that?'

'With her debit card…'

'But I thought you would have her bank cards in a locker or something?'

'No…that's her own private property. We can't remove them without permission.'

'Oh cripes! What else has she been ordering?'

'Hopefully, nothing else…Um, do you think you could arrange for the removal of all these boxes, please? They're blocking emergency access, and any other access for that matter.' James looked a bit overwrought.

'I don't think I can get them all in my car in one go. I'll have to make several journeys,' I said looking at the enormous quantity of dog paraphernalia. By the time I'd done four trips back and forth, I was shattered. Before I left

Sunnyside for the evening, I popped in to see Mum. She was fast asleep and didn't notice me sneakily taking her purse out of her handbag, opening it, and removing all her bank cards. I slipped out unseen and quietly left the building.

'Why are all these boxes here?' said William, when he came home later. I explained what had happened and he asked if we could take it to the dog rescue centre in town.

'That's very thoughtful, William,' I said, feeling pleased at this unusually kind-hearted show of empathy.

'We can charge them for it and make some money,' He added.

CHAPTER 26

In the morning, I tackled the mountain of junk mail and letters that had piled up in the last few weeks. Even before Mum went to the care home, she'd stopped opening things. When I looked at her bank account statements, I had to sit down.

'Jenny,' I said, calling her immediately, - 'Mum's been spending a fortune – we need to stop all these direct debits.'

'What are they for?'

'Well, I've counted twenty-five sponsored children in Africa, five animal charities, nine wildlife trusts, six world poverty charities, the African Locust Emergency Appeal, and the British Society for Erectile Dysfunction…'

'Good grief! That's daytime TV for you – nothing but a conduit for conning money out of old people. It's outrageous! Why that last one, I wonder?'

'Best not to dwell,' I said. 'Anyway, the thing is, that by the end of the year, Mum will have £37,000 less in her bank accounts.'

'Christ! We'll have to get her into the bank and cancel them straight away. What a nightmare! You need to get her cards off her, before she does any more damage.'

'I have.'

'How much has gone already?'

'About £5,000.'

'Bloody Hell! So, what does she have left in there at the moment?'

'£1.50. Her pensions will go in soon, but that will all disappear within the week.'

'Lord above!'

Mum was not particularly keen on going out when I went to fetch her.

'I've made an appointment with your Bank Manager. We need to get a move on, Mum.'

'I don't need to go there.' said Mum.

'You do! We need to go and sign some forms.'

'What for?'

'It's so I can help you manage your accounts – it's just so you don't have to worry about all of that…'

'I've always done it myself, thank you very much, Laura. And I'll carry on if you don't mind. You and Jenny were always terrible with money. You never managed to save it up – it burned huge holes in your pockets. Your piggy banks were always empty.'

I had to call Jenny again, later.

'She won't go to the bank, Jenny. We're going to have to get Power of Attorney.'

'But that'll take weeks! She'll bankrupt herself by then. I'll come over on Wednesday. I've got the day off. I was supposed to be going to a health spa with my friend Felicity, but I'd better cancel it now. Honestly, our mother is a bloody liability!'

I sat and looked at all the boxes in the lounge and decided to ask Gabriel to come and help me. After all, what use is a boyfriend if you can't get them to do some lifting and shifting when required.

'Oh, dear!' he said, when he arrived. 'That's a lot of money's worth… Can't you send it back?'

'No. I checked.'

'Oh. Well, the rescue place will be pleased.' We put it all into both cars and drove over to the animal centre, where it was received with open arms.

'I want to put an offer in for the Norfolk property, Laura,' said Gabriel, when we got back to Mum's. It's the ideal place – I don't want to lose the chance to get it at a good price.'

'Well, you should do that, then,' I said.

'Have you thought any more about coming with me?'

'I can't promise anything, Gabriel. I've got so much to consider. This house needs to be sold, my mother's finances are in a terrible mess, I have to find somewhere else for her to go, and I can't think about applying for another job – I've got too much on my plate right now. Your timing couldn't be worse!'

'I understand,' he said, 'but where there's a will, there's a way!'

I think I need to be philosophical about Gabriel's plans. What will be will be. I need to focus on my own priorities right now. It's ridiculous that he thinks I can just leave all my responsibilities and go and live in the back of beyond, although it's a wonderful thought! I'd love to be able to tell Jenny to deal with our mother and give my job up at school. I'd still have William to worry about, though. It wouldn't be fair to take him away from all his friends.

'You're trapped in a spider's web of complicated predicaments,' said Dan, when we went for coffee the next day.

'Hm, well, you could put it like that. But less of the spider analogies, thank you!'

'Have you had an email from the Führer about going into school next week?'

'No.'

'Well, some of us are going in to help paint a mural on the science block outside wall. It's all been drawn out – it'll be like painting by numbers. Fancy helping?'

'Well, it might be fun,' I said.

'As far as anything to do with school can be,' said Dan.

'Has she found out who the 'culprits' are, yet?'

'No, of course not. She's on a hiding to nothing there.'

'I think William knows who did it.'

'He's not going to let on, though, is he! By the way, Beth won the two tickets to go to see Larry in a couple of weeks, but she can't go. Would you like to come with me? It should be a good laugh. What do you think?'

'Yes, why not! Oh, but I've got William…'

'Can't you leave him for one night?'

'He's only fourteen, Dan. Anyway, I don't trust him – he'd invite a load of mates over while I'm out.'

'OK, well, maybe you could ask Gabriel?'

'Hm, I don't know…I'll think about it.'

'I saw Valerie the other day…'

'Oh, how is she?'

'She booted Henry out two weeks ago.'

'Right…'

'Aren't you pleased?'

'Well, I suppose so. It's a bit weird, knowing I'm responsible.'

'She's OK about it. She's glad she found out.'

'Men are such idiots.'

'Pardon?'

'Sorry – present company excluded.'

'Gabriel's OK, isn't he?'

'Well, not really. I mean, who meets someone they really like and then decides to move 120 miles away?'

'It must be really nice there…'

'Well, yes, I suppose so…'

'Nicer than here?'

'Yes - I can't deny that. It's deep in the countryside – idyllic in fact.'

'If it wasn't for your Mum, and William, and your job, would you go?'

'Yes, I would. I definitely would.'

I'm really missing Morag's yoga class now. All that box-moving and runs to the tip with Mum's stuff has given me awful back ache. I need to find another instructor before I seize up entirely. To make it worse, there was another phone call this morning from James Pilkington. He said more boxes had arrived. One of them was so big, it had to be left in the driveway. He sounded really fed up. At least there's one piece of good news: Gabriel is collecting Stanley today, so William and I can go back to the flat. I've missed it more than I thought I would.

After lunch, I drove over to *Sunnyside* to see what all the fuss was about.

'Isn't there any way you can stop her watching adverts on the TV?' I said to James when I saw what she'd been buying. He gave me an exasperated look, saying that some things were beyond his capabilities as a 'mere mortal'.

'What am I going to do with 24 solar-powered water features and a giant statue of Eros?' I asked him.

'Put them in *your* garden?'

'My garden is the size of a table, James. Anyway, I have an unshakable aversion to garden decorations.'

'Well, we don't want them either. It's a *Health & Safety* matter.'

When I expressed my surprise at that, he explained that hard surfaces and protruding artefacts could endanger the elderly residents if they fell over, which, being frail and prone to losing their balance, was a strong possibility, and he wasn't prepared to take that risk.

'*Arrgghh!*' I screamed internally.

When I rang Gabriel for his assistance in the matter, he suggested the local council might like them, and then laughed uproariously. 'I tell you what, I bet if we put them on the pavement for people to take, they'd disappear quite quickly. Things like this are always being stolen, aren't they?'

'There's a thief in this place, Laura,' said my mother when I went in to see her. Someone has taken my bank cards.'

'Have you told the staff?' I said.

'No. It could have been any one of them. They're all up to no good. Just the other day, I saw that receptionist take the bell off the front desk. She hid it when she saw me coming.'

'That's because you keep ringing it. Listen, Mum – I took your cards. You were asleep, and I didn't want to disturb you.'

'Well, you'll have to give them back, Laura. I've got things I need to order.'

'No, Mum, you can't order any more things by yourself. Gabriel and I have had to spend hours finding homes for all the things you've bought. You'll have no money left at this rate.'

'Who's Gabriel?'

'My new boyfriend.'

'Am I going to meet him, then?'

'He's outside at the moment, packing the cars with all the boxes. I'll get him to come and say 'hello' in a minute.'

'Are you moving? You can't leave me here if you're moving, Laura! It's not safe here. There are people here who can't be trusted.'

'Mum, they're very nice here. I've met them all myself. And, you've got your friend Margery to talk to…'

'She's dead.'

'Well…I mean Grace, then.'

'Who's Grace?'

When Mum met Gabriel, she said she thought he was very handsome, but he should cut his hair and dress more smartly. He smiled graciously and told her he would try harder next time.

'Sorry,' I said, when we left. 'I'm afraid she's not the person she used to be. She'd never have said those things before – not quite like that, anyway.'

'It's fine, Laura. I think I can cope with a loopy old lady,' he said, smiling. 'I'm getting lots of practice…'

'You'd better not mean me!' I said, play-thumping him on the arm.

Gabriel went in search of Stanley when we got back to my flat and found him under a cushion. He'd brought a small cage and put some food and water in it for him.

'There we are, Stanley,' he said, stroking his pet affectionately. I averted my eyes, as it made me feel ill. 'Don't worry, Laura. He's safely in his cage. He can't get out.'

'That's what you thought last time…'

'I'm just going to look for the skin moult – I don't want you coming across it when you're hoovering or something!' He found the black, wrinkly husk under the sofa and showed it to me. 'It's amazing, isn't it!'

'Er, yes, but I don't need to see it.'

'I'll add it to my collection. It's perfectly intact. I usually put these in resin if they are good ones. I could make you a paperweight or something…'

'Stop it, Gabriel! You can make one for William!'

CHAPTER 27

Jenny was late, as usual, but it didn't matter – the estate agent was late as well.

'You've made it look much bigger,' said Jenny.

'I got rid of a lot of stuff, I didn't think you'd want any of it.'

'No, I didn't. I presume you've kept photos and letters and personal things…'

'Yes, of course. I found this really funny photo of us, Jenny – look!' I got a photograph out of a drawer that showed us both covered in mud at the seaside, with buckets on our heads.

'Hm,' said Jenny, looking at it, - 'why did our mother put us in matching clothes?'

Trust Jenny to have had a humour bypass. I put it away again.

'How's life?' she asked. 'How are things with Gabriel?'

'Good; well, apart from the fact that he's leaving me…'

'What! Already? What did you do?'

'What I mean is, that he's moving to Norfolk.'

'Oh, well, that'll put the kybosh on it.'

'I don't know…'

'You're not actually thinking of going too, are you? That's insane! Norfolk is a terrible place. *No one* goes there, Laura! It's like the place that time forgot – it's all swamplands and pig farmers…'

'Jenny, it's not like that at all. Not all of it, anyway…'

'Well, I think you're mad to even consider it. No man is worth giving up everything for, especially one who has such an incredibly *weird* pastime. I mean, really Laura, you could do so much better.'

'You haven't even met him. He's a very kind and intelligent man. He makes me happy and I'm at a crossroads in my life.'

'What tosh! You've been perfectly happy until now.'

'No, I haven't. You just didn't notice.'

She went quiet for a bit. 'Well, none of us have a perfect life, Laura.'

'I know, but I'm going to try,' I said, even though it sounds a bit *insane.*'

'Hm,' she said.

'What are we going to do about Mum's money?' I said, changing the subject.

'I'm going to get her to agree to us being joint account holders.'

'How?'

'We're taking her to the bank this afternoon. If we tell her that it's to stop people stealing her money, I think it'll work. She's obsessed with people taking her things at the moment.'

'Well, the only person taking her money is herself! Honestly, she's literally throwing it away.'

'I know. Hopefully, we can put a stop to it today. We'll still have to get Power of Attorney, of course. I wish we'd thought about all of this before she went doolally.'

'Hindsight is a wonderful thing,' I said.

Typical of Jenny to be so negative about Gabriel. In a funny way, it sort of galvanised how I feel about it all, and made me more determined to go with my gut feeling. I'm sure she'd be more positive about him if she actually met him. I'm not sure if I'm really ready for that at the moment. She can be so abrasive. She'd probably be really rude and I'd be embarrassed, and then I'd have to apologise…I do sometimes wish she wasn't my sister.

The visit to the bank was not without its difficulties. It was quite hard to keep Mum on track. She dobbed me in about taking her cards as well, which almost ended the whole meeting. The woman at the bank was not impressed.

'You know that's a fraudulent act, don't you?' she said, scowling at me. 'You could be prosecuted.'

'But I didn't use them!' I said, - 'It was to stop any more irrational spending.'

'It wasn't irrational!' said Mum.

'Well, what do you call twenty-four water features, or fifteen bags of frozen peas, 30 packs of loo rolls, or fifty-five dog beds, thirty-three bags of dog food and a hundred rubber chickens – not to mention 250 metres of netting for the imminent locust invasion?'

The woman raised her eyebrows.

'And,' I continued, - 'over a hundred direct debits for charitable causes that she has set up in the last two months…'

The woman's eyes expanded like saucers. She looked at Mum's statement on her computer screen and cleared her throat. 'Well, I think it's a jolly good idea to have your daughters in a position to help with financial matters, Mrs Blewitt, as long as you are happy with that arrangement?'

'We don't want anyone stealing your money, do we, Mum?' chipped in Jenny.

'Or stealing your identity,' I added. 'Jenny and I can make sure that can *never* happen to you.'

Our mother capitulated and signed the papers.

'Phew, thank goodness that's over,' I said, when we took her back to *Sunnyside*. We gave her a card with limited funds on it to keep her happy.

'I'm on a tight schedule,' said Jenny. 'I need to get back now. I've got a meeting at 3pm.'

Out of Mum's earshot, I said to Jenny as she was leaving, 'if I moved Mum to a home in Norfolk, what would you think about that?'

'I don't have time to discuss that now, Laura. It's a hell of a long way for me to go to visit, though.'

'OK, but given that you normally only visit Mum a couple of times a year, wouldn't that be OK?'

Jenny gave me a hard stare. 'I'll speak to you about it later,' she said, marching off down the corridor.

'She never stays long, does she?' said my mother.

William was just going out as I got back in from seeing Mum.

'What are you up to this afternoon, then?' I asked him.

'Going to Blade Park skating.'

'Oh, that's quite far away,' I said. 'You'll have to get the bus, won't you?'

'Nah, I'm going in my mate's car.'

'Who do you know who can drive, then, William?'

'Just a mate.'

'Right… and Blade Park costs about £20 to get in – how do you have enough money to pay for that?'

'It's fine – my mate's paying…'

After he'd gone, I suddenly felt a nauseous, sinking feeling in my stomach. I'm pretty sure he sold his bike, so I started thinking about what else he might have been selling. I went into my bedroom and checked my jewellery boxes. It was almost as if I already knew what I'd find.

'Cath,' I said, tearfully, - 'he's taken everything valuable, plus the things I collected from my mother's house for safe-keeping. I can't believe it!'

'Oh, I'm so sorry, Laura. That's terrible. You need to call the police.'

'Oh, I can't do that, Cath!'

'Why not?'

'Because I need to give him a chance to return it all…'

'Good luck with that, Laura. I'm really sorry, but that stuff is probably long gone.'

'I don't know what to do…'

'You need someone else there when he comes back – for back-up.'

'I'm so disappointed, Cath. I thought we were getting somewhere.'

'Why don't you ask Gabriel to come over, just in case things turn nasty.'

Gabriel was very sympathetic and came over straight away.

'You need to make a list of everything that's missing, Laura. I'll help you.'

When we'd finished, there were 27 missing items of jewellery and other bits and pieces. We half-watched a mediocre film on TV to pass the time, and I drank some wine to calm my nerves. By the time William came back, we'd both fallen asleep in front of the TV. He woke us up, banging the front door when he came in.

'William, can you come here please,' I said, - 'we need to talk to you.'

'That went well,' I said to Gabriel, as we watched William hightail it out of the flat, onto the street and away into the night. 'What do we do now?'

'Call the police, I suppose,' said Gabriel.

'But they'll arrest him.'

'He's a minor and he's gone missing, so you haven't much choice, Laura.'

'No, I suppose I don't. I'd better call social services as well. I feel really foolish about this…'

'It's not your fault. You've given him a chance and he's blown it.'

The police were out searching for him all night. They finally found him at a much older man's house – a known offender, apparently. When they questioned him about the stuff he'd stolen, he denied taking anything, but they found it at the local pawnbroker straight away, who instantly identified him. It was a relief to know I was going to get it back – most of it anyway. Orla rang me the following afternoon.

'Where is he now?' I asked her.

'I'm picking him up from the station this afternoon, Laura. He's refusing to come back to stay with you, so even if you were willing to give him a chance to redeem himself, it's a non-starter.'

'What will happen to him?'

'He's going to be moved to a residential unit away from here. He needs to be kept away from the people he's fraternising with. When the police caught up with him, he had Class A drugs on him - £1,000 worth of cocaine, to be precise.'

'Oh, my God! I had no idea!'

'He's been dealing for a while. Well before he came to you.'

'Did you know?'

'No, but it doesn't surprise me. I'm sorry, Laura. You did a nice thing offering him a home, but sometimes it just doesn't work out.'

I decided I needed a shoulder to cry on and rang Cath.

'Here,' she said, when I got to her house, - 'have a tissue.' In her garden, the sun was out and the scent from the orange blossom was heavenly. I tipped my head back to feel the sun on my skin, closed my eyes, and listened to the birds singing while she made us coffee.

'I feel such an idiot!' I said, sniffing into the tissue.

'Don't be silly, Laura. You weren't to know. You did your best with him. He'll have to suffer the consequences now, I'm afraid.'

'But it's not his fault, is it?'

'No, but neither is it your job to fix him.'

'It's just so disappointing, Cath. I mean, I thought he was settling down.'

'He's obviously a very good actor! Maybe he should consider that as an alternative career option…'

I laughed. 'It's true. I've been duped spectacularly.'

'What did Gabriel say to him?'

'He was pretty angry. He tore a strip off him. He told him he'd betrayed our trust in him and that he was going to end up with a criminal record, which would ruin his chances of having a decent life. William wasn't listening, though. We just got a load of verbal abuse. Really, Cath, the language was awful.'

'Well, I guess he's made his bed now, Laura. At least you two can get on with your own plans now, can't you?'

Gabriel and I went for a long walk in the Country Park with the dogs in the evening.

'In some ways, it's a relief,' I said to him, - 'but at the same time, I just can't help worrying about what will become of him. I mean, he's still only fourteen…'

'I know, but it's out of our hands now, Laura. Maybe someone else can turn him around. There's still time. When I was his age, I got into all sorts of trouble…'

'Did you?'

'Yes, unfortunately.'

'What sort of trouble?' asked, slightly nervously.

'I stole a car…'

'You did what? Really?'

'Yes. Well, I borrowed it. I took it back, but it was too late by then. The neighbour reported it missing.'

'What happened?'

'My parents hit the roof. I was grounded for three months. The police gave me a warning. That wasn't the only thing I did, though.'

'I'm afraid to ask!'

'Well, I went through a patch of being pretty stupid.' Gabriel gave me a slightly embarrassed smile. 'I nearly killed my sister once. I made this slide thing out of cardboard and binbags and attached it to a tree branch in the garden. I told Isla to slide down it, but it broke, and she fell off.'

'Good grief! Was she OK?'

'She broke her arm. Luckily, that was all.'

Goodness!'

'Anyway, boys can be idiots, I'm afraid. William has two disadvantages – he's a daft fourteen-year-old, plus he's had a terrible homelife. He was bound to react badly to being caught out as well. By the way, is your nickname at school really *poo tits?'*

'That's not the worst one, I can tell you! Dan has a much harder time than me. With a name like Longbottom, he's developed the hide of ten rhinos.'

'God, I don't think I could teach. I'm in awe of your resilience and fortitude! By the way, and I'm not joking when I say this – how would you like to change your name to 'Shape'? I mean, it can't be worse than 'Blewitt', can it?'

CHAPTER 28

When Dan rang me in the morning, I wasn't fully awake.

'Are you coming down?' he said.

'What? Where? Sorry, I've only just woken up…'

'The school, Laura. We're painting the mural.'

'Oh, God! Sorry, I forgot.' I looked over at Gabriel who was still asleep. 'I've been a bit preoccupied. I'll get there in a bit.'

'Who was that?' Gabriel asked, rolling over and yawning.

'Dan. I'm supposed to be painting today. I completely forgot.'

'Can I help?'

'Well, I suppose so – I mean, yes, they'll be grateful for an extra pair of hands.' Gabriel smiled sleepily. 'You do know that you have me in the palm of your hand now, don't you? I'll be stuck to you like glue, at your beck and call like a sad puppy. Can you just tell me again that you've agreed to marry me, just in case I didn't hear you right last night?' He smiled and pulled me back into bed.

'What time do you call this, then?' said Dan, when we finally turned up at school.

'We were a bit busy. Sorry,' I said, grinning. Dan rolled his eyes.

'Who did the drawing?' I asked, looking at the wall. Someone had outlined an image of a tree with books hanging like fruit from every branch. There were birds flying above it and the roots were being watered by an adult on one side and a child on the other.

'It's nice,' said Gabriel.

'One of the Year 11s. We'd better get on with it before the rain comes in later today.'

'I saw you,' I said to Gabriel, when we left.

'What?'

'You put a spider next to the tree.'

'Oh, yes, well it's only a small one…'

'It was a really good mural, wasn't it?' I said. 'It made me re-evaluate what us teachers are here for. I have a sort of love-hate relationship with my job. I'd like to do something else, but at the same time, I would miss it hugely.'

'No one's making you quit, Laura. You can do whatever you want to do. It doesn't have to be all or nothing. You could teach part time, couldn't you? And do other things the rest of the time.'

'But my income would halve, Gabriel.'

'I don't think we need to worry about that,' he said. 'I'll be able to pay you double for your invaluable assistance in making this dream come true! It'll be yours as much as mine, Laura. I don't want to do it alone.'

I must say, I can't quite get my head round the idea that I'll be financially dependent on someone else, even if it's only for a short while. I've always been completely independent since I left university. The idea of spending money I haven't earned myself is going to take a lot of getting used to.

'It won't take you long,' said Fay, when we were at school the next day. Scott has always earned more than me. Spending his money is my favourite hobby!' She laughed like a drain. 'Seriously though, Laura, Gabriel is obviously head-over-heels, and he really wants you to be happy. Just jump in with both feet and stop worrying.'

I went to tell my mother the good news later that day. It took her a while to absorb it.

'What do you mean, 'getting married'?'

'To Gabriel, Mum. You know, you met him the other day.'

'Did I?'

'Yes. He was the scruffy one with shaggy hair.'

'Oh my! Well, you'd better tell him to smarten himself up if he's getting hitched. Who's the lucky girl?'

Jenny was equally bemused. 'Really? But you hardly know him! You can't be serious?'

'Well, we are. Sometimes you just know it's right. We don't need to wait.'

'Good grief! Well, I think you're being a bit mad rushing into it.'

'Just say 'congratulations' Jenny,' I said.

She sucked in her breath and eventually said she hoped we'd be happy together.

'Cath,' I said, calling her up, - 'you'll never guess…'

'Oh my God! He asked you…? And…?'

'I said 'yes'!'

She screamed down the phone. 'Get over here now! I'll call Dan and Fay. Bring Gabriel - we're having A PARTY!'

EPILOGUE

It's been a funny kind of summer. Who knew my life would change so much in just three months? We've named the house in Norfolk *Stanley House* – well, I didn't name it, obviously! Gabriel wanted to call it *Spider's Barn,* but I drew a line at that. It's coming along – I've found a new passion for DIY, just as Gabriel predicted. The grounds are slowly being transformed; a collection of huts for all the insect exhibits are being built (well away from the house with trees screening them so I don't have to look at them), a garden and café has already been created and Gabriel is expanding his creepy-crawly collection on a weekly basis. Otto is in dog-heaven here – there's so much space for him and Cleo to run wild and free.

Handing in my notice to St Jude's was the hardest thing I've ever done, but, as Gabriel says, I can always apply for a teaching job here if I want to. I have to admit, my enthusiasm for teaching has waned somewhat since I met him and moved out here, despite the fact that I had unexpectedly good GCSE results from my Year 11s (*that's one in the eye for you, Evelyn Ferrier*!) The search for the porno-doll perpetrators goes on, with little chance of success in my view, but there's never a dull moment at St Jude's. Fay told me that at the beginning of term, several rude balloon combinations were discovered in various places around the school grounds, sending Evelyn into a spin again. My replacement in the English Department is another fresh-faced energetic young woman, keen to make a difference, according to Dan. Good luck to her, anyway. She'll learn! The main thing is, I've begun writing my novel, which I'm still too shy to discuss with anyone, but Gabriel is convinced it'll be a Best Seller, despite the fact that he knows nothing about it. That's true love for you, or blind faith – whichever way you want to look at it!

William is settling into his new residential school well, and apparently has the other kids enthralled regaling them with stories of giant tarantulas invading his house, near-death experiences out at sea, and how he caught a fish the size of the Titanic.

In the end, my mother agreed to move without too much palaver, especially after James at *Sunnyside* said he was going to have to put a tracking device on her so they could check her movements. She made a bit of a fuss about that, not quite understanding the meaning. Gabriel found a lovely nursing home near our house for her, which she has taken to like a duck to water.

So, all in all, I'd say things have turned out nicely, and best of all, Cath isn't the only one about to become a new Mum! Gabriel says he wants to name Cleo's babies after famous arachnologists, but I am putting my foot down. You really can't call a puppy 'Norman Platnick' or 'Ludwig Koch', can you?

Nicola Kelsall

ABOUT THE AUTHOR

Painting and writing have always been my main passions, although the demands of earning a living have frequently got in the way of a creative life, and it's been a frustrating journey. But, despite having had to do many different jobs, I have continued to paint and to write as much as possible. I've done all sorts; from being a Chambermaid, Barmaid, Driver, Shop Girl, Secretary, Dresser for the Royal Scottish Ballet, Printer, PA, Designer, Illustrator, Singer in a Medieval Banquet, Events Organiser, Teacher, PTA Queen, and most importantly – Mother to three of our own kids and Foster Mum to several more. When times have been difficult, we've always retained our sense of humour as a family and tried to see the funny side of things.

I used to worry that some of the dead-end jobs I did represented huge amounts of wasted time and often felt trapped and frustrated. Now of course, I am grateful for this vast array of experience and all the interesting characters I've met along the way. Family life has given me another very different set of experiences, and luckily inspired my first published series, 'Diary of a Stressed Out Mother', and now my latest comedy romance 'With Both Feet'. I very much hope there will be many more to follow as I've enjoyed every minute of writing these books and I hope my readers love them too!

For more about Nicola Kelsall:

Facebook and Instagram: @nicola_kelsall
Twitter: https://twitter.com/StressOutMother

Printed in Great Britain
by Amazon

49069713R00185